A Torrent of Faith

EUGENE H. STRAYHORN JR.

A Torrent of Faith

EUGENE H. STRAYHORN JR.

Chapter 1

After hours spent doggedly tramping through the woods, searching for any recognizable landmark, I could no longer deny that I was thoroughly lost.

As I tried to work out how I had come to be in such a fix, I recalled slipping and tumbling down a rocky incline earlier in the day. Dazed and shaken, I had rested on my back, staring up at the sky. Perhaps that was when I got turned around.

I've heard of backcountry hikers who have lost their bearings in mazes of thick foliage. My predicament was different. The forest wasn't dense; the trees were spaced far enough apart to see for a considerable distance. Also, the leafy canopy was thin enough to reveal the crests of several low hills—the sloped, gentle rises common to the Hudson River Valley. Visibility wasn't my issue. My problem was that nothing looked familiar. The surrounding woods were undisturbed. The absence of human activity gave the odd impression that I had materialized in the middle of the forest rather than having hiked in from the trailhead near Lake McDougall, just off State Route 171.

My name is Paul Xavier Langdon. I lived in Trinity Falls Township in Upstate New York and sold real estate for a living. Early that morning, I had set out to explore a tract of land owned by Ian and Eva Campbell. A friend had suggested that their two-hundred-acre parcel might soon come on the market. Brokering real estate was a competitive profession, especially in a small town, so I was always looking for lucrative properties. Sadly, after half a day of searching, I had failed to locate even one boundary marker. The most likely explanation was that I had trekked straight across the Campbells' land and into the virgin forests beyond.

Glancing up at the heavens, I noted that the afternoon was fading toward dusk, which was a worrisome development. The air was growing chilly—a lingering vestige of winter. In the northeast, March was an unpredictable time of year. Late seasonal storms could sweep down from Canada, bringing snow and freezing temperatures. My denim trousers and nylon jacket would prove a poor match for such severe weather.

Feeling frustrated and angry, I again drew my cell phone from its leather pouch on my belt. No matter how many times I pressed the power button, the screen remained dark. I had forgotten to charge the blasted thing before heading out. As a result, there was no way to access the backcountry GPS app that would have guided me straight home. Relying on modern technology to keep me safe in the woods had been a mistake, and now there was a price to pay.

The anxiety mounting within me suggested that I should press on. But which way to go? I knew Lake McDougall lay to the southeast, but which way was south and which east? In the gathering darkness, finding my way would be even more difficult. My innate sense of caution declared that it was time to camp for the night.

To the right, I noted a small clearing nearly seventy feet in diameter. At the edges of the clearing stood oaks, white spruces, and birch trees. All sported new spring foliage, though the fading light robbed the forest of its color.

Spending a cold, miserable night curled up on the forest floor filled me with despair. Of course, I would build a makeshift shelter, and after clearing the ground, I would light a fire, mindful not to set the woods ablaze. I used to be a cigarette smoker and, out of habit, still carried a lighter. Both efforts would help, but I would likely pass the night shivering rather than sleeping without a blanket or warm clothing.

* * *

A panoply of stars sparkled overhead as I lay curled up on an uneven bed of pine boughs, gazing at the small fire that flickered just outside the lean-to I had constructed. My thoughts were on my family. My wife, Rachel, and my daughter, Alicia, would worry. So would my older brother, Franklin. They would assume the worst—that I was injured or even dead. It seemed too much to hope they might guess I was incommunicado because my phone was out of commission.

A shooting star sliced across the heavens, followed by another. *When was the last time I witnessed such a display?* I wondered. *Should I make a wish?* The impulse seemed reasonable, but rather than a haphazard wish, I realized that a sincere prayer might be more appropriate.

I've always regarded myself as a Christian since Franklin and I invited Jesus into our lives at the same revival meeting. He was fifteen at the time, and I was thirteen. Although my brother then served as pastor of the Maranatha Gospel Fellowship, I, on the other hand, was more lackadaisical regarding spiritual concerns. I had trouble remembering the last time I had prayed.

When I thought about what to say, I realized with alarm that I was more than a little frightened. I was lost and with minimal resources. Unaccustomed to strenuous activity, I was weak and depleted from the day's exertions. My stomach rumbled, reminding me that the small bag of trail mix I had consumed around noon had done little to slack my hunger. If I were to go without eating much longer, my endurance would suffer. Worst of all, my shivering muscles suggested that I was on the verge of hypothermia.

I rolled onto my back and closed my eyes. With deep sincerity, I pleaded, "Lord, I could use a miracle. I'm lost in this stretch of wilderness into which I have wandered. I need a clear sense of direction. Help me find my internal compass. Guide me and show me the paths I'm to follow. Give me the strength and the fortitude to continue and sustain me on my journey. Amen."

It wasn't fancy, but a decent prayer would suffice.

When I opened my eyes again to study the sky, a third shooting star streaked across the firmament. It blazed more brightly than its predecessors. As a rule, I regarded signs and omens as random events subject to the imagination. Yet the falling meteor had added an intriguing exclamation point to the end of my prayer as if God were affixing His stamp of approval. For some silly reason, I felt a small rush of pride.

That night, as anticipated, I slept little. I considered praying again, but God doesn't award extra points for excessive verbiage. For whatever it was worth, a single prayer would have to do.

* * *

The following day, when it was light enough to see farther than a few feet, I didn't wake up exactly. Instead, I quit trying to fall asleep. It had been for only a few fitful minutes if I had slumbered at all. As anticipated, the cold temperatures, the hard ground, and my anxieties had conspired to rob me of sleep.

Gradually, the tops of the trees became visible in the first rays of dawn. I flexed my arms and legs to test their mobility. My joints felt stiff, and my muscles ached, as much because of my incessant shivering as due to the previous day's exertions.

Upon rising to a seated position, I gazed out across the clearing. At first, all I could see were shadows and the gray outlines of the trees. Suddenly, I recognized a shape that sent a shiver of fear through me, a shiver more intense than those evoked by the most ardent chill of night.

A wolf sat on his haunches thirty feet away, watching me. The animal was huge. I assumed the beast was male; he appeared to weigh well over a hundred pounds. He did not move, not even a twitch. Instead, he transfixed me with an unwavering gaze.

A shaft of sunlight penetrated the forest canopy. It seemed as if a spotlight had been trained upon the animal. The beam illuminated the predator's face from the tops of his ears to the tip of his muzzle. His fur was pale at the roots but blacker at the ends, giving the appearance of ashes on snow. His tufted ears were attentively tuned in my direction. Slanted downward near the bridge of his nose, his almond-shaped eyes conveyed a look of unbridled malevolence. Even more striking, the beast's eyes were a light translucent blue. They glittered like sunlight shining through ice. The wolf kept his gaze focused intently upon me.

I froze, fearful of making even the slightest movement lest I provoke an attack. The animal remained immobile as well. For the longest time, we stared at one another. Then, with my eyes alone, I searched for a means of defense. The only sticks available were the branches I had gathered for my lean-to. Were I to remove one, there was a strong probability the flimsy structure might collapse. Finally, I spotted a rock I had shifted aside while fashioning my bed. The size of an apple, it seemed hardly adequate, but it was the only weapon at hand. Ever so slowly, I snaked my hand out to grasp the rock. The wolf did not respond.

"Well now," I said quite softly, "what's on your mind?"

At the sound of my voice, the wolf's ears perked up. I eased into a sitting position with my legs drawn up so that I might rise quickly.

"Where are your buddies?" I looked around, aware that wolves rarely hunt alone. I listened, but the forest remained still except for the scattered chirping of a few birds coming awake. A faint breeze drifted in my direction. I wasn't sure how an alpha carnivore should smell, but the wolf's scent was not entirely unpleasant, much like a shaggy dog on a damp morning.

"What's it to be?" I said with a false display of bravado. "We can stare at each other all day, but I need to get on my way."

Moving slowly, I reached out my empty hand to test the fire. The ashes were still warm. The wolf held his position as I eased to my knees. Cautiously, I began burying the ashes beneath a layer of dirt. The wolf monitored my every movement.

A thought crossed my mind. *Instead of putting it out, maybe I should reignite the fire as a defense.* But that would require dismantling my lean-to. During the night, I had burned up all the twigs I had gathered for fuel. The commotion of tearing my shelter apart might provoke an attack.

When I rose to my feet, the beast lifted off his haunches. Gripping the rock tightly, I prepared to swing it as a club rather than throw it. Yet instead of charging, the wolf regarded me silently as before. There was no snarl of warning, no bristling of hackles.

Still gripping the rock, I gathered up my day pack with my free hand. My mouth felt dry, and I longed for a drink of water. But rather than dig around in the pack for my water bottle, I decided to test the wolf's intentions. If there was going to be a battle, it should begin at my instigation instead of allowing the beast to take me by surprise.

"Come on then," I growled, my voice parched and raspy. "Show me what you've got."

The predator flinched. His muscles rippled when he moved. Though he had not yet bared his fangs, I did not doubt that he could easily rip my throat out. And even though the morning breeze flowed in my direction, with him standing so close he could smell my fear.

I took a step forward.

To my surprise, the beast backed up a pace, maintaining a consistent distance between us. Another step forward evoked a similar result. But when I took a step backward, the wolf did not advance.

"What are you up to?" I said with no small amount of curiosity. Still tightly clutching the rock, I unzipped my backpack and extracted my water bottle with my empty hand. "To your good health." I offered a toast to my visitor. After draining half the bottle's contents, I returned it to my day pack, which I settled on my shoulders.

Taking my eyes off the wolf and glancing around for the first time, I realized I was now confronted by the problem that had troubled me so mightily the night before.

"Which way should I go?" I said to the wolf. "What's your opinion?"

As if sorting out my words, the wolf cocked his head. He then turned and disappeared into the forest. I breathed a huge sigh of relief. Perhaps we weren't about to set to after all —fang versus rock.

After gingerly retrieving a small branch from my lean-to, I broke off one end over my knee. With my eyes closed, I turned in a circle several times and tossed the stick. I then opened my eyes just in time to see where it landed.

With my course now determined, I, too, headed into the woods.

Throughout the day, the wolf returned periodically—sometimes after an absence of only fifteen minutes, sometimes after several hours. Gradually, I began to appreciate his companionship. With each visit, it seemed less likely that he was about to rip me to shreds. I thought about naming him, but how do you name a wild thing that knows no master? Besides, each time he disappeared into the forest, I expected never to see him again.

As the day progressed, I changed course several times, though I was only guessing which way to go. Trusting in blind luck wasn't the wisest policy, but lacking other options, it was the best I could do. Yet everywhere I looked, the forest seemed the same. No one place stood out as being more familiar than another.

During our trek, I had expected to see a variety of wildlife: squirrels, rabbits, maybe a porcupine or raccoon, or perhaps even a deer. None appeared. Probably, the wolf's presence had scared them away.

When dusk fell, I was thoroughly exhausted. My hunger had become an emptiness gnawing at the pit of my stomach. To my great relief, I chanced upon a small, clear stream around midafternoon. There the wolf consumed his fill of water as well.

When it again came time to stop for the night, I peered into the forest. Ahead, I could make out a thinning of the trees. As I stumbled forward, the wolf paralleled my track, keeping his distance. We were fellow sojourners, not friends. Together, we emerged into a small clearing.

I regarded the wolf. "What do you think? Is this a good place to set up camp?"

The wolf advanced to the middle of the opening and lay down. I nodded in his direction. "If it's good enough for you, it's good enough for me."

As I inspected my surroundings, seeking a suitable place to pitch camp, my eyes fell upon a sight that filled me with anguish. The lean-to I had constructed the previous evening stood at the far edge of the clearing. After an entire day of trekking through the woods, I had traveled in a great circle, only to return to where I had begun. I wanted to cry, but I was too fatigued for tears.

As if in sympathy, the wolf emitted a high-pitched whine. Its mournful cry startled me. It was the first sound the beast had made other than the soft lapping up of water when he drank or the faint rustle of dry leaves as he padded across the forest floor.

"You're right." I cast a sidelong glance at the wolf. "I am probably the dumbest human you will ever encounter. Certainly, the ineptest in the woods."

After gathering twigs and branches enough to last the night, I built a small fire. For his part, the wolf ignored my activities. He might well have already been asleep.

Upon lying down in my lean-to, I closed my eyes and considered conjuring up another prayer, but what would be the point? I had already prayed once. Besides, God knew where I was and what I needed. He didn't need me to remind Him.

*   *   *

In the morning, I awoke to the sound of running water, much like a leaking spigot splashing in a puddle. I opened my eyes to find the wolf relieving himself not three feet from my lean-to, marking his territory.

"All right. I'm awake," I muttered through dry, cracked lips. "What's your problem anyway? Was I snoring?" I rose to my feet.

The wolf retreated to his customary distance. With both arms raised to the level of my shoulders, I flexed my spine at the waist. To my amazement, the wolf mimicked my movements, bowing his spine, extending his front legs, and then rocking forward to stretch his hind legs.

"Are you as stiff as I am?"

As expected, the wolf ignored my question. For him, sleeping on the ground and tramping through the woods were everyday activities.

After thoroughly extinguishing the fire, I gathered up my backpack and looked at my furry companion. "Well, what's it to be this day? Which way is home?"

As on the previous morning, the wolf turned and trotted into the forest, but this time, he stopped at the clearing's edge to look back. There, he sat down on his haunches and watched me.

About to gather another decision-making twig from my lean-to, I paused to regard the wolf.

"Really?" I said. "That's the way you want to go?"

The animal stood up and waited.

9

"All right then. We'll do it your way."

When I moved in the wolf's direction, he turned and glided into the forest at a pace just fast enough to maintain the space between us.

Twice that morning, fatigue compelled me to rest. Both times, the wolf sat patiently, waiting for me to gather my strength. Rousing the will to plod on became increasingly difficult.

An hour or two after midday, we descended into a shallow valley. The surrounding trees wore their most gorgeous spring greenery. It was a magnificent sight I might have appreciated had I not been at the end of my rope. I felt done in.

As I trudged forward, my foot caught on a root, and I sprawled face down in the leaves. Too depleted to rise, I lay with my eyes closed, waiting for oblivion to overtake me.

Then I felt something wet and rough against my cheek. A stench, like rotting meat, caused me to gag. I opened my eyes. The wolf had licked my face. As soon as I stirred, the animal bounded away.

After maneuvering into a sitting position, I regarded my companion. "Does this mean we're friends?"

The wolf's icy blue eyes remained free of even the faintest hint of emotion.

I struggled to my feet with incredible difficulty. "Lead on," I said as I took a faltering step.

The wolf turned and continued in the direction we had been traveling.

Glancing up through the canopy, I noticed clouds gathering in the sky overhead. A storm was rolling in. If the weather turned nasty, I would not survive another night. Ridge County got a lot of rain. It was said that a man in the open could drown if he fell asleep on his back.

As we crested a low hill at the valley's edge, I peered ahead, ensuring my guide was still with me. As if reading my mind, the animal halted. He turned and stared in my direction. We eyed each other for a long moment. Then, there was a blur of gray, and he was gone. I hurried to where I had last seen him as best I could. I anxiously scanned the forest, fearful that I had been abandoned.

There was no sign of the wolf.

An inexplicable sense of foreboding arose within me. Strangely, I knew that our time together had come to an end. A great sorrow inundated my soul.

I dropped to my knees. My strength was gone. I had reached the limits of my endurance. A flash of light caught my eye as I was about to pitch forward onto my stomach in a final act of surrender. Then it came again. It was not an illusion. I forced myself to stand. Straining to move one foot forward at a time, I stumbled toward the gap in the trees where I had seen the flashes.

Thirty yards farther on, I emerged from the tree line. The flash of light turned out to be a ray of sunlight reflecting off the rearview mirror of a search-and-rescue van parked at the trailhead beside Lake McDougall.

I was saved.

I began waving my arms and yelling as loudly as my parched throat would allow. Several volunteers were carrying me toward the graveled lot in no time. While being loaded into a van to be driven to the hospital, I looked back at the forest. There was no sign of the wolf, no hint of movement among the trees. With sadness, I wondered if I would ever see the beast again.

*   *   *

"You certainly know how to worry a girl," Rachel, my wife, said from the doorway to my room in the emergency department. Search and rescue had informed her that I was on my way to the hospital.

As I lay upon the gurney, I could tell that, even though distressed, she was holding herself together reasonably well. She had swept her dark brown hair into a ponytail. Strands hanging loose at the temples suggested that she had dressed hurriedly and left the house in a rush. The strain of sleepless nights and worried days showed on her face.

Drummond Memorial's emergency department was rarely busy. The muted sounds of the hospital staff going about their daily routines filtered into my room. My bedside monitor displayed a variety of numbers, only a few of which I could interpret. After several liters of IV fluids, my pulse and blood pressure had returned to normal, and I felt stronger.

"You look worn out," I said to my wife.

"That makes two of us."

"Sorry to have worried you. I kind of took a wrong turn."

Rachel stepped forward to take hold of my hand. "For real, are you okay?"

"I'm fine. Nothing that a good night's rest won't fix. Where's Alicia?"

"In the waiting room. I wanted to see what kind of shape you were in before I brought her in."

"How did she cope with me being missing in action?"

"You know, nine-year-old girls. She was upset when she heard you were gone. I reassured her that you'd be all right, and that seemed to satisfy her."

After ten years of marriage, you get to know a person. I recognized the look in my wife's warm brown eyes—an unspoken demand to hear about what happened. So I explained, "I wanted to check out the

Campbells' property and learn the lay of the land, just in case they offer me the listing. I should've told you where I was going, but I only expected to be gone a couple of hours."

Rachel scowled. She seemed on the verge of tears. "You absolutely should have told me."

"Trust me. It won't happen again."

"We had no idea where you were."

"Everything was fine until I took a tumble and lost my bearings. When I realized I was turned around, I tried to call you, but my phone was dead. I had forgotten to charge it before leaving the house. I spent most of my time walking in circles." I briefly considered sharing my encounter with the wolf, but it seemed the wrong place and time. I decided it would be best to speak of it later when we were less emotionally engaged.

Rachel shook her head and asked, "Why would you go into the woods alone? You can get lost in our backyard. I gather it was only by the grace of God that you made it out like you did. Search and Rescue told me you were on the verge of collapse."

"It felt like I was running on empty." I lay back and stared at the ceiling.

"Are you sure you are all right?" Rachel asked anxiously.

"I'm good. No, really, I am. It was a rough couple of days, but I'm here now. Look. Do me a favor. Get Alicia, would you? I need to hug her and let her know I'm okay."

My wife eyed me with concern. "Perhaps I should speak with your doctor first. See if he has any objections."

"You needn't worry. I'll soon be right as rain."

As Rachel left the room to fetch our daughter, Frank Jenkins—Search and Rescue's senior coordinator—poked his head in. "How you doing, my man? Feeling better?"

"Much. And by the way, I understand you put in some long hours looking for me. Thank you."

"That's what we live for." Frank was a rugged outdoorsman with an athletic build. "I assume you know you led us on a merry chase. Several times, we came across your trail but lost it. The tracks kept crossing. You should have stayed put."

"No doubt, but I figured I could find my way out."

"And so you did."

I remembered something my father had once said: *It is better to finish well rather than start well and finish poorly.* I looked at Frank. "By the way, how did you guys know where to search for me? I hadn't told anyone where I was going."

"When we found your car, we figured you had headed away from the river."

"Of course. That makes perfect sense. Let me ask you something, Frank. You spend a lot of time in the backcountry. Have you ever come across any wolves?"

"Wolves? Heck no. They were hunted to extinction in the late 1800s. Upstate New York hasn't had wolves for over a century. Why do you ask?"

"No particular reason. I thought I might have seen something as I trudged through the forest. Probably my imagination."

"Whatever you saw, it wasn't a wolf."

"I'm sure you're right. By the way, pass the word to your team, would you? I appreciate all the time and effort they invested on my behalf."

"Like I said, it's what we live for, but you might not feel so grateful when you get our bill."

"There is that," I acknowledged with a groan.

Frank touched two fingers to his forehead in a goodbye salute.

I lay back and closed my eyes. I had a lot of thinking to do.

*   *   *

Trinity Falls was a community with strong spiritual roots. Our town had more churches than bars. As a rule, we raised our children to believe in a strong Judeo-Christian ethic. Most citizens believed Christmas and Easter should be times of worship rather than secular holidays devoted to rampant commercialism.

This was not to say we didn't have our share of sinners. Our pews were filled with as many hypocrites as any other rural community, and we could be just as bigoted and judgmental. The difference was when we transgressed, we suffered a more profound sense of self-condemnation. Far too often, we wore our religion on our sleeves.

Take my brother, Franklin, for example. He tended to be dogmatic. I, on the other hand, was pragmatic when it came to confronting ethical issues. I believed the end could justify the means, and a favorable outcome was better than being left with nothing more than a claim of moral superiority.

The Maranatha Gospel Fellowship was a small evangelical church. Franklin served as its pastor.

When I made my way to the rear of the building, I found Franklin seated at his desk in his cramped office. He looked up with surprise. "Well, well. Look who's up and around." Twenty-four hours had elapsed since my rescue. "To what do we owe this honor?"

"I just stopped by to touch base. Is this a bad time? You look busy." I noted papers and books strewn across his desk.

"I'm putting the finishing touches on Sunday's sermon. I think I'll title it 'What to Do until Jesus Quiets the Storm.' It's a study of how the disciples must have felt huddled in their boat in the middle of a tempest on the Sea of Galilee."

"I can come back later if you'd like."

"No, no. I need a break. What's on your mind?" The look in Franklin's eyes suggested I had piqued his curiosity.

"I'm troubled by an experience I don't understand. I'd like your opinion."

"I assume this involves your time in the woods. That must have been harrowing. We were worried you might have been injured…or worse. Several times, we found your trail but then lost it."

"That's right. Search and Rescue mentioned you were among the volunteers. I was surprised."

"You're my brother. We've had our differences, but I love you. I'd have a hard time living with myself if something happened to you and I hadn't lifted a finger to help."

"Wow," I exclaimed softly. Franklin's expression of brotherly devotion had touched me, and I felt a flush of embarrassment.

Rising from his chair, my brother glanced out the window. "Looks like a nice day. If you're up for it, what say we walk while we talk? I've been sitting too long."

I nodded. "A walk might do me good, I think. My muscles are stiff, especially my legs."

"But otherwise, you're okay?"

"No worries. I'm fine."

Franklin grabbed his coat, and we left the church.

The Maranatha Gospel Fellowship was four blocks from downtown Trinity Falls, just outside the central business section. The church was a converted grange hall, barely adequate for the congregation's needs. During the conversion, the building was retrofitted to resemble a New England house of worship. The most notable addition was a towering steeple topped by a gold cross. A raised dais and stained-glass windows were also added to the sanctuary. Office spaces for the pastor and the church secretary were set at the back of the building. A small parsonage was built adjacent to the church to accommodate my brother and his wife, Ellen Rose. Altogether, it was a convenient, though somewhat cramped, arrangement.

"So what happened out there?" Franklin's breath was made visible by the chill in the morning air. He hooked a thumb toward the rolling hills north of town.

I glanced at my brother as I joined him on the sidewalk that led toward the residential neighborhoods away from town. As best I could, I recounted the first day's events and how I had gotten turned around. I described pitching camp that first night and repeated the prayer I had prayed as accurately as possible. It seemed important not to leave that part out.

"In the morning," I continued, "the most amazing thing happened. When I awoke, I discovered a huge gray wolf sitting on his haunches not ten yards away, watching me."

Franklin halted to regard me with skepticism. "A wolf, you say?"

I stopped as well. "I know this sounds crazy. You're going to point out that there haven't been any wolves in New York State since the late 1800s, and you'd be correct, except I'm convinced it was a wolf I saw. I will never forget his icy blue eyes. Not only did he watch me, but he kept me company for a day and a half." I described how the beast had tracked me through the woods, lay down nearby at night, and led me to the forest's edge near the trailhead as if he had known precisely where I needed to go.

"What you're saying—"

"Sounds impossible. Like a made-up story. I agree. But it is the truth."

"How did this wolf, or whatever it was, just happen to be there when you needed him?"

"I have no idea. That's what I wanted to talk to you about."

"Let me understand. You're telling me a wolf guided you through the woods?" Franklin seemed exceedingly doubtful.

"When I didn't insist on going my own way, yes."

"Have you discussed this with anyone else?"

"Only Rachel."

"What does she think happened?"

"She told me to talk with you."

"I see."

"I wasn't hallucinating. I know what I saw."

"No doubt, but was what you saw real, or did it exist only in your mind?"

We resumed our walk.

Half a block later, Franklin suggested, "I'm cold. This was a bad idea. Let's head back."

I concurred, and we turned around.

Franklin blew on his hands to warm them. "I'm not sure what to think. This encounter you're describing… You've always had an odd sense of humor."

The insinuation needled me a tad, but I tried to remain calm. "Look. I nearly died. I wouldn't have made it out alive if I had been forced to spend another night in the open. I'd come to the end of myself.

I had nothing left. If not for the wolf, I would have given up, and you'd be officiating at my funeral."

"So I heard. They told me you were exhausted, famished, and sleep-deprived. Not only that, but I assume you were frightened as well. I know I would have been. Wouldn't such a state increase the likelihood that you were seeing things?"

I bristled. "I wasn't hallucinating. How did my delusion lead me to the precise spot I needed to reach to be rescued? What are the odds? Besides, delusions don't smell like wet dogs. Several times, the wolf came near enough that I caught his scent." I deliberately neglected to mention that the animal had licked my face. Such an assertion would have convinced my brother I was crazy. "Can you say for sure that what I saw wasn't real?"

"No. Of course, I can't. I believe all things are possible with God, but it's not every day that He hands out a miracle."

"Are you suggesting this was a miracle?"

Franklin gave me a quizzical look. "Isn't that what you were implying?

"To be clear, when I prayed, I didn't ask for a miracle. That wasn't what I had in mind."

Franklin's eyebrows scrunched together. "If you're telling me that a flesh-and-blood wolf was sent to serve as your guide, I think that would qualify. God sent the animals to Noah two by two to fill the ark, and we consider that a miracle."

For a time, we walked in silence. Half a block later, Franklin spoke up. "What do you think happened to you out there? What's your explanation?"

"Honestly? I can't figure it out. When people ask what happened, I don't know what to tell them. I wish I could get my life back to normal. I'd like to forget the whole experience."

Franklin halted again. His demeanor became even more serious. "There is a facet to this event that we haven't discussed.

I stopped and turned to face him. "And what might that be?"

"If God did choose to save your life, He did it for a reason. And if so, it's up to you to figure out what that reason might be. In that regard, I wish I could help, but I can't."

We eyed each other as the implications slowly sank in. Then we began walking again.

Franklin regarded me with a sideways glance. "You know, there is someone who might help put things into perspective."

"Who might that be? God?"

"Precisely. Maybe you should talk with Him."

When we reached the church, I bid my brother farewell and thanked him for listening. Then I took my leave. With the subject of miracles at the forefront of my mind, I returned to my office and the showing I had scheduled that afternoon. But something else unexpected happened.

Still mulling over my conversation with my brother, I parked in the lot adjacent to Trinity Falls Realty, the real estate business I owned and managed. As I walked toward the front door, something on the ground caught my eye. The low leafy hedge that paralleled the sidewalk partially obscured the item. I had almost missed it. I recognized a brown paper sack with its top folded shut. At first, I assumed it was a bag of rubbish someone had thoughtlessly tossed aside.

With a grunt of disapproval, I bent down to collect the refuse so I could discard it properly. Upon opening the bag to glance inside, I was astonished by what I saw: bundles of ten- and twenty-dollar bills neatly encircled by rubber bands. There had to be at least ten bundles. Rather than count the money while standing on the sidewalk, I refolded the top of the bag and ensured it was securely closed.

With trepidation, I looked around, worried that someone had noticed. Trying to act as nonchalantly as possible, I scanned the neighborhood for anyone who might have dropped such a treasure. No one was in sight. There was no sign of the bag's owner.

I considered who might have left a sack of money lying at the edge of our parking lot. Instinctively, I knew neither of my employees—Linda Babcock, my receptionist and office manager, or Jack Flashman, my sales assistant—would foolishly abandon bundles of cash. Neither was that careless or that wealthy.

I could feel the bag's weight in my hand as I stood there. For some reason, it seemed heavier than I would have expected. Upon considering my options, I concluded that there was only one thing to do.

My watch informed me that if I hurried, I could run a quick errand and still make my scheduled meeting.

I hurriedly returned to my car before temptation could change my mind. I drove straightaway to the Trinity Falls Police Station to turn in the money. I figured the authorities should be the ones to keep the loot safe while I searched for its owner. Before I left the station, the officer on duty handed me a receipt for $11,907 and gave me a promise: if no one claimed the money within a reasonable waiting period, the sack and its contents would be mine.

That last bit made me laugh. No one walked away from wads of cash. It was an absolute certainty that someone was bound to step forward and demand their money.

Chapter 2

Ten days after my ordeal in the forest, I awoke in my bed with the tail end of a disturbing dream slowly slipping from my mind. I tried to grab hold of it, but it faded away. All I could manage to hang on to was the lingering sensation of swimming in a sea of green, clutching a rock like a baseball. I let the dream go and sat up.

Rachel and I slept in the same bedroom but not in the same bed. Usually, I was the early riser. I preferred to get a running start on my day. I looked over to where Rachel should have been still asleep, snuggled beneath an electric blanket and a down comforter. She wasn't there, and her bed was freshly made. The clock on the dresser informed me that I had overslept. I could hear kitchen noises downstairs.

The picture on the wall opposite my bed attracted my notice. It showed a wooded landscape with a gently flowing stream meandering through a sylvan glade. The scene reminded me of my recent ordeal. It occurred to me that a stark desert panorama might have been less jarring.

I rose to begin my morning. The aches that plagued me after my time in the woods were gone. My memories of those few days, thankfully, were also becoming less immediate, at least whenever intrusive images weren't around to remind me. I stepped into the bathroom to shower and shave. After dressing, I trotted downstairs.

When I entered the kitchen, Rachel was washing dishes at the sink. I crept up behind her and kissed her neck.

"Sorry," I said when she startled, a faint flush rising in her cheeks.

"It's good you're awake," she said without turning around. "I was about to check on you. How'd you sleep?"

"Fairly well. Am I too late to get breakfast?"

"I fried extra bacon. You'll have to scramble your own eggs. There's juice in the fridge and an English muffin in the toaster. All you need to do is brown it. Sorry, but I have to run. I wanted to ensure you were okay, but now I'm late."

Rachel was one of Trinity Fall's two librarians. She took her job seriously, especially when it came to opening and closing on time.

"Where's Alicia?" I said, glancing around.

"Already on the bus." Rachel cast her gaze toward the clock above the stove. "Or maybe at school by now."

"You should've woken me. I wanted to say good morning."

"I figured you could use the sleep."

"I don't need coddling," I snapped. I hated being treated like an invalid, and I let it show. My wife seemed offended, so I added less stridently, "Forgive me. I know it's only because you care. The truth is I need to put this matter behind me. Can we forget about my episode in the woods?"

"If that's what you want." Rachel turned to leave but then stopped to reach for a pair of professionally printed reports lying on the kitchen table. She held them up. "I was reviewing our genetic profiles again to see how similar we are."

Feeling guilty for my outburst, I said mildly, "We don't need genetic testing to tell us we're made for each other."

"So we are." She opened one of the reports and pointed to the third page. "Did you happen to notice we share the same mutation?"

"Is that a cause for concern?"

"I looked it up on the internet. It's a rare recessive gene that's thought to cause juvenile heart failure. We might have a problem."

"What's your point? We're both adults, and we're both healthy."

"But if we carry the same gene, then maybe Alicia…?"

"Oh. But she's well. She doesn't have heart failure."

"Maybe not, but I think we should get her tested."

"Tell me more about what you learned online."

"There's not much to tell. The references were rather technical, and I didn't understand some parts. From what I read, it seems the mutation is extremely rare. To be symptomatic, a child must inherit the same abnormal gene from both parents, and the probability of that is like one in ten million."

"Sounds like we don't have much to worry about. Those seem like pretty good odds."

"But what if… I mean, think about the implications if we both passed on the same anomaly."

I considered the possibility. "I suppose you're right. We still have the test kit I was going to give Franklin as a joke to confirm he's really my brother. We could use it to test Alicia instead."

"I think we should."

"Perhaps you're right. We can collect her DNA tonight, and I'll mail the kit first thing in the morning."

"Good." Rachel kissed my cheek, signaling that she was no longer feeling hurt.

"There is something else," I ventured hesitantly. "I hate to bring this up, but I did promise. I have a closing this morning, but I have to return to the woods this afternoon. I need to find that property I was told about."

"Do you think that's wise?"

"I will make absolutely certain my phone is fully charged. I'll even buy an extra battery. There wouldn't have been a problem last time if I could have accessed my GPS app. I'll even bring along a kit of emergency supplies. Besides, this time, you'll know where I am."

"Just be safe. That's all I ask." Rachel turned away but then halted and looked back. "Oh, I just remembered. While tidying up in the utility room, I noticed the water heater has a slow leak. I put a pan down to catch the drip. You might want to check it out before it gets worse." She again glanced at the clock above the stove. "Lord, I am so late." She flashed me an apologetic smile and opened the door to our attached garage.

"I'll put it on my to-do list," I called out dejectedly as the door closed behind her.

Great, I thought, *one more thing to fix. How much is this going to cost?* As a homeowner, it seemed that something was always busted, like the gate on the picket fence or the cantankerous garage door opener that tended to jam halfway up. I thought, *Maybe I should live in the woods permanently*, but then cautioned myself, *Bad idea, given your lousy sense of direction.*

*   *   *

I founded Trinity Falls Realty shortly after Rachel and I were married—I was twenty-three then. I had worked in another office for a couple of years before that to learn the ropes and prepare for my exams. As a broker, I'd served the township for ten years. My realty office was conveniently located on Broad Street, a block off Main Street, where my two employees and I shared a converted house with another company, Upstate Title. We conducted business on the ground floor. The title company leased the upstairs rooms.

Seated in Upstate's agreeably decorated conference room, I gazed out their front window. As I had informed Rachel, I had a closing scheduled for that morning. I was waiting for my buyers to arrive. I suppose I could have hung out in my own office downstairs, but then I wouldn't have been able to monitor the parking lot below.

As I watched cars glide past on the street facing our parking lot, I thought about my conversation with my wife. Was it possible that I could have passed on a genetic abnormality to my daughter? The concept seemed inconceivable. Alicia was a delicate child—innocent, undeserving of anything grim. On the other hand, one chance in ten million. You didn't get odds like that in Las Vegas. To keep from stressing, I refocused my thoughts on my impending meeting.

I used to love officiating at closings. Until recently, it was one of my favorite functions as a real estate broker. I considered it an honor to match buyers with sellers, especially when the transaction worked to the benefit of both parties. Yet, of late, the process had become tedious and more routine than privilege. Don't get me wrong. I was grateful whenever I closed a deal. When a client signed on the dotted line, it put bread on my table and paid for things like a new water heater. It was just that the ritual had lost its luster.

A late-model Mercedes coupe pulled into the lot and parked. The individual who emerged from the driver's seat was not one of the people I was expecting.

"What's she doing here?" I muttered to myself.

Helen Dunn had been a thorn in my side for years. We'd locked horns on more than a few occasions. She had often challenged my opinions at real estate council meetings. Worse, I suspected but could not prove that she was the source of unfounded rumors regarding Trinity Falls Realty that had recently begun circulating, all without merit. There was also the issue of advertising signage going missing from several of my listings.

Then an older model Buick LeSabre pulled in and parked beside Helen's vehicle. I recognized the car. It belonged to the clients for whom I had been waiting. Todd and Grace Greeley climbed out and greeted Helen warmly.

"What the hell!" I exclaimed as I hurried downstairs.

"Well, hello, Paul," Helen said as she entered through the front door. "You seem to have survived your wanderings in the forest." As I studied her face, I could almost read her thoughts: *Too bad you found your way home.*

"Helen, what are you doing here?"

"Let's not be inhospitable. I'm here to assist my clients, the Greeleys, with their closing."

When Todd and Grace entered behind Helen, both seemed embarrassed. I greeted them warmly, but neither would look me in the eye.

Helen ignored Linda Babcock, who, with her mouth agape, watched from behind her reception desk. Instead, Helen said curtly, "I assume we'll be meeting in the upstairs conference room as usual?" She immediately headed for the stairs. "This way," she called back over her shoulder. Todd and Grace dutifully fell in behind her.

When our visitors had passed out of earshot, Linda whispered, "Should I call the police?"

"Not yet," I responded, "but make sure you have their number on speed dial."

The trio settled themselves along the far side of the conference table.

Rather than sit down facing them, I gazed across the polished mahogany and said firmly, "Helen, might I speak with you privately? Now, please." Without waiting to hear her response, I turned and left the room.

Downstairs, we passed straight through the waiting area onto the front porch, where I turned to confront my nemesis.

Helen was a reasonably attractive woman, though a little on the thin side. She wore her caramel-blonde hair layered toward the back. A pearl brooch adorned the lapel of her charcoal gray jacket, and a sharp crease descended the front of each leg of her tailored black slacks. There were nicotine stains on the fingers of her left hand.

"Would you like to tell me what's going on?" I demanded. "The Greeleys are my clients, and you know that's true."

Helen smirked. "All you did was to entertain them at an open house. They've chosen Rimdale Properties to represent them."

"But I was the one showing the house they decided to buy. They never said a thing about already having a broker."

"You must have misunderstood."

"No. I didn't. I recall our conversation quite well."

"Obviously not, but now you know."

"I distinctly remember them mentioning that they were house hunting on their own."

"Ask them. They'll tell you. Before they ever met you, they'd already been to see me at my office."

"Of course, they'd say that, now that you've coached them. Look. You're not going to get away with this. I know what you're doing. It's one of the oldest tricks in real estate. You intend to kick back part of your commission so you can muscle in on a pending sale."

Helen bristled. "That's a slanderous accusation."

"It's not slander if it's true. I'll report you to the council. We'll see what they have to say."

"Don't be absurd. It would be your word against mine, and I have two witnesses."

"Then I'll take it to the newspaper," I growled. "They'll love a bit of salacious gossip."

"If you breathe one word of such tripe, you'll wish you hadn't."

"Oh yeah? What will you do?"

"Oh, I don't know. Let's see. What do you think Rachel might say if she knew you and I used to be intimate?"

I felt inclined to laugh, but I was too shocked. "Don't be ridiculous. You're not my type, and you never have been."

"Nevertheless, who do you think your wife will believe, you or me? I can be very persuasive." Helen's blue eyes narrowed. I was reminded of the wolf. "If you challenge me on this, I'll make sure your home life becomes a nightmare."

"You wouldn't."

"Test me and see. Now, should we go back upstairs and get this over with?"

With all that was in me, I wanted to throttle her, but I was afraid of the consequences. She had me over a barrel. I could submit and take a 50 percent cut in the commission I was about to earn, or I could oppose her and run the risk that Rachel would have to deal with some gruesome allegations. I knew my wife would accept my word against Helen's, but to spare her the pain of a scandal, I chickened out and let the matter slide.

"Fine, but one day, there will be a reckoning."

"Yeah, right." Helen spun on her heel and reentered the building.

I followed meekly behind.

When Linda gave me a quizzical look, I said dolefully, "Call Walter." Walter Kraft was the owner-operator of Upstate Title. He usually served at all my closings. "Let him know we're ready to go." Giving voice to that last sentence nearly gagged me.

*   *   *

State Route 171 ran north and south, parallel to the western banks of the Byrne River. If you were headed north, after passing through the middle of town, the highway began a gentle rise into the low foothills of Upstate New York.

As I cruised along, my mind was still troubled by my run-in with Helen Dunn. The woman's brazenness appalled me. She had flat-out lied, but I found my reluctance to confront her even more distressing. I had always loathed conflict. I avoided it whenever possible, mostly because I dreaded taking risks. I hated not knowing how things would turn out, and when two people fought, anything could happen.

Worse, I had surrendered half of my commission on the sale of a reasonably decent home. When you were the sole proprietor of a small business, every dollar of income mattered.

Upon reviewing the incident, I realized I should've called Helen's bluff. I was wrong not to confront her. Filled with self-loathing, I tried to put the horrid woman out of my mind and concentrate on my driving.

As I navigated a series of easy switchbacks, I could make out a narrow gorge to my right. With the windows open, I could also hear the roar of the Byrne River as it surged furiously southward over a trio of stairstep falls, hence the name Trinity Falls.

At the top of the rise, a two-lane road veered off toward the parking lot adjacent to the Eldridge Dam. Built in the late 1930s when the township was still farmland and virgin forest, the dam was intended to tame the Byrne River and keep it from periodically flooding the valley below.

The dam's construction had also led to the formation of Lake McDougall, a comely body of water popular with fishermen and boaters alike. Cruising parallel to the lakeshore, I noted stands of cattails in the shallows and sunlight ricocheting off ripples farther out. After a long winter, every tree seemed eager to don its spring foliage. The beauty of the scenery helped soothe the animosity I was feeling.

My destination was the trailhead, which was a half mile farther, near where the Byrne River fills Lake McDougall. From there, sojourners could set out for a gentle day hike or, if feeling adventurous, head into the Adirondacks to the west or toward the Catskills—a longer hike to the east. My intent was more pragmatic, having promised myself that I would find and explore the Campbells' property without getting lost.

The trailhead consisted of a carved wooden sign posted by New York foresters and a gravel lot large enough to accommodate half a dozen vehicles. Only one other car was present when I pulled in and set the parking brake. I grabbed my day pack with the emergency supplies I had added and ensured my phone was fully charged and functioning as it should. I also confirmed that my new spare battery was safely zipped into one of the pack's side pockets. Finally, I summoned up my backcountry navigation app, again noting significant landmarks and the course of the Byrne River.

Before setting out, I also retrieved the sturdy case that contained my aerial drone. Initially, I had regarded the six-prop machine as something of a toy, but as my flying skills had improved, it had become an increasingly valuable tool. Photographs taken at elevation could be invaluable when sizing up potentially marketable properties.

A crisp breeze drifted in from the northwest. The air was laden with scents of the forest. A short distance in, I paused to consult my navigation app again. It informed me that I would have to leave the well-used trail I was following to reach the tract of land I sought. The realization brought a jolt of apprehension. *I wondered how it would look if I lost my way in the same stretch of woods twice within a month. My reputation would be shattered. Rachel would see that I never ventured out on my own again.*

On impulse, I switched the navigation app from map view to satellite view. The change revealed something I had missed, something I should have noticed. A narrow dirt road veered off Highway 171 to track along the eastern edge of the Campbells' land. Rather than hike from the trailhead to reach the property, I could apparently park beside the access road and walk a hundred yards. *How could I have overlooked something so obvious?* Feeling like a complete idiot, I retraced my steps to my Jeep.

Twenty minutes later, I was exploring the Campbells' property. While trekking between trees and tramping through the underbrush, I kept an eye peeled for the wolf. Once, I thought I spied a pile of scat. It was a clump of moss dislodged from an upper tree branch, probably by a squirrel.

Upon remembering the wolf, a sense of foreboding arose within me. I looked around to see if I was being followed. The forest was quiet. That didn't mean I was alone. Perhaps it was time to launch my drone.

I set the case down on the ground and opened it. In short order, my drone was soaring above the treetops. After setting the controls to hover, I slowly rotated its camera in a 360-degree arc, alert for any signs of movement. Nothing attracted my notice. Still, I had the uncomfortable feeling that I was being followed.

After searching out two boundary markers, I was beginning to get a feel for the forest's layout around me. By studying the video monitor, I could better appreciate the terrain's topography. Looking down from an overhead perspective, I quickly identified my Jeep parked beside the access road. Then, to my surprise, I noticed that rather than continuing parallel to Highway 171, the access road veered sharply to the west, along what I presumed was the parcel's northern boundary.

This was good news. Accessing the property from two sides would add to its value. Other features were equally attractive: the land was flat and free of significant malformations, the late-growth forest looked in good health, and the surrounding properties were free of urban encroachment. I landed the drone and stowed it in its case. Feeling better oriented, I set out to identify the third boundary marker.

As I tramped along, an oddly shaped boulder caught my eye. It reminded me of Rachel's vanity in our bedroom—part of her dowry upon marrying me. I recalled our wedding ceremony. In those days, we had clung to each other like there was no tomorrow, but then life's stresses had overtaken us. Now, all we did was worry about what tomorrow would bring. We still loved each other, but how we expressed that love differed.

Odd, I thought, *how some things never change. Yet, some things do.*

I stared at the patchwork sky visible through the canopy overhead for a time. When I lowered my gaze, I recognized a faded strip of orange tape not far away. Three markers down, one to go.

Upon turning toward the center of the lot, I noted that the land sloped gently downward to the east. This, too, came as a welcome observation. As I trekked along, it became clear that more than a few vantage points afforded a fine view of the Byrne River and Lake McDougall farther to the south. This was an excellent plot of ground.

I considered brokering the real estate and performed some rough calculations. First, I would have to persuade the owner to sell. Then, I would have to track down a buyer. That I myself might acquire the property was out of the question. If I were to liquidate everything I owned, I'd raise only a tiny fraction of the likely asking price of $2 million, assuming two hundred acres of raw land would fetch something near $10,000 per acre.

However, if I were to sell the lot, I would garner a nice commission, approximately $120,000, given my standard rate of six percent on raw land. That kind of payday would go a long way toward shoring up Trinity Falls Realty's shaky finances.

My mind was still grappling with the logistics of such a significant transaction when a gruff voice sounded behind me: "Who are you, and what are you doing here?"

Taken by surprise, I startled. Upon turning around, I noticed a man holding a shotgun and glowering at me. Technically, the shotgun's muzzle was pointed at the ground, but it could be swiftly aimed in my direction. The man was stout with short gray hair. He wore a pair of denim coveralls, a white T-shirt, and calf-high boots.

"I'm Paul," I stammered. "Paul Langdon. I live in Trinity Falls. I'm just out for a day hike. I mean no harm."

"You seem to be doing a bit more than hiking. I've been watching you for a while now. You've been scouting out boundary markers."

"Yes. Yes, I have."

"You do realize you're trespassing on private property?"

"I do. Yes. But like I said, I mean no harm. By the way, who are you?"

"I'm Ian Campbell. I own this land."

"Is that right? Well, this is an honor. I was thinking that I should pay you a visit." I extended my hand and stepped forward. The muzzle of the shotgun came up smoothly. I halted in my tracks. "Easy. All I'm saying is it's nice to meet you, sir."

"You want to tell me what you're really doing here?"

"Certainly. You see, I'm a real estate broker. I own Trinity Falls Realty. I heard from a friend that you might be interested in selling. I wanted to see the property for myself to get an idea of what it might be worth. Is it true you're of a mind to sell?"

"I might be, depending upon the offer. What do you think this ground is worth?"

"At the moment, it's hard to say. I haven't fully assessed its value. Maybe $9,000 per acre. Perhaps $10,000."

"Ten thousand only? You're joking."

"Like I said, I haven't fully evaluated its marketable features or researched comparable sales. You know, two hundred acres is a sizable chunk of land. Not easy to move. A buyer would need deep pockets to purchase something this size. By the way, why the shotgun? You been having trouble with vandals or squatters?"

"I was hunting rabbits till I heard you tramping through the woods. You say you're a broker?"

"Yes, sir, and I'd be pleased to represent you if you're in the market to sell. Let me give you this." I fished in my shirt pocket and drew out a business card. I cautiously handed it over.

Mr. Campbell took a moment to read its information and then looked up. "Eva, my wife, is getting tired of winter. She's been hinting that we should move somewhere warm, perhaps Florida, be closer to the kids. That's why we're thinking of selling."

"Well, Mr. Campbell—"

"Ian. Call me Ian. I'm not a fan of formalities."

"Well, Ian, from what I've seen, this is an attractive plot of ground with many appealing features."

"That ten grand per acre, you sure about that?"

"Like I said, I won't know what a fair price is until I've done my homework. Rest assured, if I am fortunate enough to represent you, I'll do my best to get you as much as possible. That's our guarantee."

Ian shouldered his shotgun. I breathed a sigh of relief.

"Must be providence," he said, "us meeting like this. Tell you what, let me give you my address and phone number. Take your time. Look the property over. Do what you need to do, and then give me a call. We'll talk."

"It would be a pleasure." Tentatively, I extended my hand again.

The shotgun remained on Ian's shoulder as he returned my handshake. His grip was as firm as that of a younger man. We chatted for another ten minutes or so about unrelated topics, and I took my leave. My spirits soared as I waved goodbye. It seemed entirely possible that Mr. Campbell would become a client, meaning I was halfway to my goal of brokering a sale. Next, I would need a buyer.

Rather than search out the fourth boundary marker, I returned to where I had parked. Along the way, I again scoured the woods for the wolf, but he never appeared.

*   *   *

After touring the Campbells' property that afternoon, I returned to my office. Seated at the reception desk in the main lobby, Linda Babcock looked up to greet me. She was a portly middle-aged woman with dark, deep-set eyes. Her round face accentuated her large nose. Yet Linda was a compassionate soul with a knack for putting people at ease. As an office manager, she had her strengths and weaknesses. Her flair for keeping my appointment calendar up-to-date was first-rate, and she always made sure I got to where I needed to be on time. Her math skills, however, left something to be desired.

"Oh, good. You're back." Linda seemed hugely relieved.

"I told you I wouldn't get lost again. Didn't you believe me?"

"It's not that. It's Jack. He has a problem I think you'll find… interesting." Linda often relied upon code words and phrases rather than explicitly stating her thoughts. Interesting could mean there was a problem, not an emergency per se, but a difficulty outside the normal range.

I scowled. "Has Jack been misbehaving again?"

John Flashman—whom we all called Jack and occasionally referred to as Jack Flash—was the third member of our team. He was my sales assistant. I had hired him, the twenty-year-old son of a good friend, to help in the office. His duties included running errands and handling the menial tasks integral to every real estate transaction. In his spare time, Jack was studying to become a licensed sales associate. His stated goal was to one day earn his broker's license.

A tall, lanky fellow with a shock of blond hair, Jack had a flair for communicating with clients, though he occasionally tended to get ahead of himself to the point of promising results we could not deliver. More than once, I'd been obliged to pay good money to honor his overzealous commitments, but he was learning, and I liked the man, though I had a lingering suspicion that he might one day become my competitor.

"So," I said, "what's this problem Jack is up against?"

"I think it's best if he tells you himself." My office manager returned her attention to the open folder on her desk. She looked up as I headed down the hall toward the rooms at the back. "We're really glad you're safe." There was a hint of playful taunting in her voice.

"Me too," I replied sincerely.

"Come in," Jack said when I knocked on his open door.

Standing in front of a four-drawer filing cabinet, he turned around as I entered the room. His office had once been the guest bedroom. My office, however, had been the master suite with its own bathroom.

"Paul!" Jack exclaimed. "Thank goodness you're back. The Jacobys' farm is scheduled to close tomorrow afternoon, and I can't find their file. We've already delayed their closing once when you were…unavailable. If we postpone it again, it will make us look really bad."

I appreciated Jack's tactfulness. Instead of being unavailable, he might have said pathetically, wandering around in great circles.

I stepped forward and placed a reassuring hand on his shoulder. "Not to worry. The file is at my house. The day before my walk in the woods, I took it home to review but then totally forgot it was there. Do you need it right now? I could go get it."

Jack breathed a sigh of relief. "No. Tomorrow morning should be soon enough. I need to go over the preliminary title report. There was some confusion concerning a couple of the easements attached to the property. Some weren't that well written."

"You know," I commented with admiration, "I expect you will do well in this business."

"I hope so. Tell me, did you inspect the Campbells' land? What did you think? Is it all hills and valleys?"

"Actually, it's much nicer than we thought." I described what I had observed and finished up by saying, "I noted a couple dozen potential building sites. The buyer would have his pick."

"I gather that means you'd be against marketing it as an agricultural property?"

"That plot of ground is far too pretty to turn into a farm. By the way, I bumped into Ian Campbell. He confirmed he wants to sell."

"Did you secure the listing?"

"Not yet. I have to do a comp analysis and a marketing survey, but I'm fairly confident he'll hire us."

Jack seemed troubled. "We could use a major listing."

I could almost hear his thoughts. As my employee, Jack's wages were based upon two factors: a minimum wage salary plus a prorated bonus as determined by the properties he helped sell. Including the Greeleys, we had closed on precisely two listings in the last thirty days, far below our normal average. Jack's paycheck could be somewhat skimpy when closures were few and far between. Mine as well.

I nodded in agreement. "Any activity while I was out of the office?"

"A young couple stopped by. They're shopping for an agent. I have a good feeling. I think they'll be back."

"You know, the weeks after a heavy winter are always slow. Sellers are itching to sell, but buyers want to wait until they know winter is truly gone. Things will pick up. You'll see."

"Let's hope so."

In my ten years as a real estate broker, I had endured one major and several minor economic downturns. Recent forecasts were predicting another drop. Worse, there was no way of knowing how deep the next recession might be. Even so, I gave Jack an encouraging grin.

"Every roller coaster has its ups and downs. The trick is to hang on and enjoy the ride."

"I'm with you as long as I can pay the rent and put food on the table."

"I appreciate that."

Jack nodded in acknowledgment.

"Time for me to get to work." I turned and headed for my office.

A stack of folders, reports, and the usual correspondence filled my inbox. I groaned as I shed my coat and rolled up my sleeves.

Two hours later, I'd had my fill of reviewing zoning maps, inspection reports, and mortgage contracts. It was time to go home.

* * *

Five days after touring the Campbells' land, I arose early, jarred awake by my bedside alarm. Piecing together a listing for the two-hundred-acre property had become a significant challenge. Only a handful of comparable sales were available for review, and what little marketing data I could find was geared more toward agricultural properties.

The previous evening, I had lingered at the office, polishing the sales pitch I would deliver to the Campbells. By the time I'd finally made it home, my daughter, Alicia, was already asleep. That was why I had set my alarm: to ensure I would have enough time to visit her in the morning before packing her off to school. Because of my repeated absences, I worried that she might begin to wonder if I still loved her.

However, there was one unexpected consequence of my daughter having already been put to bed. My wife and I had enjoyed an interlude of sexual intimacy. In recent years, such occasions had become less frequent.

After hustling through my morning routine, I climbed the stairs to my daughter's bedroom to help her prepare for school.

When I knocked on Alicia's door, I found she was already dressed. She had chosen to wear a dark blue leotard under a pink dress with white polka dots. She had then added a multicolored scarf with a checkered pattern for effect. As a final touch, she had laced up a pair of neon blue ankle-top tennis shoes. Surprisingly, the outfit seemed to blend well, at least in my opinion.

I reached for a hairbrush lying on her mirrored vanity. "Hold still," I insisted as I drew the brush through my daughter's long honey-blonde hair. "Only a couple more strokes."

"Mommy doesn't pull as hard as you do," Alicia declared accusingly.

"Sorry…must be out of practice. There. All finished. You look great."

Her scowl turned into a grin.

"How are you doing these days, sweetheart?" I returned the hairbrush to its place on her vanity.

"Good." Alicia gathered up her overstuffed backpack. Who could know what all it carried?

"Any problems at school?"

"None that matter."

"Any of the other kids messing with you?"

"They know better than to mess with me," my daughter declared defiantly.

I chuckled. "I wouldn't doubt that a bit."

Alicia coughed as she swung the backpack onto her shoulder. She then coughed again.

"What was that?" I said. "Are you coming down with a cold?"

"I don't think so."

"Do you cough a lot?"

"No. It was just a tickle in my throat."

"Do you get short of breath, perhaps when you play at school?"

"No."

"Do you have a fever?"

Alicia shrugged.

Gently, I touched the back of my hand to her forehead. She didn't feel overly warm. "I think you're okay. Let me know if the coughing continues. All right?"

"Okay."

"Now, what do you want for breakfast?"

"Pancakes!" my daughter exclaimed with glee. "And bacon."

"Pancakes with bacon coming up." Together, we headed downstairs.

Alicia sat at the kitchen table, drawing with crayons while I fixed our morning meal. Some of her pictures were pretty good; the best ones we posted on the refrigerator with magnets. I assumed Rachel would join us, so I mixed enough batter to feed us all.

When the strips of bacon were crispy enough, I laid them out on a folded paper towel to drain. Next, I began ladling pancake batter onto the griddle. As the pancakes browned, I faced my daughter.

"So, pretty girl, what would you like to do this coming weekend? Want to go fishing?"

From the doorway, Rachel announced, "She can't…not this Saturday anyway. Our daughter has a birthday party to attend. Betty Kenyon, Tina's mom, is having a dozen kids over for cake and ice cream. It should be fun. Right, sweetie?" My wife crossed the room to kiss Alicia's forehead and then turned to join me at the stove.

Alicia glanced up from her drawing. "Tina's going to be ten. Mrs. Kenyon promised we'd have a treasure hunt."

"That does sound fun." I reached out to hug my wife. Rachel responded with more enthusiasm than usual. Then I noted the sultry, half-lidded smile on her face. I said teasingly, "It would appear someone got a good night's sleep."

Rachel playfully poked me in the ribs with her elbow. "And I suppose you plan on taking credit?"

"Well…yeah, now that you mention it. By the way, I called the plumber. A new water heater with an eighty-gallon tank will cost around $900. I thought you should know."

Rachel's mood changed instantly, causing me to regret mentioning the needed repair.

"We'll be all right," I said. "I have a good feeling about the Campbell listing. It's a great property. The right sale should bring in a hefty commission."

Alicia looked up from her drawing. "Mommy says you're a good real estate agent."

"Is that right? Is that what she says?" I rewarded my wife with an appreciative smile.

After breakfast, I accompanied Alicia to her bus stop. As the school bus glided to the curb, I asked, "Are you all set for today, sweetheart? You got everything you need?"

"I think so," Alicia replied in her most grown-up manner.

The brightness of her countenance lifted my heart. Sometimes being a dad was pure joy, if you could keep your mind off the economics of supporting a family.

When I returned to the kitchen, Rachel sat at the table, going through the stack of mail I had brought the previous evening. Upon returning home, I hadn't even bothered to sort it. One item attracted her notice—a business-sized manila envelope. She slit the flap open with a paring knife and pulled out a formal-looking document. I could tell from across the room that it was Alicia's genetic report, the one we had been expecting.

My wife hurriedly scanned the document and then looked up. Tears began forming in her eyes. "It's positive," she declared with a sob. "Our daughter has the mutation. She's inherited the mutant gene from both of us."

Chapter 3

The day after learning of Alicia's genetic malady, we went to consult with Dr. Angus McGregor, who had been our family physician for years. He practiced medicine out of a modern-style building just off the main thoroughfare not far from my office. Most days, his waiting room was crammed with patients needing to be seen. For that reason, Rachel and I were astonished when, after entering through the main door, we found the waiting room virtually deserted except for a well-dressed middle-aged gentleman seated in a corner, reading a newspaper.

I approached the sliding window and greeted the receptionist, whom I knew only by her first name. "Hi, Maggie. Any chance we might speak with the doctor for a few minutes?"

Maggie looked up with a friendly smile. "You're in luck. He's all caught up. We've had a cancellation and a no-show. He should be able to see you soon."

I cast a glance toward the gentleman in the corner.

"Oh," Maggie said, taking note of my inquisitive look. "He's waiting for his wife. The doctor is with her now. They should be done in a few minutes. Can I tell the doctor what this is about?"

"It's a family matter," I responded to Maggie's arched eyebrow. It concerns our daughter. We have some questions about her health. I'd like to see what Angus thinks."

"We can make an appointment for her if you'd like to bring her in."

"Let's wait and see what the doctor recommends."

"Not a problem. Would you like to have a seat?"

We were about to sit down when a frail-looking woman entered the waiting room through an internal door. A sling supported her splinted arm. The gentleman in the corner rose to greet her. They left the office together.

"Looks like you're up," Maggie called across the waiting room. "Come on back."

Angus himself greeted us as we stepped through the door the woman had just exited. He wore a waist-length white coat with a stethoscope in a side pocket. His tie hung loosely knotted around his neck. He said pleasantly, "Hello, Rachel. Good to see you."

"You too, Dr. McGregor. It's been a while."

I detected a quaver in my wife's voice.

"Paul, how have you been?" The doctor stuck out his hand.

I returned his handshake. "Well, a little stressed at work, but that's about to change."

"Good, good." The doctor indicated that we should follow him down the corridor. "Let's head to my office. It's more comfortable than an exam room. So, what's going on?"

Rachel answered first. "It's our daughter we're concerned about. By the way, thank you for seeing us without an appointment."

"My pleasure. Some days, it's a feast; some days, a famine. I can never predict how busy I'll be. The first couple of years, I tended to fret. Now, the slow times don't bother me. It all balances out."

When we reached Angus's private consultation room toward the rear of the building, he motioned to the chairs that faced his desk. His office setup was similar to my own.

"So you think your daughter has a health issue? Tell me what's going on." He sank into the executive high-back chair behind his desk and leaned back.

Rachel fished in her purse and pulled out the genetic reports. Her hand trembled as she handed them to the doctor. "We've had ours for a couple of weeks. Alicia's came in the mail yesterday. As you can see, they indicate that our daughter might have a genetic abnormality. We think it could be serious. That's why we wanted your advice."

Dr. McGregor accepted the reports and studied them carefully. He then looked up. "This mutation is in the same chromosome that carries the HMBS gene. As I recall, abnormalities in that gene cause acute intermittent porphyria, but forgive me, porphyria has nothing to do with this locus."

"What?" I said.

"Sorry…just remembering stuff from medical school." The doctor studied the reports again. "I'm afraid I'm not as current on rare genetic diseases as I might be. Allow me to do a little research." He turned to the computer terminal on his desk. I watched as he accessed what I assumed was a medical reference site. The information displayed changed several times as he navigated the database.

"Ah, yes. Here it is," he declared at last. The room was quiet as he studied lines of text that scrolled by on the screen. The silence seemed to drag on forever.

I was about to ask what he had learned when he looked at us. "Has your daughter been ill recently? Has she begun displaying any worrisome any unusual symptoms?"

"Such as?" Rachel said with alarm.

"Anything out of the ordinary."

"Not really," I said. A cloak of trepidation fell upon me. "She had a dry cough this morning but claimed it was a tickle in her throat. Otherwise, she seems perfectly healthy."

The doctor's demeanor became even more somber. Creases of concern lined his forehead. "Perhaps you should bring her in and let me look her over."

"What's going on?" Rachel exclaimed. "What were you reading?"

Dr. McGregor held up our genetic profiles. "If these are correct—and I'm not saying we should accept them at face value—your daughter has Lascaux Syndrome, a rare condition that involves the immune system. It tends to become manifest around the age of puberty, and it can impact the heart."

I leaned forward to peer intently at the doctor. "Lascaux Syndrome?"

"Yes. Like the Lascaux cave in France. Apparently, the syndrome was first recognized in the daughter of one of the cave's more prominent explorers. Initially, she was thought to have contracted an illness while accompanying her father underground. Later, her symptoms were proven to be the result of a genetic mutation. To develop the syndrome, a patient must be homozygous—that means they have inherited the same mutation from both parents, as would appear to be the case here. Sometime before puberty, the child's immune system gets switched on and begins to attack the heart. This can cause weakness of the heart muscle, which progressively leads to cardiac failure. Symptoms include fatigue, lethargy, dizziness upon standing, fainting, fluid retention, shortness of breath, coma, and ultimately death."

Rachel drew in a sharp breath.

I reached out to comfort her by laying my hand on her arm. "How long do we have?" I said, doing my best to hide my own distress.

Dr. McGregor reached into the top drawer of his desk and extracted a box of tissues. He passed them across the desk to my wife. "I hate being so blunt, but I think patients should hear the truth. Alicia is how old now?"

"She's nine," I replied.

"Girls usually undergo menarche between the ages of ten and fifteen. The average is around twelve. However, I wouldn't place too much stock in those numbers. The syndrome can begin at any age.

There is no way to predict." Dr. McGregor leaned forward to brace his forearms against the edge of his desk. "I know this information comes as a terrible shock. I should point out that this genetic analysis hasn't been verified. Before we accept it as gospel, we should consider having Alicia formally tested in a certified lab."

"Yes. That's what we should do," Rachel declared flatly as she fought to pull herself together. "It could be a mistake. The report could be wrong."

Dr. McGregor pursed his lips. "I should warn you—though I doubt this will be a consideration—genetic testing can be expensive."

"How much?" I blurted out without thinking. Rachel launched a scowl in my direction. "I just need to know what to expect," I protested in self-defense.

Dr. McGregor shook his head. "I'm not sure what the lab charges. I'll have my nurse inquire and get back to you."

"I don't care what it costs," Rachel stated firmly. "That's what we'll do."

I nodded in agreement, and the doctor began scribbling something on a prescription pad. He tore off the top sheet and handed it to me. "Take Alicia to the lab at Drummond Memorial. Give this to the lab tech, and she'll draw her blood. It will take about a week for the results to come back. I'll give you a shout as soon as they're in. In the meantime, try not to worry, though I know it won't be easy. Also, let me know if Alicia begins showing any symptoms whatsoever."

"What about therapy?" I asked worriedly. "There must be some form of treatment."

Dr. McGregor rocked back in his chair. "This is a genetic illness we're discussing. Typically, they're not amenable to conventional therapy."

"There must be something we can do," I insisted.

"Let me do some more research and see what's available. I'll check for what's current in the literature. Perhaps something new has come along. Hopefully, I'll have something to report by the time the formal results come back." He rose to his feet. "I know this will be hard to handle, but believe me, we will do all we can to keep Alicia healthy for as long as possible. Like I said, there's no telling when she might begin showing symptoms. It could be years from now. For the time being, let's wait and watch. I'm sure this feels entirely unsatisfactory, but at this point, there's nothing more to be done."

Rachel and I rose to our feet as well. We were both in a state of shock as we thanked the doctor for seeing us. Numbly, we left his office.

After leaving Dr. McGregor's clinic, we drove straight home. En route, we hardly spoke. Rachel was too distraught to return to work. Instead, she called in to request the afternoon off without mentioning why. Cindy Charlton, Rachel's coworker at the library, graciously agreed to cover for her.

Mostly out of habit, we migrated to the family room. Neither of us touched our coffee, though I had brewed a fresh pot. For a time, we sat quietly, dealing separately with our agonies.

Then Rachel blurted out, her voice laden with anguish, "It's not fair. It feels like she's been handed a death sentence."

"That is not going to happen," I replied. "We'll find some way to fight this."

"How?" Rachel exclaimed. "This isn't a run-of-the-mill infection. We can't just give her a pill and make her all better. Her DNA is corrupted. It's what she's made of. It's who she is."

"I realize that, but medically speaking, they're doing amazing things these days. There have been major advances in fighting cancer and treating heart disease in the last couple of years. Surely, someone must know how we can help our daughter. Genomics has become a medical specialty unto itself."

"That reminds me…" Rachel looked across the room from her recliner to where I was seated on the couch. "Do you think McGregor knows what he's doing? He's a good family doctor, but I can't help feeling that Alicia's problem might be out of his league. I guess I'm saying, shouldn't we seek a specialist?"

"I've had the same thought, and knowing Angus, I doubt he would mind. I'm sure he'd even recommend somebody if we were to ask, which would be the right thing to do. Having his blessing would be better than going behind his back." I sipped my coffee. It had grown cold. I set the mug aside. "Anyway, let's wait to see what the formal testing shows. Then we can ask him."

Rachel rested her hands in her lap. "Will you take Alicia to the lab tomorrow, or should I?"

"I will. I'm meeting with Ian Campbell tomorrow afternoon, but my morning is free."

Rachel squeezed her eyes shut. A shadow of grief crossed her face.

"Are you okay?" I said with concern.

"I was imagining what lies ahead. Every time she sneezes, every time she feels tired, I'm going to worry that her immune system is damaging her heart. Not knowing is going to be terrible. More than that, I'm not sure I can handle the guilt. We didn't intend to, but we gave her this condition. You're going to protest that it's not our fault, and morally, you're right. That doesn't change the fact that she's going to get sick and die because of us, because of the mutant genes we passed along. We are responsible."

I said softly, "We also gave her life for as long as she gets to live it. Until now, her life has been wonderful—for her and us as well. Our challenge at this point is to ensure she lives for as long as possible. Do you want to know what troubles me? And I don't mean to be crass by saying this. I can't help worrying how expensive her care will be."

Rachel gasped as if offended by my callousness. "How can you even begin to reckon our daughter's illness in terms of money?"

"You misunderstand. I will spend every penny we have to keep our daughter alive. What troubles me is that we won't have enough to provide for her care. Something tells me we will need to spend much more than what we've put aside. If I'm right, it will fall to me to make a ton of money in a very short time."

"And how do you plan on doing that?"

"I don't have a clue yet."

"What about the Campbell property? You said it could bring in a hefty commission."

"Yes, if I get the listing and can find a buyer. Even then, it won't be nearly enough—not after paying overhead and expenses, especially if I'm required to split the commission with another broker. No, I'm going to need more, something…bigger." I struggled to envision what that might be.

"Should we tell her?" Rachel said softly.

"Tell who?"

"Alicia. Should we tell her she has Lascaux Syndrome?"

"Do we know of anything at this point that will improve her chances of survival?"

"No," Rachel admitted with apparent sorrow. "Not as things stand."

"Then what's to be gained?"

"You're right. Telling her would only distress her. It's hard deciding the right thing to do."

"I doubt it will get much easier. This won't be the last decision we'll have to make."

"I wish there was someone we could talk to, someone with a clear understanding of what we're up against."

"Who did you have in mind? God?"

"Well…yes. Now that you mention it."

I held a hand up, palm out. "Don't look at me. I'm not qualified. I'm not a spiritual person."

"Perhaps that should change."

"Really? How?"

"I don't know. Why don't you consult with Franklin and see what he recommends? Besides, he'll need to know about his niece's condition sooner or later."

"I suppose you're right. First thing, however, it's vital that I meet with Ian Campbell and secure that listing."

Rachel stood and looked to where I sat. "I'm tired. It's been a horrific morning. I'm going to lie down for a while." She turned and left the room, leaving me to ponder the days, weeks, months, and hopefully years that lay ahead.

*   *   *

I trailed behind Ian Campbell as we tramped through the woods. We had agreed to meet on the property because I wanted to draw upon his familiarity with the land. Sellers often acutely appreciate the parcel they bring to market. Their insights and anecdotes can frequently be used as practical sales tools. Besides, only a foolish broker would ignore a seller's expectations when structuring a real estate transaction.

"Over there is where we thought we'd build our house." Ian pointed to a gentle rise. We were in the southeast quadrant of the property. "As the years went by, we never seemed to get around to it." I detected a hint of melancholy in his voice.

We trekked up a gentle incline to the top of the rise. The view was impressive. We could see the Byrne River and most of Lake McDougall farther in the distance. "This would make a tremendous building site," I confirmed. I had noted more than a few such locations, several dozen at least.

As if reading my mind, Ian confided, "It was hard to decide. There are many to choose from, but Eva likes this location best. I think it's because of the sycamores and that stand of red oak over there. Those trees are especially colorful in the fall."

"That's something I wanted to ask about. The forest seems to be in excellent condition. Have you done much to maintain it?"

Ian shrugged. "We thinned out some dead wood a few years back. Before that, we had to take down a bunch of elms. They up and died because of Dutch elm disease. It hit us pretty hard in the late '70s. Otherwise, we've left it alone, allowed it to become the forest it was meant to be."

We turned to our left and headed north, keeping the property's eastern boundary in view. Again, I was impressed by the land's potential. "What about the water table? Would you happen to know the depths of your neighbors' wells?"

"As best I can recall, they are mostly between seventy and a hundred feet. I've been told a giant aquifer spans this entire section. It's good water, too, clear and unpolluted."

"Why is it you never drilled for water?"

"We always expected that we'd put in a well when we got ready to build. But like I said, we never seemed to get around to it."

As we walked along, I looked around again but found no sign of the wolf. I asked Ian, "Is there much wildlife on the property?"

"Deer mostly and small animals, squirrels, skunks…an occasional raccoon."

"No predators?"

"Like what?"

"Wolves?"

Ian chuckled. "Shucks no. No wolves around here."

When we neared the northern boundary, Ian turned west and said, "Down this way, there's something I need to show you." A hundred yards farther on, he paused to look around as if gathering his bearings. "Yes, here we are. You see that tree?" He pointed to an American mountain ash. It was a fine-looking, mature specimen.

"I see it."

"That marks my forty-foot easement. Way back years ago, shortly after I bought this property, Walter Drake—he's my neighbor to the north—helped me cut in Argyle Road. We did the surveying ourselves. We thought we laid it out so the road would run between our properties, but we screwed up. Later on, we found out that we had sliced off about thirty feet of Walter's land. Rather than leave me high and dry without a secondary access to Argyle Road, Walter granted me an easement across the sliver. I already had a right-of-way to Argyle Road along the eastern edge of my property, but it's always good to have a back door, so to speak. Like with the well, I intended to clear-cut the easement when it came time to live on the land. Anyway, I was thinking you should know it's there."

"I appreciate your telling me." From a sales standpoint, having two accesses was a plus. "By the way, did you ever consider developing this parcel yourself?"

"Develop? How?"

"Subdivide it, create a multifamily community."

Ian scowled. "I don't know nothing about such things."

His response told me that this was a touchy subject, which worried me. It was increasingly looking as if the most likely buyer would want to subdivide the land. There was too much acreage for a single landholder. The parcel could be turned into a huge estate, but finding the right buyer for such a transaction would be a horrific undertaking, especially in a semirural community like Trinity Falls Township. Given Ian's reaction, I decided to put aside our discussion of subdivisions.

"So," I said instead, "the last time we met, you mentioned you have family in Florida. Is that right?"

"It is. We have a son, his wife, and two grandchildren. The boy is eleven. The girl's seven. Do you have kids?"

"A daughter. She's nine."

"Then you can feature what it's like not having them around. We miss them something fierce."

"Yes, I can imagine that." My voice cracked with emotion. Ian looked at me but didn't comment. I cleared my throat and again changed the subject. "Well, sir, I think we have a pretty good handle on what this parcel is all about. So what do you think? Are you of a mind to let me sell it for you?"

"I am. You seem like a decent fellow, and I trust you will do right by me."

"I will certainly do my best, and I appreciate your confidence." The elation I should have felt was blunted by lingering images of losing my daughter. I took a deep breath to settle my internal turmoil and then reached out to finalize the deal with a handshake. "All we need now is your signature on a sales agreement. The paperwork is in my car."

"Let's get her done." Ian set off to head back through the forest.

I called out after him, "If you don't mind, could we cut across your easement and follow Argyle Road back to where we parked? I'd like to see the property from that perspective."

"Not a problem."

Again, Ian led the way. Twenty minutes later, I was on my way back to the office with the signed documents. Despite my good fortune, I was in a bitter mood.

*   *   *

Twenty-four hours after securing the Campbells' listing, I pulled into the parking lot of the Maranatha Gospel Fellowship. My brother was out front, cutting the grass. His faded jeans and New York Jets T-shirt seemed a far cry from the dress shirt, slacks, and sportscoat he customarily wore on Sundays. He smiled and waved as I set the emergency brake and shut off the Jeep's engine.

I called ahead, above the roar of the lawn mower, "I thought the church had volunteers to do this sort of work?"

Franklin shrugged and cupped a hand behind his ear. He then bent down to switch off the motor.

I said, "Don't you have a guy who takes care of the lawn and does the gardening?"

"He's been sick for a week." Franklin mopped his brow with the hem of his T-shirt. "The grass was getting a mite thick. The grounds need to look nice for the ladies' auxiliary meeting tomorrow. So, to what do I owe the honor this time?"

"I need to tell you something, and I could use your advice again."

Franklin eyed the uncut portion of the lawn.

I volunteered, "I'll finish what's left while you wash up."

Franklin motioned toward the lawn mower. "She's all yours. I'll go make myself presentable."

When he returned, I was completing the last section of the lawn.

I finished not far from the church's front entrance and killed the engine.

Franklin nodded in appreciation. "Thank you for that."

"Not a problem. It feels good to do a little lawn care. I haven't been gardening much recently." I noted that my brother had put on a clean shirt, changed his shoes, and washed his face and hands. "You shine up pretty good."

"Now I feel more like a pastor. So where do you want to go to have our conversation?" Franklin gripped the lawn mower's handle and began pushing it toward the storage shed at the rear of the building. I tagged along.

"I don't know. Someplace where we don't have to be around a bunch of people."

"I gather this is serious?"

"It is."

"Then let's talk in the sanctuary. Nobody's around. We'll have the entire church to ourselves."

Franklin stowed the lawn mower in the shed and led the way inside. When we passed through the narthex, the building was silent, and the air was still. In the nave, light was streaming through the stained-glass windows, laying down colored patterns on the hardwood flooring. The ambiance sparked a strange sense of serenity that I wasn't expecting. We continued down the central aisle to sit in the second pew from the altar.

Seated an arm's length apart on the padded bench, we angled our bodies toward one another. Rather than immediately beginning to ask questions, Franklin waited, indicating that he had taken note of my somber mood.

After collecting my thoughts, I said quietly, "It's about your niece. Yesterday, we learned that Alicia has a genetic abnormality. She's homozygous for a mutant gene. Homozygous means you inherit the same gene from both parents—"

Franklin smiled. "I know what homozygous means."

"I had to look it up. Anyway, she's been tentatively diagnosed with Lascaux Syndrome, a rare genetic disorder that, at some point in the near future, will trigger her immune system to attack her heart. We're running tests to confirm the diagnosis, but I expect they will prove what we already know."

Franklin's eyes narrowed. "This syndrome, how serious is it?"

"Dr. McGregor indicated that it's routinely fatal. There is no known treatment or cure."

Franklin sat quietly for an extended period. "How long does she have?"

"For now, her immune system is functioning as it should, but sometime before the onset of puberty, her first symptoms will appear. After that, she'll have a steady downhill course, which can take weeks or months. Rarely years."

"How is Rachel coping?"

"About like you'd expect. We were both stunned by the news."

"I imagine it must have come as a tremendous shock. You say there's no treatment or cure?"

"Not for Lascaux Syndrome, at least none we know of. I've been reading about other therapies. There have been some encouraging results in treating patients with genetic mutations."

Franklin tilted his head back and closed his eyes. When he opened them, he said, "Does she know?"

"Alicia? No. We haven't told her."

"When do you intend to tell her? You're going to have to at some point, you know."

"We haven't decided. Hopefully, we can wait till she begins showing symptoms. That's one of the things I wanted to talk to you about. It's hard to discern the right thing to do. I could use a little wisdom if you have any to spare."

"Ah, yes. Wisdom. Spiritual guidance. Well, you've come to the right place, literally. Scriptures teach that the fear of God is the beginning of wisdom."

"So I've heard, though I'm not exactly sure what that means or how it relates to my daughter."

"What it doesn't mean is that we should be afraid of God, at least not those of us who are redeemed by the shed blood of Christ. Rather, it means we should honor God and give Him the reverence and respect that are His due. I believe the Scriptures are telling us if we put God first in our lives, everything else will fall into place."

The uncertainties that had been troubling me became more immediate. "Can a believer ask for wisdom and expect to receive it?"

"Absolutely."

"How can you be sure?"

"If God can send a wolf to lead you out of the forest, He can show you the right path to follow in your current situation."

"You're still convinced that what happened to me was God's doing?"

Franklin grinned. "Aren't you? What other explanation is there?"

I shrugged to indicate that I couldn't offer an alternative theory.

Franklin reached over to touch my shoulder. "You've always been the timid one, but you can trust your judgments, you know. You have a good head on your shoulders. You'll recognize the right way to go when the opportunity presents itself."

"Oh, how I wish that were true. I have so many uncertainties."

"Other than Alicia, what else is going on?"

"Well, take this real estate deal I've been working on, for instance. It has me troubled. I just signed a listing on a fantastic two-hundred-acre parcel of ground. It has great views and ideal terrain. I'll probably wind up selling it to some developer who will subdivide it and make a fortune. Instead, I've been thinking maybe I should subdivide it myself. The problem is, I'm afraid. The risks are enormous, and you know how I hate taking chances."

Franklin withdrew his hand and regarded me with great seriousness. "Let me ask you this: What would be your motive for subdividing the land?"

"To provide for Alicia's medical care. From what little I've read, treating genetic illnesses can be horrendously expensive. Our insurance doesn't cover experimental therapies."

"If you decide not to take a chance on this real estate venture, what would be the result?"

"We'd run out of money. Even if we sold everything we own, we still wouldn't have enough."

"And if you take a chance but fail, what happens then?"

"We'd be broke, and Alicia doesn't get her medical care."

"So if you do nothing or if you do something and fail, the outcome is the same: Alicia doesn't get treated. But if you try and you succeed, there's a possibility, no matter how remote, that she could be cured. It doesn't seem like a difficult choice."

"Since you put it that way…" I turned my face toward the altar. The light reflecting off the gold cross had a mesmerizing effect. Long-buried memories suddenly came rushing to the surface. One dreadful event stood out from the rest.

Looking at Franklin, I said, "Do you know why I'm so afraid of taking risks? I've never told you, have I? It's because of what happened to Thomas." Thomas was our younger brother. He had died at age thirteen when he fell into the Byrne River and was swept over Trinity Falls. "I was there that day, you know, the day he drowned. I watched him disappear into the raging torrent."

"I knew that. That's what you told our parents."

Yes, I thought. *That's true. I told them how he drowned, but I never revealed why.* With all my heart, I yearned to speak up, to finally explain what had happened, but I couldn't. The memories were too painful. Unbidden tears began to flow.

My brother slid closer and wrapped me in a supportive embrace. "I don't blame you, and you shouldn't blame yourself. I know Mom and Pop would feel the same if they were alive. You can let go of the guilt. This burden is not yours to bear." Franklin continued to hold me as waves of agony washed over my soul.

After a time, I realized I wasn't crying just for my departed brother only but also for my daughter and the suffering that was to be her future.

*   *   *

Eight days after visiting with Franklin, I found myself lingering on the sidewalk in front of the Byrne River Bank, staring at the polished brass nameplate bolted to the bank's brick façade. To say I was nervous would have been a massive understatement. My knees were shaking. My stomach was tied in knots. For the past week, I had spent nearly every waking moment stewing over the Campbell property.

My original plan was to broker a quick sale, take my commission, and be done with the deal. However, after speaking with Franklin, it had become increasingly apparent that my only logical course of action was to subdivide the property myself, despite the risks. Having never subdivided a property before, I was horrified when I considered the number of things that could go wrong.

My first task, I had decided, should be to convince a small group of wealthy investors to form a limited partnership to purchase the Campbells' land. Then, with me serving as a managing partner, it would be my responsibility to subdivide the property, oversee the preparation of the land, and build homes on individual lots. Spearheading such a partnership would demand considerable time and effort. Not only that, but it would require a level of expertise I wasn't sure I possessed. I knew a lot about buying and selling real estate, but creating a small community out of nothing was entirely different. For someone who was pathologically risk averse, the prospects were terrifying.

From a financial perspective, however, the deal made perfect sense. Properly managed, the partnership should be highly profitable for everyone involved. Besides, I knew for sure that this would be my only opportunity. As hard as I tried, I could not conceive of any other way to raise the cash to provide for my daughter's medical care. My calculations indicated that from start to finish, it would take a year to build out the subdivision. In that same time frame, if I were to broker houses one at a time, I could never accumulate the funds needed to maximize Alicia's chances of survival.

In the final analysis, one of my brother's comments had awakened within me the will to proceed. His reference to the wolf and my recollection of how the beast had led me to safety moved me deeply. Picturing my time in the woods, I remembered the fear that had consumed me. Yet, despite being afraid, I ignored my own impulses and followed the wolf. Now, for this project to succeed, I would again need to rely upon divine providence. This represented a tremendous leap of faith, reaching a level of trust far beyond any I had previously attained.

After ardently praying for wisdom, I had finally resolved to move forward. Forty-eight hours earlier, I had begun my campaign to form a limited partnership by contacting Winston Fordyce III, one of the wealthiest men in Trinity Falls Township. Winston had served as the Byrne River Bank president for seventeen years, ever since the bank's inception. After shoring up my courage, I had approached him with an outline of my idea. Intrigued, he had agreed to contact three of his wealthiest friends to see if they would be willing to listen to my presentation.

This small group of potential investors was assembled and awaiting my arrival in the bank's conference room.

Chapter 4

For seven years, Janet Dungee had held sway as Winston Fordyce III's executive secretary. A demure middle-aged woman with a polite but professional manner, she had screened his calls, greeted visitors, and organized his days to ensure that everything ran smoothly. What I liked most about Janet was that she could be tough when the situation demanded. I had once watched her tell a persistent huckster to get lost in no uncertain terms. The man had doggedly insisted that the bank had a moral duty to sponsor his destruction derby entry at the Ridge County Fair. She forthrightly showed him the door when he refused to take no for an answer.

Doing my best to remain calm, I trailed Janet down the corridor toward the conference room and thanked her politely when she announced my arrival. Four unsmiling faces greeted me. The metaphor of Daniel entering the lion's den came to mind.

Like a king holding court, Winston presided from the head of the table. He had the air of a man willing to argue even the most trivial point to assert his dominance. The way he carried himself—back straight, chin thrust forward—gave testimony to his ego. My broker instincts told me I should tread softly where Winston was concerned.

Two of the other three men present were also known to me.

Marcus James Durham, editor of the *Byrne River Times*, our local newspaper, was a surprisingly good journalist with a well-earned reputation. He had a keen nose for news and could sniff out chicanery where less discerning journalists could not. He would be all over me if I displayed a hint of subterfuge.

Seeing that Dr. Angus McGregor, our family physician, had also been invited was a welcome surprise. His intellect was razor-sharp; as a matter of principle, he weighed his facts carefully before rendering an opinion. It seemed likely that, in a pinch, he would make a valuable ally, so I was glad to see him. On the other hand, I would have to trust that his medical ethics would prevent him from discussing Alicia's condition. Explaining her genetic mutation to the other men present would do nothing to promote the business. More than that, Rachel and I had decided that we would keep our daughter's medical issues private for the time being.

The fourth man, I did not know. Older than his companions, he seemed somewhat detached. Perhaps he had already concluded that he was wasting his time.

Remaining seated, Winston announced, "Good. Our guest of honor has arrived. Paul, I believe you know Marcus and Angus?"

"Indeed I do. Marcus, it's good to see you. I've been following your editorials regarding the upcoming mayoral race with interest. You're right that Charlie Quinn is fighting an uphill battle."

Marcus nodded. "He certainly is, and the slope gets steeper every day."

"So it does. And Angus, how are you? Caught any big ones lately? I read that a lucky angler pulled a twenty-pound brook trout out of Copper Lake. I'll bet that was a tussle." I had intentionally avoided referencing anything having to do with medicine. Hopefully, Angus would take the hint.

"Sadly," Angus confessed, "I haven't had the opportunity. Perhaps come summer."

"When you do get some time off, give me a shout. I'd love to go fishing with you." Silently, I breathed a sigh of relief. For the time being, it seemed my daughter's secret was safe.

Winston cleared his throat. "Paul, I don't believe you've met the Honorable Reginald Tolliver, one of our town court justices."

"Judge…a pleasure." Shifting the briefcase I carried to my left hand, I reached across the brightly polished conference table to offer a greeting. With Winston enthroned at the head of the table, Angus sat to his right, nearest to where I stood. Marcus sat to Winston's left, across from Angus. Reginald sat across from me, next to Marcus.

"Call me Reggie," the judge said. "We're not in court. No need for formalities." His hand felt bony, and his skin was cool, but his grip was firm. "Winston told us you have an interesting proposal to share."

"I do." I undid the clasp on my briefcase and extracted five presentation packets. I had spent a considerable sum having them printed on the highest-quality glossy paper with four-color illustrations. I handed one packet to each potential investor, keeping one for myself.

"Gentlemen," I said, pausing to steady my nerves, "allow me to introduce you to the Spirit Wolf Estates."

"Catchy moniker," Angus commented. "Where'd you come up with that one?"

Despite myself, I smiled. "It just came to me. I trust Winston has already informed you that I recently negotiated a listing agreement with Ian Campbell. He has authorized me to sell his two-hundred-acre parcel of prime real estate. I'm proposing that we form a limited partnership to buy Ian's property and subdivide it into fifty individual lots, each approximately four acres in size. On each lot, we will build an upscale single-family home. These estates will be sold incrementally, meaning the last ones sold will be the most expensive. After all fifty have been sold, we will dissolve the partnership and distribute the profits."

Marcus leaned forward. "Did I understand Winston correctly? You're asking each of us to invest $750,000?"

"That is correct," I confirmed with a nod. "That's why I suggested Winston invite only people he believed could afford to participate."

There was a general stirring around the table.

"How much will you be contributing?" Judge Tolliver said, cutting straight to the issue I most dreaded discussing.

I held up my copy of the proposal. "As indicated here, I will not make a direct monetary investment. However, I will provide my services as a managing partner for free. Also, I will not share in the profits that flow from the sale of the estates. The only monies I expect to earn will be my standard commissions, payable when the partnership acquires the raw land and when each home is sold."

"At what rates?" Marcus said skeptically.

"Six percent on raw land and four percent on developed properties. I think you'll find that these rates are in keeping with industry norms. Bear in mind that at the end of eighteen months, you can legitimately expect to have doubled your initial investment. That's an annualized return of approximately forty-seven percent per annum."

I paused for a moment and allowed that number to sink in. I said, "Perhaps we should start at the beginning and work our way through the proposal. Hopefully, that way, many of your questions will be answered."

For the next ninety minutes, we discussed finances and strategies. I explained that the project would be completed in three phases: Phase 1 would involve forming a limited partnership and acquiring the Campbells' property, Phase 2 would involve subdividing and improving the raw land, and Phase 3 would involve building homes and selling individual estates.

I detailed how the limited partners' combined investment of $3 million would take us to the end of Phase 2 and how, upon entering Phase 3, we would apply for a short-term construction loan to begin building houses. Thankfully, Winston indicated that he could foresee no reason why such a loan should be denied, assuming the two hundred acres of subdivided and improved property would be offered as collateral.

Next, we reviewed risks, both tangible and theoretical. We explored a variety of potential hazards, such as market fluctuations, legal hassles, construction accidents, natural catastrophes, forest fires, etc. One man even worried about unearthing an ancient Indian burial site on the property.

When we ended our discussion, I could tell that Angus and Marcus were enthusiastic. Winston seemed less so, but his attitude was generally positive. The judge, however, was impossible to read.

Winston had come to the same conclusion. He looked at me and said, "It would seem we need more time to consider your proposal. Today is Friday. What say we meet again on Monday? Would that suit you?"

"Absolutely. Take as much time as you need. Let me remind you, however, that the Campbell property is an active listing. If an offer comes in, I will be honor-bound to present it, and I can't guarantee how Ian will respond."

"We understand." Winston looked around. "Gentlemen, anything more?"

"I have one question," Judge Tolliver announced.

"Sure," I replied. "What's on your mind?"

The judge turned to a page near the middle of the proposal. "Here, you indicate that at the inception of Phase 2, before the land is subdivided, the partnership will apply to the town council to have the property annexed to Trinity Falls Township. Why?"

"Ah, yes. Three reasons. First and foremost, annexation will expedite the approval process for our subdivision plat because we will deal with the city council rather than the county commissioners. Second, after annexation, the property will be eligible for city services, including police and fire protection. Third, the city will do a far better job of keeping the roads plowed in winter, which I'm sure will be appreciated by our future residents."

Judge Tolliver nodded. "I see. Thank you." The look on his face remained enigmatic. I reminded myself never to play cards with the man.

"Good." Winston stood up. "Thank you, Mr. Langdon. We'll see you again in three days." He leaned down to press a concealed button under the edge of the conference table. In short order, the door opened, and Janet entered.

"Ms. Dungee," Winston said. "Would you show Mr. Langdon out and bring us a fresh pot of coffee, please? We have a lot to discuss."

*   *   *

Later that night, my wife and I sat in our family room, Rachel in her recliner and me on the couch. Alicia had just been put to bed. My meeting with the Spirit Wolf investors was still foremost in my thoughts. My wife was wrestling with her own issues. I sensed she was eager to talk, though she had delayed voicing her concerns until our daughter was out of earshot.

Rachel switched off her tablet computer and looked at me. "How did your presentation go today?"

"I'm not sure. Angus and Marcus seemed to support the project. Winston was more reticent. Judge Tolliver is an enigma, impossible to read. Have you met the man? He's one of our town court justices."

Rachel shook her head. "I don't believe I have. I can't put a face to the name."

"He's a dour man, completely devoid of humor. He asked me to call him Reggie, but for the life of me, I can't. I mean, calling a sitting judge Reggie… It doesn't feel right."

Rachel tugged on her earlobe. I recognized the gesture. It was one of her tells, an indication that she was feeling insecure, which was confirmed when she said, "Are you sure we should go ahead with this project?"

"We don't have a choice."

"What do you mean we don't have a choice? Of course, we have a choice."

"No. We don't. Angus phoned while I was on my way home. Alicia's genetic test results are back. Her diagnosis has been confirmed. She definitely has Lascaux Syndrome."

Rachel recoiled. She seemed on the verge of tears. We had anticipated a positive result, yet we both had clung to the tenuous hope that our daughter's genetic tests would be declared normal.

To lessen the impact of the bad news, I suggested, "Look, I'm sure something favorable will turn up. Modern medicine has come a long way. New therapies are being introduced all the time, but to access those therapies, we will need lots of money. The Spirit Wolf project is our only hope of raising the funds we'll need. I have to make this endeavor work."

"Do the investors know why you're taking on this project?"

"No, and I'm not going to tell them. As far as they are concerned, my only motive is greed, and I'm certain that Angus will protect our privacy. I'm confident that he won't say a thing."

Rachel steepled her fingers. "I hate worrying about what's going to happen. What if this partnership thing doesn't pan out? Or what if our daughter gets sick before the money is available? Will I have to quit my job to care for her? And if she dies, what will we do then?"

I could not answer these questions and had a thousand more of my own. As I struggled to find some source of comfort to cling to, a necklace lying on the end table beside the couch caught my eye. It was my daughter's favorite amethyst pendant. Instantly, I was transported back in time. Two years earlier, for a brief span, Rachel and I had endured what many parents would consider the most horrific of all tragedies.

The episode had begun while I was working in the garden…

* * *

The loamy earth felt spongy as I sifted it between my fingers. The hole I had prepared for our new rosebush was precisely the correct size. A faint glint caught my eye as I reached for the plant I had purchased from the nursery that morning. I set the pot down and edged farther along the flower bed to investigate. A silver necklace lay partially covered by peat moss and soil. I recognized it; the amethyst pendant was my daughter's favorite piece of jewelry. I remembered she had mentioned losing it. She had seemed quite distressed when she found it missing from around her neck. Surely, she would be thrilled to have it returned.

I retrieved the necklace and brushed it free of dirt. After carrying it inside, I searched the house but did not find my daughter. I returned to the kitchen where Rachel was baking bread, as she often did on weekends.

I said, "Have you seen Alicia? I have something she'll be glad to get back."

Without looking up from the dough she was kneading, Rachel replied, "Shouldn't she be in her room?"

"I checked. She's not there. Where else could she be?"

"In her bathroom?"

"Nope. It's empty as well."

"The family room?"

"Not there either, and the TV is off."

"Is her bike in the garage? She might've gone for a ride."

"Without telling us?"

"She's seven. She doesn't always follow the rules."

"I'll check."

A minute later, I returned. "Her bike is there. She's not. I even called her name up and down the street. Where could she be?"

"This isn't like her." Rachel stepped to the sink to wash the dough from her hands. "I'll help you look."

Ten minutes later, we returned to the kitchen, having found no trace of our daughter. Both of us were beginning to worry.

"I can't imagine that she would simply wander off." There was an edge of panic in my wife's voice. Then she suggested hopefully, "Do you think she might be visiting one of her neighborhood friends? Let me call around and see."

Fifteen minutes later, we had contacted every family with small children within a two-block radius. No one admitted to having seen our daughter.

Struck by a flash of inspiration, I suggested, "Hide-and-seek."

We searched the house again, paying special attention to Alicia's favorite hiding spots. Still, she was nowhere to be found. As we stood in our daughter's bedroom, Rachel and I stared at one another.

"Should we call the police?" Rachel suggested with a look of dismay.

Despite my reticence, I nodded. "Perhaps we should. It's been over half an hour, and there's no sign of her."

"You don't imagine someone could have abducted her, do you?"

"Let's not assume the worst. She'll turn up. After all, she's a bright child. She knows her address and her phone number. Tell you what, why don't we notify the authorities? They can start looking, and we'll put our heads together. Maybe we can think of where else she might have gone."

Thirty minutes later, a police detective was seated in our family room asking uncomfortably personal questions: Was our marriage in trouble? Was Alicia happy and well-adjusted? Had she ever run away before? Had she been injured recently? Both my wife and I understood that the police were looking for signs of abuse. It was hard not to take offense. We repeatedly assured them that such was not the case.

A succession of uniformed officers came and went. At any given instant, two or three patrol cars were parked in front of our house. Police radios emitted a punctuated stream of background chatter.

As the afternoon dragged on toward evening, our anxiety mutated into fear, which became a smoldering terror. Every rational explanation had been exhausted. Every lead had been investigated. And though the chief detective hadn't voiced an opinion, his thoughts were plain: we were dealing with a kidnapping, and at any moment, the phone would ring with a ransom demand. No one dared voice what we all feared, that the outcome would be the most horrific of all tragedies. With each passing second, the tension increased until it became nearly unbearable.

At length, we had gathered in the family room, waiting. Rachel was beside herself. Her red-rimmed eyes were moist with tears. On the other hand, I had built a wall around my emotions, a shell within which to hide, though a hollow had formed in the pit of my stomach, and my legs trembled whenever I stood. What would I do if my daughter was…? I refused to even consider the word.

"I'm hungry," a small voice announced from the entryway. Mommy, what's for dinner?" Our daughter had entered through the front door unseen. She seemed genuinely dumbfounded by the commotion that confronted her.

With joyful tears streaming down her face, Rachel leaped up from her recliner and rushed to sweep Alicia off her feet. Wrapping our daughter in a tight hug, she nearly forced all the air out of the girl's lungs. I, too, hurried over to confirm that Alicia was uninjured and to kiss her face.

"Are you okay?" Rachel burbled when she was again able to speak. "You're not hurt, are you?"

"No," Alicia declared decisively.

Rachel checked her over from head to toe. "Where were you? We've been so worried. Where did you go?"

Alicia smoothed the front of her dress in a very ladylike fashion. "I went to visit Ms. Sullivan. She grows flowers in her garden as Daddy does. We had tea together."

Grace Sullivan was a kindhearted neighbor who lived three doors down. An elderly spinster, she had no children of her own. It had never occurred to us that she might have invited our daughter into her home.

Sadly, it's often impossible to appreciate what we've been given until it's taken away. Having our daughter safely returned to us was the greatest gift I had ever received.

*　*　*

The silver necklace lay on the end table. Its amethyst jewel sparkled as it caught the light of a nearby lamp.

As I stared at the prophetic pendant, I realized I had been granted a glimpse of what losing our daughter would entail. In that instant, I understood that we must draw upon a power greater than our own to endure the ordeal ahead. If not, the anguish would overwhelm us.

I stood and stepped forward to take hold of Rachel's hand. "Next Sunday is Easter. Let's go to church and keep going every Sunday thereafter. You have worries. So do I. Something tells me that without help, we won't find the answers we seek."

Rachel rose from her recliner. I could tell she was trembling. As I opened my arms to embrace her, she confessed, "I'm frightened. I don't know if I'm strong enough…considering what's coming."

I stepped back to hold my wife at arm's length so I could gaze into her eyes. Mustering my resolve, I declared, "Together, we will ask God to see us through this nightmare. And together, we will fight until our daughter is free of her affliction. We will never quit. We will never surrender."

Rachel bravely squared her shoulders. "I'm with you. Whatever comes."

*　*　*

After what seemed like an exceedingly long weekend spent stewing over what the investors would decide, it was finally Monday. This time, rather than gather in the Byrne River Bank's conference room, Winston had convinced the others to meet at the Encounter—a members-only dinner club with a back room for private functions. As a nonmember, I was admitted as Winston's guest.

The club's reputation was well-established. Its cuisine was equaled by its posh decor. Linen tablecloths and sterling silver cutlery graced each table, with a fresh flower in a small vase. I had dined at the Encounter once or twice before when meeting with clients. The food was generally first-rate, especially the prime rib, which is what I ordered.

Usually, I preferred to meet with clients over lunch and have dinner at home with my family, but Winston had insisted. I suspected we were gathering at the Encounter because he wanted to impress his friends.

A team of white-gloved waiters removed our soup dishes and served our main entrées.

"So, Paul," Judge Tolliver said, "we've been reviewing the project's financials, and I have a couple of questions."

Apparently, the time for small talk had come to an end.

He continued, "After the partnership acquires the land, you've indicated that you expect land improvement costs to run somewhere in the neighborhood of $4,250 per acre. That's in addition to the $10,000 per acre purchase price. That land development number seems high. Could you share how you came by such a figure?"

"Certainly." I looked at each man in turn. "Actually, you're right. That figure might be slightly inflated. Hopefully, we can do better. However, I've always believed it's best to underestimate your income and overstate your expenses. That land improvement figure includes multiple items"—I ticked them off on my fingers. "A detailed property survey; road construction; laying in the underground utilities—power, phone, cable TV; drafting an environmental impact statement; conducting a hydrology survey—"

"Does that number include the cost of drilling the wells?" Winston said.

"No. The wells aren't figured on a per-acre basis. They are calculated separately. And let's not overlook the expenses related to submitting a subdivision application to the planning board. There could also be other costs, depending upon how Phase 2 unfolds."

Angus flipped through several pages of my proposal. "What other expenses might you foresee?"

"Mainly those that the planning board will require. For instance, they could demand that we do an initial preparation of each building site or tell us to install sidewalks and curbs along our central roadway, though I doubt they'll be that demanding. Yet, in my experience, government agencies will always find additional work to be done. That's the nature of bureaucracies. The more deficiencies they cite, the more they can justify their existence."

"Right on," Winston affirmed. "That's especially true in the banking industry."

"I'm curious," said Marcus Durham. "How many projects like this one have you managed where a large property was being subdivided?"

"This will be my first as a controlling partner," I admitted truthfully as I regarded my prime rib, which was growing cold. "However, I have sold several homes in subdivisions under construction. From a realtor's perspective, the principles that apply are very nearly the same."

"Are they?" said Marcus musingly.

Judge Tolliver spoke up. "Another point. Your commission rate of four percent, as applied to the sale of newly constructed homes, seems high, given that you will be guaranteed fifty estates to sell. We think two percent would be more appropriate."

"Two percent! Seriously?" I rocked back in my chair. "Don't forget that I'll serve as the managing partner for free. It will take a lot of work to bring this project to fruition. If you had to pay me for my services, it would cost almost as much as I'll receive in commissions."

"No doubt," Winston replied, "but remember that you won't be hustling properties to sell. As the project moves forward, buyers will come to you. As the broker of record, you'll have to officiate at closings. With that in mind, two percent seems entirely adequate."

"One more thing." Angus dabbed his mouth with his napkin. "We're concerned that you're not investing your money in this project."

"What Dr. McGregor is saying," Marcus interjected, "is that it bothers us that you don't have any skin in the game. You're asking us to come up with three-quarters of a million apiece, but you're not risking any of your own funds."

I looked directly at Winston. "What are you suggesting?"

With his fork halfway to his mouth, Winston paused and then set the fork back down on his plate. "We've talked it over. We feel you should contribute at least a third of what you're asking us to invest. Of course, our way you will proportionately participate in the profits rather than garner commissions. We've redone your calculations to indicate these changes."

He produced a typed spreadsheet with the proposed revisions annotated. He handed it to me. The four investors already had their copies.

"As you can see, you'll do slightly better this way than you would have done at a four percent commission rate. It all works out in the end."

Slowly, it sank in that the limited partners demanded that I invest $250,000. "These are your terms?" I said, feeling more than a little shell-shocked. Again, I looked straight at each man. They all nodded.

"I'm afraid these conditions are not negotiable," Winston declared. "If you want our cash, you must share the risk."

"I see." I regarded my uneaten meal and discovered that I had lost my appetite. I pushed my plate away. "I'll need time to think about this."

"We assumed you might." Winston smiled. "Take all the time you need, but as you reminded us, the Campbell property is an active listing. If a buyer turns up…"

"I am well aware of that. Now, if you gentlemen will excuse me, I should consult with my wife." I rose from my chair and shook hands with each man before leaving.

On the drive home, I thought about what the investors were demanding. To my surprise, I sensed that I could appreciate their point of view. In financial affairs, it is easier to trust the integrity of someone with something to lose. But for me, $250,000 was an enormous sum. There was no way I could come anywhere near laying my hands on that much equity.

More to the point, this was a decision I could not make alone. Even if I could somehow raise that much capital, I'd be putting my financial future at risk, as well as Rachel's and Alicia's. To move forward with the Spirit Wolf Limited Partnership, I would need my family's blessing, not to mention another miracle.

*   *   *

Later that evening, my wife sat on the sofa in the living room with one leg drawn up beneath her. "Be honest with me," she said. "How do you really feel about all this?"

We had migrated to the living room after the dinner dishes had been washed, dried, and put away. Alicia was playing in her bedroom upstairs. Chatting in the family room had seemed fine for small talk and confronting the challenges of daily life. The living room was more appropriate for making decisions that could impact our lives for decades.

"Honestly, I'm terrified. As you pointed out, it's difficult to imagine myself managing such a huge project."

We had reviewed what forming a limited partnership would entail. I felt it was only fair that my wife should have the same information as the investors. With deliberate candor, I had described each peril in unambiguous terms. Rachel had listened thoughtfully and had asked several questions. As I sat facing her on the opposite end of the sofa, I could tell she was processing our discussion. Her facial expression, however, remained unreadable.

Rachel draped her arm along the back of the couch and turned her face toward me. "Can we afford to invest a quarter million dollars?"

"I don't know," I answered truthfully. "I'm still doing the math. I would've said no this afternoon, but then I recalled that I'll be earning a $120,000 commission when the partnership closes on the Campbells' land. I doubt the investors would object if I were to apply that sum toward my contribution, meaning we'd have to come up with only $130,000."

"Only $130,000? Really?"

"I know. If we sell all our investments, borrow against our IRAs, and take out a second mortgage, I figure we'd still be $30,000 short."

"So that means we can't do it."

"What it means is I'll have to ask Franklin for a loan."

Rachel recoiled. "Franklin? Why ask your brother? Why not get a loan from the bank?"

"Everything we own will be tied up in the limited partnership. We'd have nothing to offer as collateral. Besides, Winston isn't about to risk the bank's money on a real estate venture of this sort. His own money perhaps, but not the bank's."

"What you're telling me is—"

"Exactly. If this project goes south, we lose everything, and Alicia won't get any therapy at all. It would be a calamity from which we might never recover."

Rachel folded her hands in her lap and sat quietly, staring off into space. She was struggling with the same worries that were haunting me.

"You do realize," she said, "if this deal doesn't work out, we won't have even enough to pay for Alicia's supportive care."

"I do."

Rachel's eyes narrowed. "If we proceed, will we have enough to live on?"

"We should, barely, assuming I can broker a few properties to keep us afloat until the estates begin selling. We'll hold back a little."

"Do you think Franklin will loan you the money?"

"I don't know. I'm not even sure he has that much equity. He's had to make do on a pastor's salary all these years."

Rachel became deadly serious. "Do we want to take this risk?"

"That's the question, isn't it? There's so much at stake, but there's also much to gain. If this deal unfolds the way I believe it will…"

"And if it doesn't?"

I pursed my lips and tried not to dwell on that possibility.

* * *

The following evening, Rachel and I stood in a serving line at the Maranatha Gospel Fellowship. Every Tuesday, volunteers from the congregation prepared a hot meal for the community's needy. The large multipurpose room and attached kitchen in the church basement functioned as the perfect venue for this act of charitable kindness. Franklin had called to suggest that since we were thinking of officially joining the fellowship, we might wish to consider helping out.

We readily agreed because we needed Franklin to be in a giving frame of mind when we hit him up for a loan. What better way to earn his goodwill than by supporting one of his favorite ministries?

As I watched people gratefully accept the food I ladled onto their plates, I was moved in a way I had not experienced before. The joy of selflessly serving others came as a novel sensation. As the meal progressed, I almost forgot why we had come, but dinner for people in need ended, and it was time for the volunteers to partake of what remained.

I whispered to Franklin that I wanted to speak with him privately, so we migrated to a table away from the others. Rachel sat with Alicia and several new friends. I could tell she was monitoring our conversation out of the corner of her eye.

Franklin swallowed a healthy bite of meatloaf and then said, "Let me understand. You're asking me if you should risk everything you own for a chance to get rich. Is that the size of it?"

I reviewed in detail the mechanics of forming a limited partnership and what was involved in subdividing the land and building houses to sell. I also revealed that the partners insisted that I invest a quarter million dollars. I neglected to mention that I would need to borrow $30,000 from him to make it happen.

"Technically, yes, but not for our sakes. Remember that if we choose to do this, it will be so we can pay for Alicia's medical care."

"Sounds to me like you're in a tough spot," Franklin mused. "I can sympathize, but how is it you need my help?"

The ten or so volunteers who remained in the room seemed to be in good spirits. The noise level made quiet conversation difficult, which was good since I wanted to keep our chat private. "I was hoping to hear your opinion."

"I assume you've evaluated the pros and cons, the financial risks and the benefits?"

"In great detail, yes."

"Of course you have. And I'm sure you've also considered the time and effort this partnership will demand of you."

"I have," I confirmed.

Franklin sipped his iced tea. "But still, you're worried that other considerations apply."

"That's right."

"Could you be concerned about the moral and ethical issues? No doubt such questions are important, but they aren't the real reason you wanted to speak with me. You can figure out the right and wrong of a thing on your own."

"Astute as always," I said with genuine respect. "There is a larger issue in view. I need to understand what God expects of me. I thought I knew when I set out to create the limited partnership. I felt I could trust God, and He would lead me. But the ground rules seem to have changed. Now I'm not so sure. You've said many times that God has a plan for every life. Is the Spirit Wolf project part of His plan for me, or am I doing this alone?"

"You want me to ask Him for you?"

"No, of course not. I can do my own asking, and I have prayed for guidance. My problem is I'm not hearing an answer. It's frustrating and more than a little unnerving. This venture is serious business. I'm afraid to think how it will turn out if God is against me. Maybe it's just that I'm not listening as I should. I was hoping you could teach me how to recognize the answer when it's given. How do I know what God is telling me? How do I hear Him?"

Franklin put down his fork. He then leaned forward and rested his forearms on the table. "Do you remember when we were kids? You were thirteen, I think. You had trained all summer to make the cross-country team. But just before the season started, you broke your leg. You were furious and kept asking why God was punishing you."

"I remember. What's your point?"

"Wasn't that the year the school bus crashed on its way to a meet? Several kids were injured, fortunately none seriously. I'm convinced that if you'd been on that bus, you would've been critically hurt or killed. I do not doubt that God heard your prayer, but He answered it in a way you could not understand at the time. Sometimes, it's only in retrospect that we can appreciate God's involvement in our lives."

"How does this help me decide what to do about the limited partnership?"

"You must know that God is always with you, even when you can't sense His presence. You need to trust Him. You must have faith. Faith is belief put into action. Oftentimes, we are called to act even in periods of uncertainty. That's the nature of faith. This partnership seems like one of those occasions."

"So you think I should move forward?"

"Ask yourself a simple question: Will this project glorify God? If the answer is yes, then proceed and trust that our Heavenly Father will see you through."

"Is that what you'd do? Would you invest everything you own in something so overwhelming?"

"Given what you've told me and considering your motives, yes, I believe I would. I think God would regard your goal as worthwhile."

I sat quietly for an extended interval. Then I made my decision. "I believe your reasoning is sound." I slapped the palm of my hand on the tabletop for emphasis. "I'll do it. So now we come to that huge favor I mentioned."

"I was wondering when we'd get there." Franklin ate a bite of mashed potatoes.

Over the next ten minutes, my brother and I discussed finances—

his and mine. Initially, he bridled when I relayed that I needed to borrow $30,000, but his attitude changed when I reminded him that God seemed to be calling me to undertake the project. At length, he relented and announced that if I could put my faith in God, he could put his faith in me. I found his declaration of familial support incredibly humbling.

But then he delivered the bad news. My brother was not a rich man. With a flush of embarrassment, he admitted that all he could loan me was $19,000, his entire life savings, which meant we would still be $11,000 short.

After helping clean up in the kitchen, Rachel, Alicia, and I drove home. En route, I was mostly silent, overcome by a sense of failure. We had come so close, but things being what they were, there was no way we could move forward with the Spirit Wolf project.

Forty-eight hours later, my family and I were having our evening meal in the dining room, just off the kitchen. We had decided that, as a family, we would no longer eat separately or sit in front of the television. Dining together had seemed a small but significant lifestyle change. We hoped that regularly sharing a meal would bind us closer to one another. It would also allow us to spend additional time with our daughter before…before we couldn't.

Alicia had been describing her school day and the science experiments her fourth-grade teacher had performed in class. She continued, "Then Ms. Forsyth added baking soda to the vinegar, but she poured too much. The bubbly stuff went all over the place. It just kept coming." My daughter began giggling and then couldn't stop.

I was reminded how animated a nine-year-old girl could be, given half a chance. For fifteen minutes, Alicia had talked virtually nonstop. Several times, Rachel and I had exchanged looks of amazement.

The expectation that, in a year or two, her heart would start to fail tormented me like a needle in my brain. Even worse was the knowledge that I was powerless to alter the progression of her affliction. I had repeatedly done the calculations, looking for a way to raise the funds to satisfy the investor's demands. No matter how many ways I manipulated the numbers, the truth was unavoidable: contributing a quarter million dollars was beyond my reach.

Then the front doorbell rang.

"I'll get it," Alicia responded brightly. Without hesitating, she surged out of her chair and left the room.

Rachel regarded me from across the table. "Are you expecting someone?"

"No, but I wonder if it's Jack. He has a habit of showing up when there's food to be had." I heard muffled voices from the front entryway, but I could not distinguish the words. Alicia returned as I was about to see who might be calling during the dinner hour.

"It's a man who says he's a policeman," she announced. "He wants to talk to you, Dad."

I cast a questioning look toward my wife. She shook her head to indicate she was as much in the dark as I was. I rose from the table and stepped to the front door.

A middle-aged gentleman with close-cropped sandy-colored hair stood on our front porch. He was wearing civilian clothes and carrying a package under his arm. "Mr. Langdon?" he said. "Good evening. I'm Detective Hodges. I'm sorry to be calling at such an hour, but I just finished my shift. I wonder if I might have a minute of your time."

"Come in," I responded, feeling ill at ease. The man's face seemed familiar, but I couldn't place where we had crossed paths. He stepped inside, and I ushered him into the living room.

"You don't remember me, do you?" the detective asked. "I was called to this house about two years ago when your daughter was reported missing."

"Oh, yes. Of course. Now I remember. That was a horrible experience. I mean, it was horrible not knowing where she was, not your being here." I felt my cheeks grow warm.

"I understand. Fortunately, everything turned out for the best. I wish all my cases could be so satisfying."

"Indeed. My wife and I certainly appreciate the kindness the police showed us that day. So, what can I do for you this evening?"

"It's more like what I can do for you." He produced the package that he had been carrying under his arm. I recognized the brown paper sack with its top folded tightly closed. He held it out to me. "I believe this now belongs to you. The waiting period has passed, and no one has stepped forward to claim it. Therefore, it's yours."

I accepted the paper bag, opened it, and looked inside. The bundles of money were just as I remembered them. "Really? I can't believe someone would walk away from this much cash."

"We think a drug dealer must have lost it. They'd rather take a financial hit than get involved with the police." He produced a folded sheet of paper from the inside pocket of his sportscoat. "If I can get your signature on this receipt, I'll let you get back to your dinner. It smells delicious." He fished a pen out of his shirt pocket.

"You're welcome to stay and have a bite."

After scanning the document, I bent over to sign it on the coffee table. The sum being returned to me was listed as $11,907. I saw no reason to count it to verify the amount. I returned the pen and the receipt to the detective.

"Thanks, but my wife will be waiting for dinner. She wouldn't appreciate it if I returned home having already eaten."

"As you wish, but you're welcome anytime, especially if you keep bringing us such good news."

The detective chuckled. "Like I said, I wish all my cases could be so satisfying."

After waving goodbye and closing the front door, I turned around to find Rachel eyeing me with intense curiosity.

I held up the paper bag. "You are not going to believe this."

Later, when we were again seated at the dinner table, and Alicia had been excused to play in her room, Rachel demanded, "Why didn't you tell me you'd found a bag full of money?"

"I sort of forgot about it. I figured someone would claim it."

"You forgot about finding nearly $12,000?"

"Well, yeah." I shrugged. "You do realize what this means?"

Rachel nodded. "It means we're going ahead with the limited partnership?"

"Can there now be any doubt that it's what we're supposed to do?"

"Not to my way of thinking," Rachel said with a look of certainty. "By the way, I'm curious. How much was our new water heater, precisely?"

I consulted my phone's online banking app to refresh my memory. After keying in a series of commands, I read the amount. "Nine hundred and seven dollars."

My wife and I numbly gaped at each other across the dinner table, awestruck by a fantastic example of divine providence.

Chapter 5

Four days after being handed a paper bag filled with cash, I again found myself near the center of town. A misty May rain had begun falling around noon. I parked my Jeep in front of the Byrne River Bank. After switching off the engine, I grabbed my briefcase and hurried inside. My meeting with the investors was scheduled to begin at one o'clock, but I was running late. The investors had agreed to hire an attorney to assist in launching the Spirit Wolf Limited Partnership, and my consultation with him had taken longer than anticipated. The delay, however, had been worthwhile. I now carried with me what I hoped would be the final version of our partnership agreement. I was feeling optimistic as I entered the bank.

"Morning, all," I chirped as I stepped into the conference room. "I apologize for keeping you waiting." I noted that the four men occupied the same chairs as before. In my experience, people tended to repeat behaviors rather than try something new. Angus and Marcus returned my smile. The judge remained stone-faced as usual. Winston scowled, probably because I'd kept him waiting.

"I hope you've brought us something we can finally agree upon," Winston blurted out from the head of the table.

"I believe I have," I stated with confidence. "I think you'll agree that we've settled the points of contention rather nicely." Before sitting beside Angus, I opened my briefcase, took out a packet of folders, and passed one to each investor. "Gentlemen, this is the partnership agreement we've been discussing. Take a moment to review the revisions the attorney has suggested. You'll find those sections flagged with sticky notes. I can then answer any questions."

The room remained quiet for the next five minutes except for the usual noises emanating from the bank's public spaces.

Angus was the first to look up. Since he was naturally trusting, I wondered if he had read the disputed sections or was prepared to accept the proposed revisions on faith.

Marcus was second. I assumed he had learned to speed-read as a newspaper editor.

Winston finished third. When he closed his copy and sat back, he was nodding to himself. Many of the changes had been at his behest. I gathered that the suggested modifications were to his liking.

Judge Tolliver came in last, though he was first to speak. "I know we've been over this before, but this section still troubles me. It's the one that explicitly states that the limited partners shall have no individual authority either to authorize the expenditure of money or exercise control over the partnership's daily operations. Why is this clause necessary?"

I leaned forward and spoke calmly and reassuringly. "This section relates to why we're forming a limited partnership. Your exposure to financial loss is substantially restricted if you are not involved in daily operations. As I'm sure you're aware, in the event of a lawsuit, you cannot be held liable for more than your initial capital investment. Also, when it comes to spending money, remember that the limited partners must approve all expenses greater than $20,000 as a group. This gives you considerable authority over how the money is dispersed."

Marcus looked toward Judge Tolliver. "The clause seems reasonable to me. As a limited partner, I like being protected if this deal goes south." Angus and Winston indicated that they agreed.

Judge Tolliver dipped his chin slightly, signaling that he would accept the wording as written.

I moved on. "Before we formalize this venture, I need to emphasize a point that's already been made—just to ensure everyone understands. Your initial investments must remain with the partnership, at least until we enter Phase 3. This ensures the project remains viable and will not falter due to a lack of funds. No one will be permitted to request their money back until the partnership has secured its construction loan. Once estates begin selling, a buyout might be permitted depending upon cash flow. As sales continue, your investments will be returned incrementally, and the profits distributed proportionately."

Winston spoke up from his place of honor at the head of the table. "We've already agreed that this provision is necessary and appropriate, so let's move on. Does anyone have a problem with the revised sections?" He waited to see if any of his colleagues would voice an objection. When no one did, he announced, "Each of you has deposited your capital contribution with the bank. Since we've agreed to proceed, we will now transfer those monies into the partnership's account." Winston again waited to see if anyone would protest.

At that moment, I was reminded of what was at stake. Not only had I invested my entire life savings, but so had my brother. If the venture were to collapse for any reason, we would both be ruined, and Alicia would be left to the ravages of her genetic heritage. Fearful of what lay ahead, I very nearly cried out that we should walk away and forget the whole idea. Then I recalled the money in the paper sack. God had provided a way for us to proceed. The least I could do was trust Him going forward. I kept my peace. So did the others.

Winston buzzed for his secretary, who promptly entered the room. "Ms. Dungee, you may transfer the funds as we discussed."

Janet nodded efficiently and departed.

Angus looked at me and asked, "What happens next?"

I fished in my briefcase for another sheath of forms. "We sign and notarize these documents. Then, I'll file a limited partnership certificate with the state. Once we receive our EIN and state ID numbers, the Spirit Wolf Limited Partnership will be open for business."

Judge Tolliver's brow furrowed. "Do we know that Ian Campbell will follow through on his agreement and sell us the land for $10,000 an acre?"

I responded, "I believe Ian is a man of integrity. I have his word."

"And what if he doesn't keep his word?" Winston said.

Having already considered the possibility, I declared, "I seriously doubt that will happen. If it does, it's unlikely that we can force the Campbells to sell, not without a formal buy-sell agreement, which, without a functioning limited partnership, we are precluded from negotiating. If Ian has changed his mind and refuses to sell, I assume we will disband and give each man his money back. But like I said, Ian strikes me as an honorable man. If everything goes as planned, we should close on the property within a week. The title search has already been completed, and a preliminary survey to confirm the boundaries is underway."

"Sounds good!" Winston exclaimed. His demeanor had brightened considerably.

I nodded, and Winston pressed his buzzer twice. The bank's notary entered the conference room. After producing the proper identification, each investor, including me, signed the requisite documents.

"It's done." I stood and gathered up the completed paperwork. As I snapped my briefcase shut, I commented, "By the way, gentlemen, you should know that earlier this morning, I spoke with Bruce Stewart, chairman of Trinity Falls Township's city council. Without revealing details, I mentioned that some guys I know were considering buying a certain parcel of land and were wondering how hard it would be to have the property annexed to the city. At first, Bruce seemed as if he could not care less. His attitude changed remarkably when I mentioned they planned to build an upscale residential community with fifty homes. He became downright enthusiastic when I pointed out that the city's boundary line already passed along the property's edge. I doubt we'll have trouble annexing Spirit Wolf Estates to Trinity Falls Township."

"Excellent news indeed." Winston beamed. "Paul, on behalf of the rest of us, I'd and like to thank you for your hard work and for bringing this project to our attention."

"Here, here," Angus agreed.

"Trust me, gentlemen," I said. "The hard work is only beginning. Now, if you'll excuse me, I should prepare for tomorrow's meeting with the Campbells to finalize the sale of their land."

*   *   *

Having visited with Ian and Eva Campbell several times, I had learned quite a bit about them, but this was the first time I had been invited to their home. The previous day's storm had finally ceased. As I traveled north, cruising just above the speed limit, I thought about what lay ahead. By the time I drew near my destination, anticipation had tied my stomach in knots. The real estate venture I had initially deemed an unrealistic fantasy was becoming a reality. This meeting would decide the project's fate.

The Campbells resided in a modest ranch-style house seven miles north of the property they were selling. For most of his life, Ian had worked as an auto mechanic in Fairline, a sedate, unincorporated village close to the Canadian border. Upon retiring at age sixty-five, he and his wife had relocated to their current residence.

Slowly, I rolled through the gate and parked in the gravel lot. As I crossed the front yard, I noted half a dozen vehicles in various stages of repair. The most appealing was a classic 1970s Ford Mustang painted fire-engine red. A black racing stripe crossed the hood to trail along both sides.

I rang the doorbell.

Eva greeted me with a smile. "Oh, good!" she exclaimed. "You're right on time." A stout woman with an ample bosom and broad hips, Mrs. Campbell fit my mental image of a farmer's wife. Her gray hair was swept into a bun at the back of her head. A natural ruddiness colored her cheeks. Her brow was lined with creases.

Eva led me into the living room, where Ian rose from his recliner to shake my hand. He gestured toward the armchair beside the brick fireplace. Sadly, no blaze was burning. A crackling fire would have driven the chill from the air. Ian was wearing a T-shirt and denim coveralls. I sat down and made myself comfortable. Eva disappeared into the kitchen only to return with a cup of coffee and a plate of sliced banana nut bread. She set both down on the end table beside my chair. I thanked her cordially.

"You have a cozy home," I said as Eva took her place on the couch. "I'll bet this fireplace is handy when the snow falls."

"It is," Ian affirmed, "but I'm getting a little long in the tooth to be chopping firewood."

Both Ian and Eva had immigrated to the United States as teenagers. Originally from Ardrossan in Ayrshire County, Scotland, their residency in the States had done little to blunt their Scottish brogues.

I said pleasantly, "Soon, you'll be living where homes don't need fireplaces. Instead, you'll be soaking up the sun beside your pool."

"Soaking up the sun, I would hope so," Ian commented. "As for the pool, I think not. The important thing is we'll be close to our children and our grandchildren. They're the reason we're moving."

"So you've indicated."

We engaged in small talk for a few minutes, and then Ian commented, "To be honest, I think both me and my wife will miss living here, especially in the fall. I understand that the trees don't change colors in Florida, unlike ours."

"I believe that's right," I replied. "I've never lived there myself, but I hear the countryside is fairly green, depending on rainfall."

Eva spoke up. "Seasonal changes are one thing that's special about the land we're selling. The colors are amazing. In autumn, we love hiking in the forest."

"Not long ago, I found myself doing that very thing." I fashioned a half smile.

"About the property," Ian said. "We understand the buyers intend to develop the land. Is that true?"

"That is correct—"

"And they plan on building a bunch of houses. That's what someone told me." Ian scowled.

My realtor's instincts switched into overdrive. In a mild tone, I replied, "You're worried that they're going to ruin the aesthetics of your land."

"That's exactly right," Ian affirmed. "We bought that property way back when it was fifty bucks an acre, and we've enjoyed its beauty all these years. The thought of it being cluttered with a bunch of track houses makes my blood run cold. I'm thinking maybe we should sell to someone else."

Talk about blood running cold; a shiver raced up my spine. I hurriedly collected my thoughts. "I suspect there are several things you might want to know. I certainly understand your attachment to the land. I feel the same. I, too, would hate to see it desecrated, and being men of principle, so would the investors, by the way. They have no intention of creating something ugly."

I took a short breath and quickly continued to maintain my momentum.

"If we step back and look at the potential uses for your property, I think you'll agree that these men represent a viable alternative.

"First off, the land isn't suitable for farming. Two hundred acres might make a decent hobby farm, but it would never be financially viable. And talk about harming the aesthetics. Imagine how a barn with corrals and pastures would impact the land's beauty.

"As a second option, the land could be listed as a nature preserve, but again, two hundred acres is too small to be much of an attraction, not with the Adirondacks and the Catskills so close by. If you were an outdoorsman and you wanted to spend time in the woods, which way would you go? Like most, I'm sure you'd head for the major recreation areas. Also, remember that you'd have to give the land away. Nobody is going to pay you to create a nature preserve.

"Then there's the possibility of selling to one person, but only that individual and his family would enjoy the land's beauty. The public would be denied access.

"Finally, there's the option of improving the property and creating a residential community. I can assure you that the people asking to buy your land have no intention of degrading its natural appeal. That's why they plan on building only fifty homes instead of a hundred and fifty or more. Green belt areas will be set aside throughout the property where no structures can be built. Only a few trees will be removed, and only those absolutely necessary to preserve the health of the forest. The rest of those magnificent trees will be treated as a sacred trust to be enjoyed by future generations.

"With the creation of a small community, fifty families—plus their visitors and guests—will enjoy the property year-round. Like you, many of the families will have children and grandchildren." I reached for my coffee cup to take a sip. My mouth had gone dry, but I also wanted my last comment to have an impact.

"That really doesn't sound so bad," Eva volunteered.

"No, it doesn't," Ian admitted reluctantly, his scowl fading slightly.

I continued. "I think you'll find that the buyers are offering an excellent price for your land."

"I see." Ian leaned back in his recliner and thought for a time. "Is there any chance I could meet with these fellas?"

"There is that possibility, certainly, but I would strongly advise against it. You work with a broker to guarantee that both parties get a fair deal and that one side doesn't take advantage of the other. Negotiations always run smoother when there's a negotiator. Besides, there is something else you need to know." I hesitated for fear that what I would reveal would be poorly received, but state law and my code of ethics obliged me to proceed. "I will be serving as the project's managing partner."

"You're one of the investors?" Eva exclaimed with a look of surprise.

"That's right. I am. And because I'll oversee day-to-day operations, I can guarantee that we will make every effort to protect the land and keep its aesthetic beauty intact. I give you my word."

Ian lapsed into silence. He then sat forward. "You know, it's not for ourselves that we're selling. If I had my way, we'd keep the land forever. It's for our children and grandchildren. We will use the money to benefit them, to help pay for their education."

"I can totally relate. I believe I've mentioned before that I have a daughter. Alicia is nine years old and the apple of my eye. I'd love to see her grow up in a community like the one we're discussing."

Again, Ian sat quietly. I held my breath; I could tell he was making his decision. To keep from staring at the man, I allowed my gaze to roam around the room. In so doing, I noted several religious artifacts—an empty cross on the wall and a well-used Bible on the end table. "I gather you are people of faith," I said, realizing I was taking a considerable risk. One of the major taboos of selling real estate was talking about politics or religion.

"We are," Eva declared.

"So am I. I can assure you that I've prayed about this project. I'm convinced that God wants us to move forward. Normally, I wouldn't share this information with a client, but I assume you've also prayed for guidance. Am I correct?"

"You are," Ian confirmed. "We've prayed repeatedly to know what to do."

"If I thought this project would harm your property in any way, my faith would oblige me to tell you."

"Is that so?" Ian transfixed me with a penetrating stare as if to gauge my sincerity.

"It is."

"Well then." He squared his shoulders and glanced at his wife for confirmation. "We'll sell, and the sooner, the better."

Eva nodded her agreement.

"Good," I said, feeling an immense sense of relief. "In anticipation of your decision, I've scheduled a closing for this Friday. You'll soon be millionaires, and I'm sure your children and grandchildren will someday thank you."

Ian and I shook hands to seal the deal. I then produced the sales contract I had brought along, and the three of us signed it.

As I was leaving, I grabbed a few slices of banana nut bread. "For the ride back to town," I told Eva with a wink.

While driving south along State Route 171, I realized that I had just brokered the most significant transaction of my career.

*　　*　　*

Ten days later, the project was coming together nicely. The partnership had closed on the property without a hitch. Ian and Eva had received a fair price for their land, and the investors had taken ownership of a splendid tract of real estate. My sales fee had gone directly into the partnership account to flesh out my required investment. Also, a week after closing, the city council voted to annex Spirit Wolf Estates into Trinity Falls Township. Not a single councilman or Trinity Falls citizen had voiced an objection.

When the property fell under the jurisdiction of the county commissioners, it was zoned A—agricultural. Now that we were officially part of the township, to proceed with building our subdivision we would have to change the zoning designation to R1—residential/low-density. To that end, I was visiting the zoning board's offices in city hall to submit an application. As with the annexation, we anticipated that the rezoning process would move ahead quickly and without incident. Approval of our application would signal the end of Phase 1, and I was eagerly looking forward to beginning Phase 2.

My thoughts were elsewhere as I exited the zoning board's offices after completing our paperwork. Unlike the annexation and rezoning procedures, subdividing the property during Phase 2 would be much more involved.

Distracted by my thoughts, as I stepped into the main corridor, I collided with a woman who also seemed preoccupied.

"Excuse me," I said with a flush of embarrassment. "How clumsy of—oh, it's you."

Helen Dunn recovered her poise with surprising alacrity. "Why hello, Paul. I didn't expect to bump into you today. What's going on?"

"Nothing that would interest you."

"On the contrary, I'm always interested in my colleagues' work."

"So I've noted. You also like to involve yourself in their business dealings."

"Come now," Helen smirked. "You're not harboring a grudge because of that Greeley thing, are you?"

"What you did was unethical, and you know it. By the way, I told my wife about the threat you made. You know what she said?"

"No. What did she say?" Helen's faux smile never flinched.

"Bring it on. Those were her exact words."

"You know, come to think of it, perhaps my comments were a bit unprofessional. I won't do it again. I promise."

"I hope you mean that."

"Absolutely, I do. So, what have you got going on in the zoning office?"

Helen's sincerity seemed as deep as a puddle on a hot asphalt road in the middle of July. Even so, I could not help but brag a little, maybe remind her that she wasn't the only realtor in town. "I'm representing a limited partnership. They're rezoning a two-hundred-acre parcel to R1."

"You don't say?" Suddenly, it seemed I had Helen's full attention. "To what end? I assume it's vacant land?"

"It used to belong to the Campbells…two hundred acres just off Route 171. I doubt you're familiar with the parcel, but we just had it annexed to the north end of the township. We plan on building fifty four-acre estates."

"Who is we?"

"The limited partnership I'm forming."

"Is that a fact? Any chance the rest of us might get in on the action?"

"The partnership is closed. We'll be handling sales internally."

"What a shame."

"Sorry," I said curtly as I struggled to keep from gloating.

"No matter. Anyway, good luck with your subdivision."

I could almost hear the gears turning inside Helen's head. As she walked away, I thought, *You devious conniver. What's going on in that twisted soul of yours, I wonder.*

* * *

Mark Tyrell, the project's surveyor, glanced away from the eyepiece of his transit and straightened up. For the better part of a week, he had been marking the boundaries of individual estates and staking out the access roads that would serve them. It was grueling work, tramping through the woods, clearing underbrush, sighting property lines, and setting corner stakes. Having just caught up with him, I was highly interested in his progress.

Mark looked at me and smiled. "This is the last of the lots. We're nearly finished collecting the raw data. Most of the coordinates have already been transmitted to my office. They can print out your subdivision plat once they get this last batch of numbers. I'd imagine they'll have it for you sometime this afternoon."

"Fantastic. I intend to submit our subdivision application to the planning board immediately. Hopefully, this approval process will also move ahead quickly—a week, maybe two at the most. That's what I was led to expect."

Mark's smile faded. "Getting a subdivision plat approved is not like requesting an annexation or rezoning a tract of land."

"Is there a problem?"

"Do you know Logan Smallwood? He's the guy they just promoted to planning board chairman."

"I don't believe we've met. Why?"

"Word is he can be something of a butthead, and that's being polite. He's a young up-and-comer with political aspirations. They say he's out to prove himself. Don't be surprised if he is less than cordial when you speak with him. Some even question how he got his job."

"Splendid. Just what I need, a self-important bureaucrat to complicate my life."

From the gentle rise where we stood, I gazed down upon the parallel rows of wooden markers that indicated the course the subdivision's central road would follow. In the morning sunlight, the stakes, with their tops painted orange, stood out cleanly against the green underbrush. I tried to imagine how the road would look when it was finally graded and paved.

I turned to face Mark again. "Show me where this lot's building site will be."

"This way." He headed to a spot fifty yards distant. I followed.

The same orange-topped stakes that defined the road marked the footprint of a three-thousand-square-foot home. We were near the southeast corner of the Spirit Wolf property, and the views were phenomenal. Lake McDougall shimmered like an azure mirror. I could even make out Eldridge Dam through the trees. It was exciting to think that some lucky family would call this lot home one day.

"Pretty nice, huh?" Mark said.

"Gorgeous. Look. I'm sure you're anxious to finish, so I'll take my leave. What time do you think I should pick up the subdivision plat?"

"Probably around three o'clock. It shouldn't take my secretary long to print it out after she has the last data set."

"Sounds good."

"I'll also instruct her to prepare your bill." Mark grinned.

"Yippee." I made a sour face but refrained from asking how much he intended to charge the partnership. I figured I would find out soon enough.

*   *   *

The township's planning board occupied an ample, multi-office space on the third floor of city hall, one level above the zoning board. Even though I had brokered real estate locally for more than ten years, this was only my third visit. The need had hardly ever arisen in the normal course of my business activities.

Looking around as I stood just inside the entrance, I noted that a square of four cubicles commanded the center of the spacious room. Walled offices lined the periphery. The largest was in the far corner. Assuming it had to be the chairman's, I headed in that direction.

I had called ahead to schedule an appointment. Even so, when I knocked on the open door, the man seated at his desk looked annoyed. "What do you want?" he snapped.

"Mr. Smallwood?"

"Yes."

"I'm Paul Langdon. I called yesterday afternoon. I'm here to speak with you about the Spirit Wolf Estates."

"The what? Oh, yes. You're proposing to build that new housing development on the north edge of town."

"I've brought our initial subdivision plat for you to review." I indicated the long cardboard tube I carried under one arm.

Logan sighed as he regarded the piles of paperwork scattered across his desk. "Very well. Let's see what you've got."

He stood and stepped up to what looked like a large drafting table snugged up against a side wall. After shifting a stack of folders to his cluttered desk, he gestured with a sweep, indicating that I should present my material.

Out of the corner of my eye, I studied him. Logan was a wiry man, perhaps five foot ten and maybe 160 pounds soaking wet. No doubt his thin mustache was intended to make him look older, but it didn't help much. I estimated his age to be nearly twenty-seven, which caused me to wonder How he had been promoted above his colleagues. Several employees in the outer offices looked to be in their late forties or early fifties.

I removed the plastic lid from the cardboard tube and drew out the subdivision plat. After unrolling it, I spread it flat on the drafting table. To my eyes, it was a work of art. I sincerely hoped the chairman would regard it as such.

"I see," was Logan's only comment as he bent over to study the plat.

"As you will note," I volunteered, "it's a straightforward design. A central serpentine road will feed into short access roads and driveways. We're planning on building fifty estates. They will vary in size from three to six acres. The average, of course, will be four."

"Is that right?" Logan said dryly. When he turned his head to glance at me, his facial expression implied I was a dimwit.

"Of course, you can see that for yourself." I then shut my mouth and waited.

For several minutes, Logan inspected the details of the design in silence. His finger traced boundary lines and the placement of specific features, including the building sites and green belt areas. At length, he straightened up.

"Excuse me," I interjected before Logan could speak. "Would you mind if I record our conversation?" I produced my cell phone and keyed up my voice memo app. "I'm sort of new to the role of developer. My investors will want to know precisely what we discussed. This way, I can make sure I get everything right."

"If you feel you must, go ahead." The chairman didn't seem thrilled with the idea. Even so, I pressed the record icon and set my phone down on the drafting table.

Logan pointed to an area on the map. "What is this section here?"

I edged closer to note what he was indicating. "That's part of the green belt. We've set aside a goodly number of no-build corridors to preserve the integrity of the environment. Our Covenants, Conditions, and Restrictions will protect them."

"And these?"

"That's where we expect to drill the wells. Since the property doesn't yet have access to city water, we'll need wells to serve the community. There will be ten in all, one for every five houses. Our hydrologist has advised us that these are the best drilling sites, the ones most likely to produce a steady flow."

"I see." Logan again studied the map for a brief interval. "Where are your fire mitigation resources?"

"Our what?"

"Your water storage features to be accessed during a fire. It would be irresponsible for a project this size not to have at least two."

"Water storage features? You mean like holding tanks?"

"You could use tanks if you wish, I suppose, but I was imagining something more aesthetically appealing, like ponds. They wouldn't have to be large, perhaps twenty thousand gallons each, twice the size of your average swimming pool, though they would have to be easily accessible so the fire department can quickly fill its pumper trucks."

"Why do we need storage ponds? Lake McDougall is a stone's throw away."

"But the only suitable place where the fire department can directly access the lake is near Eldridge Dam, and we can't allow that, having fire trucks coming and going. It would risk public safety. No, you'll need to dredge two ponds on your land. Otherwise, I'm afraid you won't get your plat approved."

I had expected an objection of some sort to be raised as a matter of course, but nothing quite so involved. Excavating a twenty-thousand-gallon pond was no big deal in and of itself, but each would need its own well. And to prevent freezing in winter, we'd have to install some type of continuous recirculation capability. The partnership was looking at a significant expense. When I studied the chairman's face, I could tell his mind was made up.

Bowing to my fate, I said sourly, "Anything else?"

"Not at present. I'll have my team go over this plat. They will look for anything I've missed. We'll get back to you."

"Thank you." I stuck out my hand.

Logan's grip was remarkably unenthusiastic as if he resented the formality.

I gathered my phone but left the subdivision plat unfurled on the drafting table. "I'll await your call."

Upon leaving city hall, I considered what to do next. The obvious course of action was to call our hydrologist and have him meet me on the property. There, we could discuss where to place the ponds.

*   *   *

Russ Talbot, the project's water expert, smiled as he inspected what, to my eye, seemed nothing more than a shallow bowl-shaped depression in the earth.

"This should do nicely," he announced with confidence. After again reviewing the contour maps he had brought from his office, he pointed to a small ridge of rocks almost entirely buried by forest duff. "That's a cleavage plane. Beneath it, the aquifer should be nearer to the surface. This would be a good place to sink a well."

For the past twenty minutes, Russ and I had been searching for a fit place to locate our second pond. We had already identified an appropriate site for the first water storage feature at the opposite end of the property. Adding fire mitigation resources to the subdivision plat would require a realignment of the boundaries of adjoining estates, which would evoke another bill from our surveyor. The good news was that it was beginning to look as if the partnership could satisfy the planning board's requirements.

I glanced up at a patch of sky visible overhead. Evening was coming on. The clouds that were rolling in suggested a chance of rain. I again looked at Russ. "If this works for you, it works for me. I'll contact our surveyor—"

"Mark Tyrell?"

"You know him?"

"We've worked together on several projects. He's a good guy."

"I think so, and I'm sure he'll be glad to make the necessary revisions to our subdivision plat. Again, let me say how much I appreciate your willingness to come out on such short notice."

"You're welcome, though I must say I'm somewhat surprised."

"Surprised? By what?"

"It's unusual for the board to require two ponds. In my experience, one would've been more than sufficient. Two seems like overkill."

"For real?"

"Absolutely, assuming your pond is supported by a high-volume well with adequate flows."

Russ was a qualified hydrologist with impeccable credentials. He had come highly recommended. I valued his opinion. "Should I file a protest?"

"That wouldn't be the most prudent thing to do. I'm sure the chairman has his reasons, and it's unlikely you'd change his mind. At this stage, it would be unwise to provoke a dispute."

"I imagine you're right. So, what are we talking about pricewise?"

"To install the ponds? In this locale, the average cost of a well runs around $15,000. From there, digging a pit, preparing the ground, laying in a waterproof bed liner, plus plumbing in the necessary piping… I'd estimate it all will cost another $10,000. That's $25,000 a pond. Fifty grand for both."

"Are you serious?" My heart sank. After covering our budgeted expenses, the partnership would still have enough to pay for this unexpected expenditure. However, every dollar spent on development meant one less dollar of profit. It galled me to realize that I was at the planning board's mercy. I swallowed my anger and declared grudgingly, "Well, if that's the way it is, that's the way it is."

I was in a foul frame of mind as I accompanied Russ back to his car, though I tried not to let it show.

Later that evening, I was alone in the house. After meeting with Russ Talbot, I was feeling grumpy and exhausted. Sensing my mood, Rachel and Alicia had elected to take in a kids' movie at the theater. I was thrilled that they hadn't insisted I tag along. Watching cartoon characters with ray guns chase each other around impossible landscapes didn't seem like my idea of fun.

Wrapped up in my musings, I almost didn't hear the front doorbell's chimes. Rising from the couch in the family room, I set aside the notepad upon which I had been outlining the most efficient ways to move my project forward.

I found Jack Flashman fidgeting on my stoop when I opened the front door. He seemed troubled. Usually, I would have welcomed an opportunity to gab, but this night, I was in ill humor, and I almost told him to get lost, though not in so many words. I would never have been that blunt. Instead, I would have invented some minor crisis that demanded my immediate attention. However, the troubled look in Jack's eyes suggested that I should hear his story and find out what was going on.

"Come in," I said, opening the door wider.

"Sorry to bother you at home." Jack stepped inside. "Something has come up. I need your input."

I had watched Jack grow up since he was four years old. As an only child, he was an intelligent, hardworking lad endowed with a well-developed sense of integrity. He was also a surprisingly good athlete.

As the high school football team's halfback, he had set the school rushing record, not because of his size but because he was quick. After graduation, his involvement in sports had dwindled, replaced by the need to earn a living.

"Can I get you something, Jack? Coffee, water, juice?" I led the way to the family room. "I'd offer you a beer, but you don't drink, as I recall. Have you eaten? We had spaghetti for dinner. I think there's some left if you're hungry?"

"I'm fine."

"If you change your mind, let me know. Say, I haven't inquired recently. How's your dad? Is he well?"

Jack slumped down on the far end of the couch, away from the paperwork I'd strewn about. "He's good. He says moving to North Carolina was one of the wisest decisions he's ever made. He golfs three to four times a week. He would play more often if not for the arthritis in his shoulder."

I shifted some of the papers aside to sit down. "And your mom? How is she?"

"Content. Did you know she joined a writers' guild? She claims she's working on a Hollywood screenplay, a chick flick, or something. She wants to stay busy while Dad's out golfing."

"Next time you speak with them, give them my best, will you? I miss them."

"I will." Jack's somber frame of mind seemed unfazed by my mention of his family.

"How are your studies coming along? You test in what, a week and a half? Will you be ready?"

"I've been reviewing zoning restrictions and rights-of-way. The statutes are fairly technical."

"Tell me about it," I recalled more than one sale where similar issues had proven a distraction.

"To answer your question, yes. I think I'll pass."

"Excellent, though I gather the certifying exam isn't why you're here. Whatever it is, it must be important for you to sacrifice a date night." Jack had a reputation for being a ladies' man, not a womanizer but instead a guy who enjoyed the company of the opposite sex.

Jack sat up straighter on the couch. "Helen Dunn called yesterday afternoon. You were out on the property with your surveyor."

Internal alarms began signaling code red. "What did she want?"

"She offered me a job."

"Did she now?" In the back of my mind, I had anticipated that this day might come. Jack would make a valuable addition to any real estate office as a sales associate. Unsurprisingly, my main competitor was attempting to snatch him up. "What did you tell her?"

"That I'd have to think about it."

I interpreted his response as a small ray of hope since he hadn't said yes immediately. "What did she offer you?"

"Perks, plus a promise to double my current salary, contingent upon my passing the qualifying exam, of course."

"Of course." I looked directly at Jack. "That's an attractive offer."

I had thought about what would be involved if Jack decided to move on. He was a reliable asset. Without him to fill in whenever I was out of the office… Well, it was impossible to be in two places at once. With his sales license, he would become become an even more valuable commodity, and his leaving would prove a significant hardship. Besides, I liked the kid a lot.

Jack nodded. "That's the reason I'm here. I'd like to know my prospects if I stay with Trinity Falls Realty."

There it was, that most troublesome issue: money. With the entirety of my financial reserves now tied up in the partnership, there was no way I could match Helen's offer, and I told Jack as much. "However," I continued, "a year from now, the situation will look considerably different once the residential estates start coming on the market. Until then, we'll have to make do with what we have." This last thought was delivered more as a plea than a statement.

Jack seemed unconvinced. "How likely is it that the Spirit Wolf Partnership will go bust?"

"That's right to the point. It's a real possibility. The odds are against it, but when the dust settles, there's a chance that Trinity Falls Realty might be bankrupt."

"That's what I suspected. I must say, I appreciate your candor. You could have told me everything will be fine and let it go at that."

"You have a right to know where we stand. You are about to make an important decision, and you need facts. So, what do you think you'll do?"

Jack tossed his head back to gaze up at the ceiling. "And here I thought I'd already made my decision, but now I guess I'll give you the same answer I gave Helen: I need time to think about it." He rocked forward to look at me. "It all boils down to this, I suppose. Is your partnership viable? Do I trust you to make this venture of yours work?"

"That is the size of it. You should know I want you to stay, but if you feel you need to move on, I won't hold it against you."

"Again, I appreciate your honesty."

"You deserve nothing less."

Jack rose to his feet, and I showed him to the door. With a deep foreboding, I watched as he disappeared into the night.

Chapter 6

Ten days after Jack's visit, toward the middle of a Monday morning, I was again seated in Dr. McGregor's waiting room, doing my best not to let my anxiety show. For the most part, the patients waiting to be seen ignored me. For that, I was grateful. To keep from fretting, I tried to focus my attention on the events of the preceding week.

Jack had not decided whether to hire on with Rimdale Properties or stay with Trinity Falls Realty. The thought of losing him had pressed down on my consciousness like a heavy weight.

Work on the property had been proceeding at a steady pace. We had submitted our revised application to the planning board. The project's fate was now in their hands. Their rulings would determine the future of the Spirit Wolf subdivision. In addition, the second draft of our environmental impact statement was being reviewed by the subcontractors who would prepare the land in anticipation of building houses.

More than that, I had begun the process of selecting an architect to design the estates. I had solicited bids from several prominent firms, both local and regional. Judging by the initial responses, there seemed to be considerable enthusiasm for the project. Several prestigious firms had indicated they were interested. Their responses had strengthened my confidence that we would ultimately hire a top-tier individual to do our subdivision justice.

However, none of these issues were worrisome enough to keep me from again wondering about my daughter and how she was getting on with Dr. McGregor in his exam room.

An hour earlier, the school nurse had called me at work. In a matter-of-fact tone, she had informed me that Alicia was running a low-grade fever. Rachel and I had previously left instructions with the nurse to contact us immediately if our daughter began showing any symptoms of illness. To reduce the risk that Alicia might learn of her genetic anomaly, we had refrained from explaining the reasons for our concern. It was, therefore, understandable that the nurse had seemed unfazed by Alicia's fever.

In a rush, I drove straightaway to the school, where Alicia was waiting for me in the nurse's office. When I spoke with her, she confessed that she had felt unwell the previous evening but had chosen not to mention her symptoms. She had assumed she would be better in the morning. When I questioned her further, she also admitted having a sore throat and dry, itchy eyes. Only then did I notice that the whites of her eyes were pinkish-red, and her eyelids were puffy. It galled me to think I had missed such an obvious sign while helping my daughter prepare for school.

I checked my watch against the clock on the wall. Alicia had been in with the doctor for forty-five minutes. I had pleaded to be allowed to be present during her exam, but Angus had gently rebuffed my request. Perhaps he had sensed that my distress would upset my daughter. Instead, he had consigned me to the waiting room, where I now sat.

When I had phoned Rachel to report Alicia's illness, my wife had cited her duty to be with her child, even if it meant abandoning the library in the middle of the day. Repeatedly, I assured her nothing was to be done except wait and worry. Finally, I convinced her that it would be best to stay busy at work and not allow her idle mind to imagine a litany of dreadful scenarios. If only I had the discipline to heed my own advice.

Minutes ticked by while I struggled to avoid thinking about what lay ahead, but try as I might, my thoughts kept envisioning the future I so dreaded. I pictured my daughter as her health failed, as she grew progressively weaker and struggled for breath as her heart succumbed to the attack her immune system would mount against her. I had read extensively about heart failure and the way it ravaged the body. Fatigue and lethargy give way to weakness, then a coma, and then death. Fluid builds up in the lungs. Each breath becomes an agony as the lungs labor to take in enough oxygen. One writer had equated the sensation to drowning slowly over weeks and months.

Unbidden, another train of thought rumbled into my awareness. *How can God, so perfect in mercy and grace, allow this to happen? What purpose will be served by my daughter's suffering? What can possibly be gained by her progressive deterioration and inevitable death? It's not fair!* I screamed silently inside my head.

The more I dwelled upon the injustice, the angrier I became. But then I remembered the wolf and the bag of money. In both instances, God had provided, not in ways I would have imagined, but according to His devising.

It occurred to me then that my only alternative, other than surrendering to utter despair, was to trust that Alicia's illness would turn out similarly and that our heavenly Father would arrange a solution. However, mustering enough faith to quiet my fears at that moment seemed impossible. I felt too lost and too unworthy. How could I trust that God would heed my prayers? In my whole life, I had never done anything to deserve His love.

The insufficiency of my faith filled me with sorrow.

"Paul," said a male voice at the edge of my awareness.

I looked up to find Angus motioning for me to come to him. I stood and crossed the room.

"The nurse is with your daughter," Angus said. "She's getting her dressed. Why don't we talk in my office?"

Numbly, I followed his lead.

"I have good news," Angus declared as I seated myself in one of the chairs that faced his desk. "I'm pretty sure your daughter has an adenovirus. It's nothing more than a common cold. She should be well in a few days if it runs its normal course. We did an electrocardiogram. There is no sign of inflammation of her heart muscle."

The profound relief that flowed through me was indescribable. "Then it's not…?"

"No. It's not Lascaux Syndrome. Her genetic mutation hasn't kicked in yet."

"She's going to be all right?"

"She may manifest a few more of the usual viral symptoms, but by the end of the week, she should be right as rain."

"I need to call Rachel. She's as worried as I was."

"By all means. Would you like to use my phone?"

"No. I'll call on my cell phone. But thanks." An insight struck me. "Is this what it's going to be like being fearful every time she sneezes, panicking whenever she runs a fever?"

"I understand what you're going through. Nothing is worse than being afraid for a child and unable to help."

The thought of helping my daughter reminded me of a topic I had been studying. I said, "Have you ever heard of gene replacement therapy?"

Angus's eyes narrowed. "I've heard of it but don't know much about it. It's hard to keep up with all the advances in modern medicine. Why?"

"I've been doing a little research. They've had some encouraging results with other illnesses."

The doctor seemed troubled. "Be careful where you look for help. There are people in this world who prey on other people's distress. They promise the moon and deliver nothing. It would not be wise to cling to a false hope."

"I hear you."

Angus's medical assistant poked her head inside his office and announced, "She's ready."

"Thank you." Angus nodded to the nurse but then looked at me. "I've written a couple of prescriptions. They should help ease Alicia's symptoms." He fished in the pocket of his white lab jacket and handed me two slips of paper. "You can have these filled at any pharmacy."

I accepted the prescriptions and stood up. "Once again, thank you. I really appreciate your seeing us without an appointment."

"Any time, day or night, call me if you think there's a need."

We finalized our goodbyes, and I hurried off to collect my daughter.

I took it as a sign of the seriousness of the matter that Angus had neglected to mention the Spirit Wolf project.

*   *   *

After dinner that evening, Rachel and I were in the kitchen when a knock sounded at the front door. We had been discussing Alicia's visit with Dr. McGregor and our incredible relief that our daughter would recover from her viral infection. We had deliberately shied away from speculating on what we would do if and when her genetic mutation finally declared itself. It was a topic both of us dreaded. I rose to see who had come calling.

Jack Flashman stood on the front stoop sporting an apologetic smile. "Sorry to bother you at home again, but I have good news."

"Wonderful," I said brightly. "We can always use more good news. Come in." I cautioned myself not to speculate as to what his glad tidings might be.

Jack seemed confused. "Has something happened I don't know about?"

"It's our daughter. We thought she was on the verge of being really sick, but it turned out it's merely a cold—nothing too serious." I led Jack into the living room since Alicia was watching TV in the family room. "Can I get you something? Have you eaten?"

"I'm fine. I grabbed a burger after work."

Jack wore a thin nylon jacket over his button-down dress shirt. He didn't bother removing the jacket before sitting on the sofa. This suggested he didn't plan on staying long, which made me wonder. Could the news he intended to share be good for him but bad for me? Had he accepted Helen Dunn's offer? Would he be leaving Trinity Falls Realty?

Rather than press the issue, I said mildly, "Tomorrow is the big day, right? The day you take your qualifying exam. Do you think you're ready?"

"As ready as I can be. I'll be glad not to have to bury my nose in a textbook every night, studying."

"This exam is only your first step. Once you pass it, you'll have to begin preparing for your broker's license."

"Not right away, certainly."

"What's to be gained by waiting? Speaking of waiting, what's on your mind?"

"Two pieces of news. A retired CPA stopped by while you were out of the office. He and his wife are thinking of relocating to a smaller home. I took them to see the Benson property. They're interested. The place doesn't carry a hefty price tag, but it'll be our first sale in a couple of weeks if they buy it."

"It might also be your first closing, assuming you pass your qualifying exam. That would be kind of cool. And your second bit of news?"

"I spoke with my dad. He is definitely in your corner. He offered to help fund my living expenses until business picks up again. That means I can stay with Trinity Falls Realty. I called Helen and told her I appreciated her offer, but I'm happy where I am. I won't be joining her at Rimdale Properties. She didn't seem all that pleased. I suspect she usually gets what she wants."

"That's a bit of an understatement. Well, now, this is excellent news. Someday, you'll be happy you made this choice. I'll see to it. I promise." I reminded myself to write Leonard Flashman and thank him for his vote of confidence and for supporting his son's career.

"I believe you. That's one reason I'm staying. You have integrity; you follow through on what you say you'll do. I don't want to take up any more of your time. I feel you have a lot on your plate right now, so I'll be going. I just wanted you to know."

"I'm so glad you stopped by. I've been worried sick that I might lose you."

I accompanied Jack to the front door and bid him farewell. As I stood on the stoop watching him leave, I gazed at the heavens and whispered, "Thank You."

*   *   *

The woods smelled crisp and clean. The earth felt spongy beneath my feet as I trekked across the Spirit Wolf property. Jack's announcement the previous evening that he planned to stay with Trinity Falls Realty was still fresh in my thoughts. However, my initial gladness had been overtaken by a more recent event.

A cold front had passed through during the night. Dew still lingered on the leaves of the trees and the shrubs on the forest floor. My pant legs were wet from brushing up against the foliage. The emergence of the midday sun promised that the afternoon's warmth would burn away the dampness. Even so, I hardly noticed. I was too busy fretting about the phone call I had received that earlier that morning. Logan Smallwood had again summoned me to his office but had refused to state a reason, leaving me free to imagine the worst. We had scheduled a meeting for the following afternoon.

In keeping with my commitment to Rachel, I had informed her that I would again be venturing into the forest. Though apprehensive, she had refrained from voicing an objection. I thought about calling her to reassure her that all was well and that I no longer needed my navigation app, having, over multiple visits, become familiar with the lay of the land.

Shafts of golden sunlight spilled down between the trees, glittering off leaves and pine needles alike. The maples, birches, and oaks were nearing a full display of foliage. The evergreens literally sparkled. Indeed, it was a beautiful day.

As I crossed the property, I was so distracted by my musings that I almost forgot I had set out to take pictures of the forest. If all went well with Logan and if the planning board approved our application, Phase 2 would move forward on schedule. If so, a crush of heavy equipment would soon throng the woods, altering the terrain forever. I intended to document the transformation.

After snapping a dozen more photos, I briefly rested on a fallen log. Seated there, I reviewed the pictures I had taken and quickly realized they would make a splendid portfolio. As I scrolled from image to image, the pristine grandeur of the property was undeniable. The promise I had made the Campbells leaped into my mind: my vow to protect the woods' aesthetic beauty. It was a promise I intended to keep.

I switched off my camera, rose from the log, and returned to my car. It was time to go. A ton of work awaited me at the office, but first, there was a stop I planned to make. A series of recent storms had swollen the flows of the Byrne River, especially the currents that surged through the Trinity Falls chasm. In a few days, the gush would wane, but this day seemed the perfect opportunity to take photos I could later use to market the estates.

*   *   *

As anticipated, strong currents rippled the waters of Lake McDougall. I watched a fishing boat with two people aboard drift toward Eldridge Dam. The fishermen cast their lines on opposite sides of the boat. I suspected they were trolling for lake trout and envied their leisure time. When they recognized their proximity to the dam, they fired up the outboard motor and sped away to continue fishing farther upstream.

Fishing was one of my favorite pastimes and one of my more proficient skills, though lately, it had been impossible to indulge my hobby. I especially liked taking Alicia with me. Witnessing her excitement when she landed a fish was such a joy. Seeing the world through a child's eyes, when everything is fresh and new, was even better than fishing.

After collecting half a dozen snapshots of the lake, I returned to the Eldridge Dam parking lot. From there, I followed the footpath to the viewing area, which overlooked the rapids. Below the overlook, a trail meandered along the western bluff of the narrow gorge through which the Byrne River frothed and churned. Along the trail, various vantage points offered excellent views of the falls. As I strolled along, a crisp spray of mist cast up by the raging waters cooled my face. The roar of the cataract would have made speech impossible had anyone been with me.

At the first vantage point, I stopped to snap more photos. Glancing around, I saw that I was the only one enjoying the spectacle. No one else was in sight. Mid-May was well before the regular tourist season.

With a sense of childlike devilry, I ignored the sign beside the trail that warned of danger and scurried over the guardrail for a closer view. A torrent of lathered water surged ten feet below where I stood. The river foamed and churned as it crashed upon the jagged rocks littering the canyon.

After gushing forth from the Eldridge Dam's spillways, the Byrne River entered a tapered canyon that gave rise to the falls. As the canyon narrowed, the river's speed and ferocity increased exponentially. Having endured eons of rushing water, the slick sides of the canyon were nearly vertical. In patches, moss grew on the rocks, but for the most part, the gorge's rocky banks were devoid of vegetation.

The panorama of the seething falls, and the fertile valley below was too much to resist. I hooked my foot in the cleft of a rock for stability. With care, I leaned out over the water for a better view. Holding myself as steady as possible—given the awkward orientation of my body—I clicked several shots with my camera, which hung from a strap around my neck. Pleased with the perspective I had managed, I flexed my leg to draw myself back to an upright posture, but my foot slipped out of the rocky cleft.

In less time than the interval between heartbeats, I felt myself falling. Instinctively, I let go of the camera and flung my arms to either side to break my fall. In slow motion, a ribbon of blue sky passed in front of my eyes as I twisted in my descent. In that instant, I realized with absolute certainty that I was about to die. Once a body hit the water, there was no escape from the canyon. A hapless victim had to endure the transit before emerging at the opposite end of the gorge where the flows slow. To my knowledge, no one had ever survived a dash through Trinity Falls.

Then it struck me. *This was precisely the spot where Thomas died. How could I not remember?* Soul-crushing terror gripped me.

When I hit the icy water, I tensed every muscle. The torrent enveloped me. My entire body went rigid. Panic flooded my soul. My vision clouded as my head plunged beneath the churning fury. I fought to resurface.

As a youth, I had read a book about surviving in the wild. The author had claimed that the best way to navigate treacherous rapids was to float on your back with your feet pointed downstream and your hands and forearms protecting your head and neck. That way, your feet would impact the rocks and debris first. The problem was that my head was aimed downstream like a body surfer riding a wave toward shore. There was no way to turn around; the force of the water was too strong.

As best I could, I craned my neck to see what lay ahead. As soon as I looked, I noticed a massive, jagged rock rushing straight at my face. Instinctively, I closed my eyes and braced for impact, but nothing happened. Instead, I felt myself being carried along like a cork bobbing on the ocean. A roaring eddy threatened to suck me under and hold my body pressed against the riverbed. Trapped by such a whirlpool, I would surely drown. Yet, as before, nothing happened. I floated serenely past.

Then, I again felt myself falling. I had reached the first of the three falls. Upon tumbling over the lip of the rocky shelf, I again braced for impact, fully expecting to be dashed and bloodied upon the craggy shards below. Instead, churning waters enveloped me, keeping me afloat. Coughing and sputtering, I rose to the surface to continue my headlong rush.

At the second falls, a similar thing happened. I felt myself falling, only to be cushioned by churning water.

The roar of the rapids was deafening. But rather than hear the noise in my ears, I felt the vibrations in my bones. Bubbling water blurred my vision, depriving me of a proper sense of orientation. Except for the force of the water on my body, it was impossible to sort out which way was forward and which was back. Periodically, when I drew in a breath, all I inhaled was water.

Time seemed to slow. My passage through the canyon seemed less chaotic. Completed in mere seconds, events felt like they were taking minutes. Remarkably, my sense of panic began to subside; the horror that had gripped me eased. In a flash, the terror vanished, leaving behind an abiding calm, like being suspended in time.

To my astonishment, a sense of utter tranquility cocooned me. Even as I approached the third falls, I did not recoil in alarm. Being the steepest and, therefore, the most violent, that hazard should have evoked an overwhelming dread. Instead, I relaxed and let the current carry me along.

As before, I tumbled over the fall's rocky lip to land in a swirling pool of water, much akin to impacting a giant soggy pillow.

Incrementally, the river's rush lessened. Floating on my back, I gazed up at a translucent blue sky. A bright yellow sun hung suspended midway above the horizon. The profound peace that had infused me remained.

I had survived. My serenity was so intense that I wanted to float in the water forever. Instead, as the reality of my predicament slowly sank in, I reluctantly paddled to shore, my camera still hanging by its strap around my neck.

After clambering up the banks of the Byrne River, I looked myself over but could find not a single injury. My hair, plastered to my scalp, was dripping into my eyes. My clothes were sopping wet, and I was shivering from what might be hypothermia. Otherwise, there was no indication that I had just navigated a headlong rush through Trinity Falls.

Glancing around in disbelief, I considered what to do next. It soon became apparent that the only reasonable course of action was to hike back to where I had parked my car. Abstractly, I wondered if my clothes would dry by the time I regained the parking lot.

The drive home from the Eldridge Dam parking lot passed in a blur. The feeling of serenity that had cocooned me continued. Never had I enjoyed such an abiding sense of peace. As I approached my home, I found it somewhat unnerving that I wasn't utterly shaken, having cheated death. Yet, internally, I felt calm and entirely tranquil—an extraordinary sensation.

Inside the house, I examined my waterlogged camera. Hoping it could be salvaged, I buried it in a bowl of rice to dry. On the other hand, my waterproof cell phone had amazingly survived its trip through the canyon and was functioning normally.

After showering and changing string clothes, I felt the need to do something. What I craved was to regain a sense of normalcy.

Gardening was one of my favorite pastimes. I found working in the soil and watching flowers grow highly satisfying. An added benefit was that gardening allowed me to work with my hands, leaving my mind free to deal with other issues. I decided it was time to weed the flower beds in the backyard.

I began by gathering my tools and wheelbarrow from the potting shed. Crabgrass was an insidious nuisance. It would invade any patch of earth it could find. Consequently, I considered it my solemn duty to eradicate the noxious weed wherever I found it.

Kneeling on a foam pad and combing the earth with a forked trowel, I yanked tufts of crabgrass from among chrysanthemums and amaryllis, careful to leave the plants undisturbed. I slowly worked my way from one end of the flower bed to the other. My world seemed perfectly normal for a brief time, everything in balance, as if nothing extraordinary had transpired.

Then, a troubling thought came to me unbidden: *Why did I fall in?* Because my foot slipped, and I lost my balance, but that wasn't the essence of my conundrum. *What had tempted me to venture so near the canyon's edge?* By nature, I am the timid sort. I do not enjoy taking risks. I shy away from conflicts, and I avoid quarrels whenever possible. I hate being a wimp, but it's who I am. *So why on earth did I take such a risk?* I sensed that I already knew the answer, but I found it too distressing to bring to mind.

Then, a corollary struck me: *How did I lose my fear?* I remembered knowing with absolute certainty that I was about to die. The outcome had seemed inevitable. At the third falls—the largest and most dangerous— my terror should have been unbearable. Yet rather than panic, a sublime sense of peace had washed through me. *How could that have happened?*

I heard a car pull into our driveway. I consulted my cell phone. It was half past five. *Rachel is home. Where did the time go?* A minute or two later, my wife emerged through the kitchen door to join me in the backyard.

"What's with your camera?" A look of puzzlement contorted Rachel's face as she bent down to kiss me on the cheek.

"It got wet," I replied innocently.

"That explains the rice. How did that happen?"

"It fell in the river."

"That's unfortunate. Were you fishing?"

"No. I was taking pictures to create a marketing portfolio."

"I see. So you dropped it in, did you?"

"No. I was holding it when I fell in."

"You fell in? Are you okay?"

"I'm fine…absolutely fine. All that happened was I got a little wet."

The most crucial question came to mind: How did I emerge *from the bottom of the gorge without a single bump or bruise? By what miracle am I still alive? Twice now, my life has been spared. Arguably, the first time, I might have made it out of the woods alive. The second time, though, I should have drowned.*

"I'm glad to hear that." Rachel consulted her watch. "You do remember that Franklin and Ellen Rose invited us over for dinner tonight?"

"Oh, right." I tried not to show that I had forgotten entirely. "Where is Alicia? Weren't you supposed to pick her up after school?"

"She's upstairs changing into her play clothes. Her babysitter will be here in half an hour. You should probably start getting ready soon."

Inwardly, I winced. I was in no mood to socialize.

Rachel went inside to prepare for our family get-together, leaving me to wrestle with my crumbling sense of serenity.

*　*　*

Franklin and I lounged in folding chairs on the small screened-in porch behind his house. Thin ribbons of smoke curled upward from the barbecue in the backyard. Franklin had insisted upon broiling our steaks out of doors. We had finished dinner half an hour earlier. The charcoal briquettes were now fading to an ash gray. Inside the house, we could hear our wives cleaning up in the kitchen. The sky was darkening, and the night's first star had just appeared overhead.

Franklin seemed at peace with the world—his hands folded over his abdomen, legs outstretched, and ankles crossed. My thoughts, on the other hand, were troubled and confused. We had been discussing local politics, but my mind kept picturing rushing rapids, swirling eddies, and cascading falls.

Franklin's brow furrowed. "Doesn't matter who's elected mayor. He'll screw it up somehow." Then he chuckled. "That sounds fairly pessimistic, doesn't it? Normally, I'm not so glum, though I wish we had better candidates. Say, are you alright? You've been quiet all evening. What's troubling you?"

I responded with an offhand gesture. "These last few days have been difficult."

My brother eyed me shrewdly. "Something in particular?"

"The usual. Money, work…family matters."

"You and Rachel? Are you two…?"

"No, we're fine. It's Alicia. She has a cold. It was diagnosed as an adenovirus, whatever that is. When she developed a fever and a cough, we got terrified. We were afraid maybe…you know." In response to my brother's questioning, I described our visit to Dr. McGregor's office.

Franklin nodded thoughtfully. "That must have been horrible, worrying that…?"

"It was. Speaking of children, are you and Ellen Rose still trying to get pregnant?"

"We are. We're beginning to believe it's not going to happen."

"Have you had yourselves tested?"

"We have. The tests say everything is a go. According to the specialist, there's no physical reason why we can't conceive. And before you make some lame comment, yes, we're doing our part, just like we're supposed to."

"How will you feel if nothing happens?"

"We trust that God will allow us to become parents, or He won't. Whichever way it goes, we'll take comfort in knowing He's in control."

"Speaking of which," I said, no longer able to ignore the concerns tormenting me, "something interesting happened to me this afternoon."

Franklin regarded me with a wry smile. "I suspected as much."

Perceptive as always, I thought. *It's spooky how my brother can sense what I'm feeling.*

In a quiet voice that would keep our conversation private, I described my transit through Trinity Falls and what it felt like: the paralyzing terror, the realization that I was going to die, and then the indescribable peace that had overtaken me.

Franklin listened with what I regarded as unrestrained skepticism. When I concluded, he said, "Is this true, or are you pulling my leg?"

"It's true, every word. Why do you think God is doing this to me?"

"You assume that surviving the falls was God's handiwork?" This time, it was his turn to play the skeptic.

"Can you think of a better explanation?"

"Random chance?"

"What are the odds?"

"Good point." My brother remained silent for a time. "If what you've told me is true—and I'm not saying I have any reason to think it's not, and considering the other miracles you've experienced—the only explanation I can fathom is that God is doing His best to get your attention."

"To what end?"

"I have no idea. Perhaps there's some lesson He wants to teach you, or maybe He hopes you will reexamine how you are living your life."

"What is that supposed to mean? I'm not a reprobate, some godforsaken sinner."

"We are all sinners, but that's not what I meant. I was rather thinking about your relationship with His son, Jesus." Franklin spoke slowly and with great seriousness. "In the core of my being, I believe that a strong relationship with God's son is the only way to make sense of our lives and the world around us. Every man is gifted with an innate appreciation for the order and structure of reality. We instinctively know we are not some cosmic accident, or the product of a chain of random events. Life has meaning, a purpose outside of ourselves. Only in Jesus, and through Him with the Father, does anything make sense. We are all called to form an intimate, personal relationship with our Creator, and scripture teaches that this can only happen with Christ as our Lord and Savior."

"I believe in Jesus. You know I do."

Franklin broached a smile intended to challenge my self-perceptions. "Yes, but are you living your life by faith, or are you relying on the strength of your own abilities to solve the problems that confront you?"

My brother's comments triggered an interlude of introspection. With absolute certainty, I knew I had been saved from the torrent by the grace of God, not by luck, not by random chance, and certainly not by my own efforts. Perhaps He was indeed inviting me to rely more fully upon Him.

"I'll consider the matter," I said softly, "but there's something else you need to know, which is difficult to admit."

"I'm listening."

I paused to inhale a deep breath. "The spot where I fell in was the exact same spot where Thomas died." My voice cracked, and I found it hard to continue.

Franklin waited until I had regained my composure.

At length, I went on, "I've shared before how our brother died, but I've never told why. It was my fault. I dared Thomas to get as close to the edge as he could. When he at first refused, I taunted him repeatedly. When I saw him slip and fall, I rushed to save him, but I was too slow. He was already in the torrent. There was nothing I could do. He would never have been so near the edge if not for me." An upwelling of shame overtook me. On the verge of breaking down completely, I stammered, "It was my fault. I killed our brother."

Franklin's mood was difficult to read. He said, "I've always suspected there was more to that story than what you told us."

Perceptive as usual.

My brother's demeanor softened. He spoke slowly in a low voice and with great compassion. "Thomas was thirteen, old enough to know right from wrong. You may have dared him, but he chose to take your dare. His passing is on his own shoulders, not yours. What you did was wrong, yes, but his dying is not your burden to bear. I forgive you, and so does God. Now, you need to forgive yourself."

For the second time in as many months, I began to cry in my brother's presence. And for the second time, he moved closer, wrapped me in a comforting embrace, and whispered in my ear, "It was not your fault." He repeated the words several times. My guilt seemed to lift a little. When my emotions settled, we separated.

"Tell me," Franklin said, "does Rachel know about your brushes with death?"

"I told her about the wolf but not about my…excursion…down the Byrne River, so please don't mention it. Not yet, anyway. I need to sort out some issues first."

Alerted by a sound behind me, I turned my head just as my wife and Ellen Rose appeared at the door that opened onto the porch. "Speak of an angel…"

When Rachel stepped outside, I noted that she was already wearing her coat. The woolen scarf around her neck indicated she was ready to leave.

She looked at me. "It's getting late, honey. We should go. We need to check on Alicia."

"Right." I stood up. When Ellen Rose joined us on the porch, I hugged her cordially. She was a smallish woman with a lively smile and a cheerful personality. "Thank you for a fine evening," I declared enthusiastically. "Next time, dinner is on us."

"We'll look forward to it," Ellen Rose responded warmly.

I turned to Franklin and said earnestly, "Thank you. I will seriously consider what you said."

He nodded. "Please do. I'm certain the effort will be worth your while."

As we stepped away, Rachel asked under her breath, "What was that all about?"

"Just brother stuff," I replied vaguely.

Rather than reenter the house, Rachel and I exited the porch onto the recently mowed lawn.

As we walked toward our car, I heard Ellen Rose ask her husband, "How'd you two get along? Did you solve the world's problems?"

Then I heard Franklin's response. "Our conversation? It was inspirational, I'd say. And poignant." I couldn't quite make out what followed, though I had no concerns that he would violate my request for confidentiality.

*   *   *

The following morning, I stood just outside the door to Logan Smallwood's office. I was running twenty minutes late. I had nearly forgotten about our scheduled meeting because of all that had taken place the day before.

The rooms occupied by the planning board bustled with activity as secretaries, appraisers, inspectors, and other functionaries went about their assigned duties. Keeping Trinity Falls Township compliant with the master growth plan required considerable bureaucratic oversight.

Logan's door was ajar. He looked up from behind his desk when I knocked on the doorframe. He did not smile but merely nodded. I stepped inside.

"You're late," he announced. "Around here, we pride ourselves on our punctuality."

"Sorry. Yesterday was terribly disorganized. I'm still trying to catch up." I drew my cell phone from its belt holster and activated the voice memo app. "Mr. Smallwood, would you mind if I again record our conversation?"

"For the life of me, I can't imagine why you'd need to, but if you feel you must, go ahead." Logan gave a dismissive wave of his hand. He did not invite me to sit down.

I sat in one of the armless chairs facing his desk. "It's just that the investors I represent will expect a full and accurate accounting of our conversation."

"Whatever. Look, this won't take long. It's just that I wanted to tell you that yesterday, I went out to take a look at your property. I wanted to see the parcel for myself and get a feel for the lay of the land."

"It is a beautiful plot of ground, is it not?"

"If you say so. While conducting my inspection, I noted several varieties of noxious weeds. In particular, I observed stands of common buckthorn and multiflora rose. Both are highly invasive species, and both are harmful to the environment. You'll have to spray the entire property to ensure you get them all."

"That's what you called me in to discuss? What about the status of our subdivision application?"

"It is still undergoing its comprehensive review. We'll let you know when we've finished."

"That's it?"

Logan glanced up from the paperwork on his desk. "Was there something else you wished to discuss?"

"No. I guess not." I retrieved my phone, switched off the voice memo app, and stood up.

As I left, Logan commented, "It would be best if you had a commercial sprayer submit an affidavit after the work has been completed. That way, I can include it in your file."

"Certainly. Happy to oblige."

As I was leaving the planning board's offices, I reflected on my multiple visits to the property. Not once had I noticed a noxious weed. It was possible I might have missed seeing them, but I felt confident that there wasn't a single invasive species on the two hundred acres. To my mind, the demand that we spray for weeds felt like another bureaucratic make-work requirement.

Upon stepping into the corridor, I had to remind myself not to slam the outer door behind me.

*　*　*

Five days later, Rachel, Alicia, and I were again helping feed the hungry at the Maranatha Gospel Fellowship. This was our second time volunteering, and I was beginning to understand the routine. One group of helpers would arrive early and prepare the food. Then, a second shift would arrive to serve the meal and clean up afterward. It seemed an efficient division of labor. As before, the Langdons had volunteered to join the second shift.

Earlier that afternoon, I had again visited the property to confirm that the spraying for noxious weeds was proceeding smoothly. As far as I could tell, the contractor was doing a thorough job, though I still could find no evidence of any invasive species. The sprayer's signed and dated certificate was now in my briefcase. I would present it to the planning board in the morning. The price tag had come in at just under $25,000 or $125 per acre—a reasonable price considering the work involved. I still thought it was a needless expense, but we were obliged to pay it if we hoped to gain the board's approval of our plat. I suppose I might have challenged the board's requirement in court, but that would have sparked a delay of months if not years—a delay I was unwilling to accept.

I ladled a spoonful of mixed vegetables onto the tray of a stout lad who looked slightly older than Alicia, perhaps ten or eleven. He made a wry face, and I countered, "They're good for you. Just ask your mom."

The woman trailing behind the youth nodded in agreement. I could tell she appreciated my comment. The warmth of her smile lifted my soul. It made me feel as if I was paying God back for His great mercies in some small way.

In addition to mixed vegetables, the main entrée was Swedish meatballs served over a bed of rice. A dinner roll and a glass of punch rounded out the fare. The cuisine wasn't lavish, but the servings were nutritious and filling.

Alicia was responsible for handing out the dinner rolls, one per tray. This was because she had asked to help. It warmed my heart to think she was learning the worth of serving others, a lesson I myself was only now beginning to appreciate.

In the first days after falling into the Byrne River, I struggled to make sense of my experience. Against all odds, I had been miraculously spared from physical harm, though my rescue was no longer the focus of my introspections. What intrigued me even more was the sudden peace that had come upon me. Repeatedly, I had relived that instant in which the terror had vanished, replaced by a sense of absolute serenity. *How did that happen? By what means did I transition from petrifying dread to utter tranquility?*

As I pondered the moment of my transformation, I recalled that time had seemed to dilate, and the forward rush of events had slowed to a crawl. Straining to remember, I pictured myself approaching the third precipice. *What,* I wondered, *was I thinking in that instant? What captivated my consciousness so that I was no longer terrified?*

Then it struck me. I remembered being swept along by the torrent, but rather than focus on my impending doom, I had imagined myself serenely floating on my back. An unambiguous image of deliverance had formed within my mind. I had visualized myself as I would emerge from the cataract unscathed. In fact, I had anticipated my own survival.

But where had that image come from? Had it been given to me as a vision, a prophecy, or had it arisen within me like a prayer? Or could there be another explanation, something even more mysterious? Could thinking that I would be saved have caused it to happen? Was it possible that my thoughts had altered reality and triggered my salvation? Might I have been saved simply because I had foreseen that I would be saved?

The concept rocked me to the core. The notion seemed so fantastical. My mind roiled, inundated by a flood of tangential possibilities as I considered the implications.

"Dad?" said a girl's voice to my right.

Startled, I looked to see who had spoken. Alicia stood pointing to a teenager on the opposite side of the serving table. He was regarding me with a censorious look. Flushing slightly, I resumed my serving duties and ladled a spoonful of mixed vegetables onto his tray.

Chapter 7

A week after meeting with Logan Smallwood, I was again back in his office, having been summoned to discuss a deficiency in the subdivision plat. As before, the planning board chairman had declined to address the problem over the phone. I wondered if Logan might be attempting to nickel-and-dime our project into insolvency.

Having endured the chairman's curt demeanor on two occasions, I dispensed with the usual pleasantries. Instead, as I entered his office, I produced my phone and activated the voice memo app. "Would you mind?" I asked, setting the phone down on the corner of his desk.

The chairman scowled. "Do we have to go through this every time? If you feel you must record our conversation, go ahead. In fact, from this point forward, I give you permission to record any and all of my conversations without limitation. Does that satisfy you?"

"Yes, Mr. Smallwood. Thank you. I assume you've found another issue I'll have to deal with?"

"Indeed, we have. Let me show you what we've uncovered." Logan rose from behind his desk and stepped around to the drafting table. I joined him there. Pointing to where Argyle Road paralleled the eastern edge of our property, he said, "According to this plat, this is the only access road that serves the Spirit Wolf Estates. Is that correct?"

"It is." The chairman's reference to our sole route of ingress and egress worried me, and a lump of uneasiness formed in the pit of my stomach.

He pointed again. "And here is where Argyle Road branches off from Highway 171. Right?"

"Yes, as you can see. Though I do believe the road is a public right-of-way, and we have unrestricted access."

"Yes, according to the title deed and other documents I've reviewed, that is true."

"So, what's the problem? Our surveyor assured me that Argyle Road can handle whatever traffic the subdivision might generate."

"Concerning width and grade, that is correct, but Argyle Road is woefully deficient when it comes to surface structure. It's a dirt road, and for the amount of use your project will demand, that's unacceptable. We project that the dust kicked into the air will reach intolerable levels. Furthermore, a dirt road's surface integrity degrades rapidly with increased traffic, especially in bad weather."

The knot of apprehension in the pit of my stomach tightened. "What are you saying?"

"We're saying that the portion of Argyle Road that parallels the northern boundary of your property will only need to have its potholes filled in. However"—he pointed to the map again—"this segment that extends along the eastern edge must be paved with asphalt."

"Which section specifically?"

With his finger, the chairman traced a line on the map. "This stretch of road. The one that extends from the property's northeast corner to where it intersects Highway 171."

"To what width?"

"To a width proportional to your right-of-way, thirty feet minimum."

Mentally, I did some rough calculations. The results were mind-numbing. The expense would be enormous at three dollars per square foot for asphalt. "You're telling me you want us to spend at least a quarter of a million dollars that's not in our budget?"

"So it would seem."

"We can't afford that!" I exclaimed.

"That's your problem, not mine. I'm telling you that as drafted, this plat cannot be approved without blacktopping Argyle Road."

I was stunned. The expenditure would exceed our reserve funds and demand additional contributions. I tried to picture how the investors would respond. For sure, Winston Fordyce III would blow a gasket. Judge Tolliver might have a stroke.

The chairman tapped the map. "Let me know what you decide to do."

"I don't suppose we have any recourse?"

"You could appeal to the city council, though I doubt you would find them sympathetic." Logan nodded toward the door. "I'm sure you can find your way out, so I'll bid you good day." He returned to his desk and buried his face in his paperwork.

I numbly gathered up my cell phone, toggled off the voice memo app, and returned to my car. On the way, I decided that the first thing I should do was return to my office and review the project's budget. Perhaps there were areas where we could shave expenses to compensate. I also briefly considered having the partnership apply for a temporary loan. Still, Winston had made it clear: the earliest we could hope to borrow money would be after our plat had received its final approval. It seemed a classic catch-22.

One thing was apparent, though I hated to admit it. From the investors' point of view, they were wise to have insisted I contribute to the project. Otherwise, the financial impact of the planning board's chairman would have been significantly more severe.

* * *

I became increasingly worried as I sat at my desk at Trinity Falls Realty. No matter how I manipulated the numbers, I could reach only one conclusion: there wasn't enough money in the partnership's bank account to cover the cost of paving Argyle Road. The funds simply weren't available. To take the edge off my frustration, I folded my hands over my abdomen, rocked back in my chair, and stared up at the ceiling.

"Is there a problem?" Jack Flashman said from the doorway to my office.

Startled, I rocked forward. "It's the partnership. We seem to have a lack of operating capital."

"There's a lot of that going around." My newly promoted sales associate stepped fully into my office. "I have just put a tiny dent in that problem."

"You finalized your first solo closing. Congratulations. How did it go?"

"Smoothly. The Benson property was listed below market value, so the commission wasn't all that great, but every little bit helps. Right?"

"Yes, it does. Tell me, how do you feel having nailed your first sale?"

"Encouraged. And happy, especially since the buyer and the seller were satisfied with the deal. Actually, it was fun. I enjoyed the sense of completion, seeing it through to the end." Jack's body language mirrored his words. He seemed at ease, content. I envied him.

"That's why we call it a closing. You know, I remember my early days, and you're right. It is fulfilling when each party walks away in a good frame of mind. So, what's next on your agenda?"

"I guess I'm back to beating the bushes for new clients. Have you developed any leads lately?"

"Not really. I've mostly been focusing on partnership business. However, that teacher from Iowa who's looking to move to the area called again yesterday. He indicated that he might be out for a visit next week. We'll have to wait to see if his intentions are genuine."

I eyed Jack closely as I considered broaching a topic on my mind of late. I decided to give it a shot. "Let me ask you something, and I know this might sound more than a little strange. What do you think determines the future?"

Jack's brow furrowed in confusion. "What do you mean?"

"It's hard to explain. As we live our lives, events follow one another in a continuing sequence, like pearls in a necklace. This happens, and then that happens, and so on. But what determines the nature of each event? Is it a random chance, cause and effect, or something else? I guess what I'm asking is, is there an unseen force that determines the events we will experience?"

Jack seemed intrigued. He sat down in one of the armchairs that faced my desk. "I guess I'd vote for cause and effect. Suppose I take a hammer and drive a nail into my tire. The tire goes flat. Now, my future is that I'll have to change the tire if I want to drive my car. Cause and effect."

"Right, but what happened before you struck the nail with the hammer? You thought about what you were doing. In your mind, you visualized the tire being flat. Wouldn't it be fair to say that what you thought became what was real?"

"Perhaps in that example, yes. But what if I'm driving down the road and run over a nail? My tire goes flat even though I wasn't thinking it would happen. In this case, I certainly didn't imagine the flat tire into existence."

"Maybe not at that moment, but had you ever thought about having a flat tire?"

"Are you suggesting that what we think determines what's real? I find that hard to accept. I've often imagined myself winning the lottery, but so far, no luck."

I grinned. "Not yet, anyway."

"I'll admit it would be nice, dreaming pleasant thoughts and having them come true." Jack tilted his head to regard me with a look of curiosity. "This seems an odd conversation. Where is all this coming from?"

"I've been mulling over my dealings with the planning board and their latest demand that we pave Argyle Road. Right before meeting with Logan Smallwood, I worried that something bad would come my way. I had this strong image in my mind. I couldn't shake the impression that I was about to face a major challenge."

"A premonition?"

"Perhaps, though, it felt more like a memory of something that hadn't happened yet."

"This is getting weird."

I chuckled. "You're right. It is. Look. Let's not spend any more time on this. We have more important things to think about. For one, I must call the Spirit Wolf investors and arrange a get-together. Believe me, it won't be fun telling them I need more of their money."

"I would imagine not." Jack stood up. "And I need to familiarize myself with the latest MLS listings, just in case someone stops in today." He turned to leave but then looked back. "I hope you solve your puzzle. If you do, let me know how it turns out. In the meantime, think happy thoughts." He grinned.

"Right."

After Jack left my office, I reached for the phone to begin summoning the investors to a meeting I wished to avoid. As I dialed the first number, my thoughts were anything but happy.

*   *   *

The collective mood of the four gentlemen seated around the glossy conference table was easy to read. Dismay and apprehension, clouded by a healthy indignation, were evident on each of their faces. I had laid out the facts as succinctly as I could. Without embellishment, I had explained the planning board's decree that either the partnership paved Argyle Road or our subdivision application would be denied. There could be no appeal, no reversal of the board's ruling. As far as we were concerned, it was either comply or abandon the project altogether.

The most contentious moment came when I delivered the project's revised budget.

Our road construction subcontractor had set the cost of paving Argyle Road at $270,000. That meant that, after installing the ponds and wells and spraying for noxious weeds, we would fall $95,000 short of having funds enough to satisfy the board's demands. When I informed the investors that covering the shortfall would necessitate an additional contribution of $25,000 per man, howls of protest erupted around the table.

"You assured us this wouldn't happen," Marcus proclaimed, evoking outbursts of agreement. And he was right. In my original presentation, I confidently predicted that our initial contributions would sufficiently cover all expenses.

"How could I have foreseen that the planning board would throw us this curveball?" I protested in my defense.

"You should have anticipated that possibility," Winston Fordyce III hissed ominously.

I sat quietly, waiting for the uproar to subside. In the process, I tried to think positively, hoping that an optimistic attitude would result in an equitable solution to our predicament.

Eventually, as the clamor died down and the investors began to think logically about our options, Judge Tolliver said, "How do we know this will be the last call for additional funding?"

"We don't," I admitted, "not with absolute certainty. However, as you can see from the spreadsheets I've provided, I've tried to account for every possible contingency. It really boils down to this: Are you willing to spend another $25,000 to protect your initial investment of $750,000?"

"What about you?" Winston said. "How much are you going to contribute?" A flush of anger still colored his cheeks.

"Regrettably, nothing. I had to borrow money to make my initial contribution. I have nothing left to contribute except my time and energy."

"Is this an elaborate scam?" Marcus sputtered with blatant hostility. "You entice us with promises of riches and then gradually bleed us with these unexpected difficulties?"

"Don't be ridiculous," Angus blurted out. "I've known Paul a good many years. He's a man of integrity. He would never deliberately cheat a man out of his money. Your premise is absurd."

I regarded the doctor with heartfelt gratitude for coming to my defense, but then I looked at Marcus. "I can appreciate your suspicions. I know how this must appear. If I were in your shoes, I'd probably feel the same. However, I assure you I have done everything I can to resolve this situation without coming to you and asking for more money. Unfortunately, that seems to be the only way forward if we hope to keep the Spirit Wolf project alive." I sat back in my chair and waited.

Winston looked from man to man. He then addressed me directly. "I think we'll need a few minutes to consider our response. Would you mind leaving us while we talk this over?"

I stood and left the conference room. Behind me, I could hear muffled voices as I took a chair in the outer office, but I could not discern individual words. Janet watched me closely out of the corner of her eye. Ten minutes later, the door opened, and Winston ushered me back into the inner sanctum.

"We've made our decision," Winston announced as I sat down. "We're not going to invest any more money in this project. Yes, we understand there is a risk that we might lose our initial contributions. However, we are willing to take that risk. Instead, we will give you one week to resolve this problem. You will have to find a way to satisfy the planning board's demands without our help. If you can't, you'll be replaced as managing partner, and we will sue you to recover as much as we can, even if it means seizing your home, your business, and whatever collateral you have in this or any other bank."

So much for holding happy thoughts. I felt compelled to point out that I had reviewed the numbers dozens of times, but it was apparent that a protest would accomplish nothing. The investors' minds were made up. Instead, I nodded to signify my acceptance of their decision.

"Gentlemen, thank you for considering this matter," I said as I gathered the paperwork before me and stuffed it into my briefcase.

"One week," Winston called out behind me as I turned to leave.

*   *   *

Twenty-four hours after meeting with the investors, I again toured the Spirit Wolf property. Franklin was with me this time because I had invited him to come along. And since it was Saturday and Sunday's sermon was already prepared, he had agreed. This was his first visit to the land, which surprised me when I thought about it. After all, he, too, was an investor and, therefore, had a financial stake in the management of the project.

It was a beautifully clear day in early June. Sparrows and finches twittered in the trees. A red-breasted robin landed nearby to scout the ground, hunting worms. On impulse, I had brought my drone along. It was currently soaring a hundred feet overhead. Franklin and I were watching its video feed on my handheld monitor.

"Yes, I do see." Franklin enthusiastically pointed at the screen. "If I'm reading those bright orange stakes correctly, that's the main road that runs through the center of the property, and that depression right there is destined to become one of the two ponds you've been describing."

"You are correct. Well done. You seem to have an eye for picking patterns out of the chaos. You would've made a splendid real estate developer."

My brother chuckled. "Thank you, but I already have a calling."

A loam-scented breeze drifted by. I listened intently, but except for the twittering birds, I could only hear the faint hum of the drone's motors. I should have been listening to the sounds of heavy equipment reshaping the surrounding terrain, but all work had been put on hold.

After maneuvering the drone until it was directly above the clearing where we stood, I brought it down for a smooth landing. As I stowed the drone in its hard-sided case, I thought about the other panorama we had just viewed.

Motivated by despair, I had flown the drone along the length of Argyle Road, monitoring every detail as if studying the road from above might magically offer a solution to my paving dilemma.

"What's wrong?" Franklin said with concern. "You seem troubled."

Always perceptive, I thought. "I have a problem, and it's a big one. I invited you to come with me today because I need your advice again. Of late, I've done this a lot, but it helps when I talk to you."

Trying to control my inner turmoil, I described the planning board's edict and the limited partners' refusal to contribute additional funding. I finished by saying, "Bottom line, I'll need just under $100,000 to comply with the planning board's demands. The partnership will have to be dissolved unless I can raise that much capital. The land will be sold. The investors will be paid back at pennies on the dollar. You and I will lose everything. Worst of all, I won't have enough money to pay for Alicia's medical care."

My brother's eyes went wide. "You're telling me I could lose every cent I loaned you?"

"Regrettably, that's what I'm saying unless I can fix our capital shortfall."

Franklin massaged his chin with his thumb and index finger. "How did you think I could help? I'm tapped out. I don't have any money left."

"I understand. I'm not asking for money. What I'm asking for is your counsel. I'm at my wits' end. For the life of me, I can't see any way to raise the capital I need."

"What about bringing in another limited partner?"

"I discussed that with the investors. They refused. They say my failure to anticipate caused this mess; therefore, it's my problem to fix. I suspect they think I'm holding out on them, and I have resources I haven't disclosed, which is absurd. But that's how they feel."

Franklin remained silent for a time and then said, "Have you tried praying for divine guidance? Prayer works miracles, and we know you're keen on those."

"Those things that happened to me," I protested in self-defense, "they weren't my doing." Then, with genuine uncertainty, I added, "At least I don't believe they were."

"Meaning what?" Franklin said, picking up on my hesitation.

"Lately, I've been wondering how such extraordinary events happen. By what means do they come to be? Tell me, what is prayer exactly?"

"You're asking me?"

"You're the expert. How would you define prayer?"

Franklin cocked his head to study me for a moment. He said, "In the simplest terms, prayer is how we communicate with God."

"I get that, but how does it work?"

"The Scriptures are clear as to how it should work. We present our petitions to God with thanksgiving in faith that we will receive what we ask for. Philippians chapter 4 also says we should be anxious for nothing. In my mind, that means we are to believe wholeheartedly that our prayers will be answered. The key is to have faith. Fear—and, by extension, anxiety—is the antithesis of faith. They are polar opposites."

I snagged a leaf off a nearby birch. A tracery of veins ribbed its surface.

"Doesn't scripture also teach that if we have faith the size of a mustard seed, we can move mountains? In effect, isn't that like saying that what we believe will become what is real? In other words, can what we think define what is?"

Franklin scoffed. "Are you serious? Are you implying that our minds create reality rather than merely experiencing it?" He became quite serious. "Though perhaps from a certain point of view, you might be onto something. Second Corinthians chapter 10, verse 5 warns that we are to take every thought captive so that we might be obedient to Christ. Elsewhere, it also says we are to think only pure and noble thoughts. I've always held that these instructions were intended to steer us away from evil. That's because evil deeds exist in the mind before they are manifest."

"So you agree with me?"

"Only to the extent that our thoughts precede our actions. We control our actions. What we can't control are the consequences of those actions. It's not up to us how things will turn out. As with prayer, outcomes are determined by the power of God as projected by the Holy Spirit. It would be ludicrous to imagine that men structure the fabric of the universe simply by their thoughts. We're not that potent.

"Also, keep in mind that faith demands an object. We must have faith *in* something. Faith cannot stand alone as a state of being divorced from our relationship with God. On the contrary, it is precisely that relationship that defines the world in which we live. If you're looking for the wellspring from which reality flows, you must look only to your Lord and Creator."

I crumpled the leaf in my hand and threw it on the ground. "So if I pray to God to solve my dilemma and adamantly believe that He will, it should come to pass. But what if it doesn't? How do I deal with that?"

"Prayer isn't a celestial vending machine. You don't put in a nickel's worth of supplication and get back a divine dispensation. Faith implies trust. You must trust that God will answer your prayer. Sometimes the answer is yes, sometimes no, and sometimes the answer is to wait. God is in control. His will is sovereign. It's our duty to embrace that truth and structure our lives accordingly."

I stared into the distance while mulling over what my brother was saying.

Franklin rested his hand on my shoulder. "Does this aid you in any way?"

I turned my face toward him. "It helps me tease apart some of the notions I've had. I'm unsure if it will help solve my problem with the Spirit Wolf partnership."

My brother tightened his grip. "Pray that God will answer your prayer. Believe He will, and don't stop believing. Keep your faith strong. Then, whatever the outcome, you can be assured it will be according to God's plan for your life. It may not be the answer you anticipate, but it will be best for you. That's the guarantee."

"Easily said. Difficult to do."

"I know, but faith is like a muscle. It only grows stronger when struggling against resistance."

"If by resistance you mean doubts, then I have an overabundance." I swept my hand toward the forest. "Anyway, would you like to see more of the property, or are you ready to head home?"

Franklin let his hands fall to his sides. "I think I'm done. Besides, I need to go over my sermon for tomorrow again. You've opened up several new concepts to preach about."

"Glad to be of help," I declared with sincerity.

We both looked at each other and laughed.

*   *   *

After touring the property with my brother that evening, I was on my knees in the family room when Rachel returned home. I was so engrossed in my conversation with God that I had failed to heed her arrival. Startled, I looked up into her face and blushed.

"What are you doing?" she demanded.

"Praying," I responded sheepishly. Only then did I remember that I was doing nothing wrong. "Asking God for His help," I said with greater conviction.

My wife seemed unsure how to respond. Her eyebrows knit together. "Should I be worried?"

I rose to my feet and crossed the room to the couch. As I sat down, I patted the cushion beside me. "There are some things I need to tell you."

As my wife joined me, I noted that her dark brown hair hung loose to the tops of her shoulder blades. That morning, upon leaving home, she had worn it tied up in a ponytail. The fact that her coffee-colored locks were now hanging free indicated that she was anxious to be done with work after a stressful day. I feared I had caught her at a bad time, but having taken the first step, I was obligated to tread the path.

I began, "The partnership is in trouble." I summarized the planning board's edict and the partnership's financial difficulties.

"What does all this mean?" Rachel said when I finished.

"It means," I explained as gently as I could, "that unless a miracle happens, we're going to be broke, and our daughter will die from her genetic mutation."

Rachel gasped.

"I'm sorry to be so blunt, but I've been dealing with this for several days, and it is tearing me apart. I've come at it six ways from Sunday and can't see a solution. I'm at the end of my tether. The only thing left to me is prayer."

"And you sincerely believe that God will hear you?"

"I do, especially since He's already favored us with three miracles."

"Three?" Rachel exclaimed.

"That's right. There's something else I need to tell you." I described my immersion in the Byrne River and transit through Trinity Falls. Rachel listened without interrupting, but I could see that she was flabbergasted. I knew it was a lot for her to absorb all at once, especially when I reminded her of how Thomas had died. I did, however, refrain from revealing that I had dared him to get close to the edge. That part was only for my brother and me.

Rachel's eyes narrowed. "So when I came home that day, and you were weeding the garden, you had just survived a near-death experience, and you said nothing about it. I'm your wife!" she shrilled. "How could you shut me out from something so monumental? We don't keep secrets from each other."

"That's why I'm telling you now. Besides, like I said, I was in a state of…I'm unsure what words to use—almost like suspended animation. It was all so surreal. It's been hard for me to process what happened. And I suppose I felt embarrassed that I had been so foolish, but you need to know. God protected me then, and if we trust Him, He will protect us in the future. Of that, I am certain."

"And if He doesn't?"

"Then we will trust that whatever comes is part of His divine plan."

We talked a while longer until Alicia came down from her room, having changed out of her school clothes. Then, as parents do, we changed the subject, unwilling to let our daughter shoulder the woes we were now carrying.

Dinner that night was a somber affair.

*   *   *

Three days later, I was back visiting the Spirit Wolf Estates.

"Do you think he's forgotten about us?" Jack said impatiently. We had been waiting for Russell Talbot, the project's hydrologist, to arrive for fifteen minutes. Russ had called as we were about to close the office for the day and had requested that I meet him on the property.

Jack, having become increasingly comfortable in his role as a sales associate, had asked if he might tag along. I had reluctantly agreed. At first, I had felt inclined to say no, but something within me had cautioned me not to refuse. Later, I would wonder if it was the Holy Spirit.

Jack accompanied me on several occasions while I conducted business partnerships. He was beginning to get a feel for the project, which I regarded as a plus. It had occurred to me that if anything untoward happened, Jack should be able to step in and take over, assuming that the project was still moving forward, which wasn't a given since I hadn't yet solved the paving dilemma. For the time being, however, it was business as usual, but only for activities that didn't require an expenditure of funds.

"Relax," I said. "Russ is always late. He'll be here."

A midsize SUV pulled up and parked on the shoulder of Argyle Road, just below the hillock where we stood waiting. Russ climbed out and waved.

After trudging up the rise to greet us, he said breathlessly, "Sorry I'm late. I wanted to ensure I had this region's latest well-flow figures. It took longer to download them off the internet than I expected."

"Not a problem," I said. "Russ, I'm not sure you've met Jack Flashman. He's my new sales associate. He just passed his qualifying exam." When I glanced at Jack, I noted the broad smile spreading across his face.

Russ nodded to Jack. "Weren't you already working for this guy? I think I recall seeing you in his office."

"It's quite possible you did," Jack answered. "I used to be his assistant, but I've been promoted."

"Congratulations. And welcome aboard. So," Russ said, turning to me, "thanks for meeting me here. I haven't been able to stop thinking about your subdivision plat. The design I proposed has been nagging at me. Something didn't feel quite right."

"Oh lord," I groaned. "Not another problem. I don't know how many more I can handle."

"On the contrary," Russ said, "I think you'll be pleased with what I'm about to suggest, though it might be best to show you rather than try to describe it." He summoned up a topographical map on the tablet computer he carried. After orienting himself, he declared, "The first one should be this way."

Russ began trudging through the forest. Jack and I followed. To say the hydrologist had piqued my curiosity would have been an understatement.

The sun hung just above the horizon. A cloud bank was settling in, blurring the trees' lengthening shadows. I watched with mounting interest as Jack wove his way through the forest. In passing, out of habit, I glanced around to see if there were any wolves nearby. There weren't.

When we reached our destination, Russ halted and pointed. "This depression is where one of the two ponds will go—"

"How large will this pond be?" Jack interjected as he stepped up beside the hydrologist.

Russ consulted his notes. "Forty yards across and approximately… eh, nine feet deep in the middle."

Jack's eyebrows knit together in a look of dismay. "That's not very large."

"We don't need a lake," I proclaimed tersely. "This pond and its companion will easily provide enough water to fight any fire threatening the community."

"What I meant was, aren't they kind of small for fishing?" Jack clarified. I had previously informed him we would be stocking the ponds with fish as a recreational attraction.

"Kids will think they're great," Russ responded. "Adults can fish in the easily accessible lakes scattered throughout the countryside."

"We're not here to discuss fish," I reminded my new sales associate.

"Sorry." Jack shut his mouth.

Russ grinned. "What we are here to talk about"—he pointed again— "lies sixty yards in that direction."

"And what might that be?" I said, still not comprehending where our conversation was headed.

"Well number 7. Currently, it's slated to provide water to estates 31 through 35."

"And?" I gestured for Russ to continue.

"When we amended the subdivision plat to include the ponds, we were going about it backward. Our mindset was that we were adding to what already existed, but so far, no wells have been drilled. Everything is still in the planning stage. What I'm proposing is that we relocate well 7. Shifting it thirty yards in this direction can serve both the pond and the estates. That way, we can eliminate the stand-alone well we'd tasked with keeping this pond full.

Concerned, I asked, "Do you think well 7 can handle the extra load?"

"Absolutely," Russ declared with conviction. "The only real stress on the well will be when we fill the pond for the first time. After the pond is full, it will need to be topped off only periodically. That's a low-flow process. The homeowners shouldn't notice any impact whatsoever."

"Seriously?" I exclaimed. "I assume we can do the same thing with the other pond."

"And you would be correct." Russ grinned again. "Eliminating two wells will save you $30,000."

"You sure about this?"

"I am."

I draped my arm around Russ's shoulders. "My man, you are a genius. Well done. Well done indeed."

"Thank you. That's what you pay me for. By the way, I just recalled what I'm supposed to tell you. Josh called this morning. He has a scheduling problem."

Josh Unger was lead foreman for Bartlett Wells, the firm we had hired to do the drilling.

"What scheduling problem?" I said with a sense of uneasiness.

Until that moment, I had forgotten that Josh was scheduled to begin drilling at the end of the week. In dealing with the financial issues associated with paving Argyle Road, it had slipped my mind that I was supposed to call Josh and put his services on hold. Drilling wells for a project that might have to be abandoned would be foolhardy.

Russ explained, "The sanitation department called. There's a situation at the sewage treatment plant. They need help replumbing one of their drainage fields. It's a major undertaking. Josh expects the Bartlett crews to be tied up for at least a few months."

"We can't wait that long," I blurted out. "If we solve the Argyle Road issue by some miracle, we'll want to immediately submit our subdivision plat for final approval and not be forced to wait a few months. When we go back to the planning board, both ponds will have to be full of water and functioning, not to mention that the other eight wells will also have to be operational."

Russ smiled. "Not a problem."

I gave Russ a questioning look. "Easy for you to say. It's not your project. Being delayed a couple of months while we wait for our wells to be brought in, how can that not be a problem?"

"You can have a tanker fill the ponds. It will have to make multiple trips, but after the ponds are full, they only need to be topped off periodically."

"Won't the planning board assume we're trying to pull a fast one?"

"Not at all." The hydrologist donned a confident grin. "To approve your plat, all the board needs is to see a high probability of finding water when you drill. They will accept my report in that regard. After all, a huge aquifer spans this entire region. I'm telling you it won't be a problem."

"Are you sure?"

"One hundred percent. And since you brought it up, what are you going to do about Argyle Road? I heard the planning board insists that you lay down paving along its entire length."

"Only along the section that fronts the eastern edge of our property," I corrected, "which is bad enough. But to answer your question, we're working on it. You wouldn't happen to have a hundred grand lying around you'd like to loan us, would you?"

Russ laughed.

"I'll take that as a no."

Then Russ said, as his levity faded, "So what are you going to do?"

I squared my shoulders. "We're going to trust that God will provide a way forward. Right, Jack?"

My sales associate nodded. "Absolutely."

"I see." Russ consulted his tablet computer again. "Let's check out the other site. If we agree, as soon as you give the go-ahead, we can have the crews open the access corridors and begin digging the ponds."

He headed off through the forest. Jack and I fell in behind the hydrologist.

As we tramped along, Jack spoke up. "I wonder if the planning board feels the same about the other wells serving the homesites. Could they be brought in *after* the final plat has been approved?"

A flash of inspiration stopped me dead in my tracks, and a sense of elation flowed through me. At that moment, I understood why God had coerced me into bringing my new sales associate along.

*   *   *

An icy reception awaited me when I entered the main conference room of the Byrne River Bank. Janet Dungee must have sensed it, too. After escorting me into the room, she politely announced my arrival and beat a hasty retreat, obviously anxious to be away.

I had personally called each investor to summon them to this urgent meeting, but I had refrained from informing them why, preferring to deliver the good news in person. As it turned out, this was probably a mistake. I'd received warmer greetings from the snowmen Alicia built in the dead of winter.

A brief silence accompanied my arrival, but then all four men began talking at once.

"I can't believe I let myself fall for this scam," Judge Tolliver said. He seemed thoroughly depressed.

"We're not going to stand for this!" Marcus Durham exclaimed. "Fraud is a criminal offense. We'll get to the bottom of the chicanery. You mark my words."

I wondered if all newspaper editors were born suspicious or if such a mindset took years of on-the-job training.

"I knew I should have insisted on being appointed managing partner," Winston Fordyce III blustered. He seemed genuinely hostile. I suspected that was because someone else, namely me, was making the business decisions.

Angus sat quietly and said nothing. When we made eye contact, I detected what I assumed was sincere sympathy. I could almost read his thoughts: *I know why this project is so important to you and what it means to Alicia's future.* I returned a look that I hoped he would interpret as gratitude.

I allowed them to carry on for a time, but rather than sit down, I stepped to the far end of the table and remained standing. Gradually, the four investors fell silent.

"Gentlemen," I began, "I appreciate your willingness to assemble on such short notice. I understand how traumatic recent developments have been for you. The possibility of losing all or part of such a sizable investment would rattle anybody, even men of your stature, and I am grateful for your forbearance. It can be difficult, trusting someone with whom you have no track record to draw upon."

The mood around the table softened ever so slightly, so I continued. "For the past five days, I have been racking my brain, figuring out what to do about our Argyle Road problem. I've been going cross-eyed from manipulating numbers. As you well know, we were handed a formidable problem to solve. The planning board's edict put us in a serious financial bind. However, I am pleased to report that I think I've found an elegant solution."

I repeated what I'd learned from Russ Talbot: that the wells didn't need to exist physically for the subdivision plat to be approved. Instead, all that was required was a hydrologist's certification that the wells were likely to produce a sufficient flow of water when drilled.

"So, as you can see, by delaying the installation of the wells, we will free up an additional $150,000, which we can apply toward the paving of Argyle Road."

I pulled the signed certificate out of my briefcase and held it up for the investors to see. "Believe it or not, this unassuming document solves our dilemma." As a sweetener, I mentioned that we would reduce the number of wells from twelve to ten, thereby reducing our expenses by $30,000. This evoked a unified murmur of approval.

I concluded by saying, "Also, it seems we can delay paving Argyle Road if we post a bond in the amount of what the work will cost. Doing so will allow us to pave Argyle Road when we pave the road that crosses our property. This will save additional cost because we will use crews and materials efficiently rather than doing two jobs separately."

I then gestured that I was done but remained standing. The investors' responses followed quickly.

"This is good news, I think." Judge Tolliver's smile seemed uncertain.

"It would appear that our concerns were for naught," Marcus added with noticeable relief.

Winston slapped the table with the palm of his hand. "Paul, I knew you could do it given the right motivation. Never any doubt."

When I looked at Angus, his worried expression had molded into a satisfied grin. "What do you need from us? Where do we go from here?" he asked.

"A motion to proceed with the plan I've outlined would be appreciated." I tried not to show my elation. I had prayed long and hard for a favorable outcome, and now it was at hand. Inwardly, I thanked God for His merciful kindness.

The vote was unanimous.

I returned the hydrology certificate to my briefcase. "It will take several days to flesh out the remaining details, including posting a paving bond. Early next week, I'll meet with the planning board. Hopefully, we will have our final approval soon thereafter if all goes well."

Little did I know how severely the distressing days ahead would test my faith.

Chapter 8

A pleasant, late-spring breeze rippled the surface of Lake Murray, a picturesque forty-acre body of water located twenty miles north of Trinity Falls Township. Alicia and I had hiked in from the rest area on Route 171. It had been an easy, unhurried ramble over gently rolling terrain with only a slight rise in elevation. Even so, Alicia had asked to stop to rest twice. I assumed her weariness was because she insisted on carrying an overloaded backpack and her fishing gear.

Upon awakening that morning, I had still been feeling elated. My meeting with the investors the preceding afternoon had gone exceedingly well. The Spirit Wolf project was back on track, and I wanted to celebrate. So, I spontaneously elected to take a day off. In deciding what to do with my unanticipated leisure time, I had recognized a perfect opportunity to spend time with my daughter. Straightaway, I had called Alicia's school and informed the attendance secretary that my daughter would spend the day with me. Alicia, of course, had jumped at the chance to go fishing with her dad.

We halted at a small hollow on the eastern edge of the lake. There, we set up our day camp and prepared our gear. The county's fish and game wardens stocked the lake with trout annually. There was an excellent chance that one or both of us might land a decent-sized rainbow since it was still early in the season.

"What size hook should I use?" Alicia said as she rifled through her tackle box.

"A ten or perhaps a twelve might be a good choice," I responded. "Best not to be overly optimistic until we see if the big ones are biting."

Alicia tied a hook onto her line with a fisherman's knot and reached for the cup of night crawlers we had purchased at a convenience store. With care, she impaled a worm on the hook, which evoked a twinge of pride within me. When baiting her hook, she was even less squeamish than I.

Alicia stepped to the edge of the water and drew back her arm.

I cautioned, "Don't forget to add some weight to your line, or it will be hard to cast."

"Right." Alicia retreated to her tackle box and clamped three split shot onto her line with a pair of needle-nose pliers.

"Also, did you put on sunscreen? The sun is at our backs now, but come noon, it will begin reflecting off the water. Your mother would never forgive me if I brought you home with a nasty sunburn."

"The fault would be mine," Alicia declared forthrightly. "I should have remembered." She fished in her backpack and pulled out a tube of SPF 40. She lathered the white cream on her face and forearms.

After readying my gear, I stepped to the water's edge, twenty paces from where Alicia stood. Drawing my arm back, I cast out into the middle of the lake. It wasn't my finest cast, but it felt damn good to be doing something I loved with someone I loved even more. Twenty minutes later, I was still lost in the moment.

"Whoa," Alicia murmured. The timbre of her voice alerted me that something was wrong.

"Sweetheart, what's the matter?"

"I don't know. I felt kinda dizzy." A look of concern had widened her eyes.

I laid my pole down on the pebbly shore, not bothering to reel in the line, though I did place a large rock on the cork handle to keep a big fish from dragging the pole into the lake. I hurried over to see what was wrong.

"Are you okay?" I placed my hand on my daughter's shoulder.

"I think so. I kind of thought I might pass out. It's better now."

"Has this happened before?"

"Not really."

"You did eat breakfast this morning, didn't you?"

"You fixed it, remember?"

"That's right. I did. Maybe you should drink some of the juice we brought along. You could be dehydrated."

I stepped to my backpack and drew out a thermos of orange juice. I poured some into the thermos lid and handed it to her. She took a sip.

"Maybe a little more?" I suggested.

"I'm not thirsty. I feel kinda sick to my stomach."

"Are you going to throw up?"

"It doesn't feel like it. I'm just sickish."

"Let's get you out of the sun. You should sit down and rest." I led Alicia to a shady spot and had her sit on a rock. "What else do you feel? Do you have any other symptoms?"

"I'm kind of achy, like my muscles are sore from overdoing it in PE."

I touched the back of my hand to her forehead. "You're warm. I think maybe you have a fever again. We need to pack up and head for home. I'm going to take you in to see Dr. McGregor."

Alicia groaned.

"What's wrong?" I said with growing uneasiness.

"It's the thought of walking all the way back to where we parked. I'm not sure I can."

"Don't worry. I'll carry you piggyback."

"What about our gear?"

"I'll carry that too—a pack and a pole in each hand."

"Are you sure you can do that? I'm not as tiny as I used to be."

"No, you're not. You're growing up, but I'm tougher than I look. We'll make it."

"Dad?"

"Yes?"

"When are you going to tell me what's going on? I hear you and Mom talking in whispers like there's something wrong, and you don't want me to know."

"We'll discuss it later after we hear what Dr. McGregor has to say."

After hastily gathering our stuff, I packed everything as efficiently as possible to reduce the number of items I had to handle. I tried not to think about what might be wrong with my daughter.

"I can walk," Alicia protested when I turned so she could jump up on my back.

"Not if you're dizzy, you can't. Climb on." Despite my resolve not to, I exhaled a puff of air when her full weight settled onto my back.

"I told you so. I'm not as little as I used to be."

I joked, "No more pancakes and bacon for you, young lady."

I bent my knees cautiously to grab the packs and poles I had stationed on either side. Straightening up, I headed down the trail with Alicia on my back, her arms around my neck and her legs around my waist. Along the way, I repeatedly whispered prayers of supplication, asking the Lord to take care of my daughter and to give me the strength to bear my load.

By the time we reached the rest area, I was thoroughly exhausted, but I didn't even notice. The only thing on my mind was that I needed to get my daughter to the doctor's office as soon as possible.

Midmorning four days later, I was back in Dr. McGregor's office. Rachel insisted on coming with me and now sat beside me in Angus's consultation room. We had passed an anxious weekend, afraid to even think about Alicia's lab studies and what they might disclose but desperate to know the results. Angus had labeled the tests urgent and requested expedited processing.

When I brought Alicia in for an emergency evaluation, Angus had prescribed analgesics for pain and something for her fever. Over the weekend, she had improved to the point that she insisted on attending school that morning. Angus had suggested that we make her life as routine as possible, so we agreed to let her go with the provision that she ask the nurse to call us immediately if her symptoms returned. Alicia had promised that she would.

Angus sat facing us from behind his desk, intently studying Alicia's chart. I had known the good doctor long enough to guess he was distressed by what he was reading. The all-too-familiar uneasiness in the pit of my stomach became a knot of foreboding.

Angus looked up. He did not smile. "I assume because Alicia isn't here, she's feeling better?"

"She is," I replied. "We considered bringing her in for this follow-up, but she swore she was much improved. Also, if the test results are bad, we didn't want her to learn about her condition in this environment, not to cast aspersions on your bedside manner. We want to tell her in our own way."

"I completely understand. As you suspected, I'm afraid it's not good news."

Rachel gasped. "It can't be. Not this soon. She's too young."

I reached out to take hold of my wife's hand.

Angus continued, "I wish there were an easy way to put this, but there isn't. So, I'll be blunt. It appears that something has activated her genetic mutation."

Stabbed by a shard of guilt, I groaned. "It was our hike to Lake Murray. I knew we should have turned back when she first complained of fatigue. I should have brought her home right away. Why didn't I heed my instincts?"

"Physical exertion wasn't the trigger," Angus corrected gently. "True, a brisk hike may have contributed to some of her symptoms, but something else has prematurely switched on her genetic anomaly. I suspect the viral illness she suffered three weeks ago is to blame. Fundamentally, Lascaux Syndrome is caused by an aberration of the immune system. White blood cells are reconfigured to produce antibodies that target the heart and occasionally other organs. We're still in our infancy when it comes to understanding genetic processes. Yet, I can tell you this: Neither of you is responsible, not for the activation of her disease or for the fact that she's homozygous for a genetic mutation. It's not your fault, either of you."

In a pleading tone, Rachel said, "Are you sure her syndrome is active? Couldn't this be another viral illness?"

"I'm afraid not." Angus tapped a sheet of lab results in Alicia's chart. "Her cardiac enzymes are elevated, only slightly, but they are definitely abnormal. And we found antimyocardial antibodies in her blood. In layman's terms, her white blood cells have begun attacking her heart, causing it to become inflamed."

A solitary tear rolled down my wife's cheek.

Looking at Dr. McGregor, I said as matter-of-factly as I could, "All right. Assuming her condition has become active, where do we go from here?"

"I'd like to refer you to an immunologist. Medical rarities like Lascaux Syndrome are best treated by a specialist. I, of course, will remain available for any other problems your daughter might encounter."

"Who did you have in mind?" I said.

"Dr. Albert Sullivan. I'll have my nurse call and schedule an appointment. She'll get you in sooner than if you were to call on your own. By the way, don't let his youthful appearance fool you. He's sharp as a tack and one of the best in the region." Angus stood and stepped around from behind his desk. He paused to look down into my face. "One more thing. Have you told her yet—about her condition?"

Rachel and I exchanged glances. After a deep breath to quell her emotions, my wife said, "We're doing that tonight. We've been putting it off till we were sure."

Angus nodded. "An entirely reasonable approach, but she'll need to know soon if she hasn't already figured out what's happening."

I stood to face the doctor. "She has her suspicions, but she doesn't yet know the seriousness of her illness."

"Paul, I can appreciate how traumatic your conversation will seem, but I've found that children can be incredibly resilient. Oftentimes, the best approach is to be open and completely honest. Sometimes, they handle hearing the truth far better than we adults do. In any event, I'm sorry. I wish there were something more definitive we could do."

Rachel stood as well. We prepared to leave.

Angus grasped my forearm. "This is irrelevant considering what you're going through, but I meant to tell you that was an elegant solution you devised for the Spirit Wolf conundrum. Thank you. I just wanted to say how grateful I am."

"It worked out well for all of us, I think."

I suddenly realized that for the last four and a half days, I hadn't once considered the partnership or meeting with Logan Smallwood to inform him that we were now in compliance with the planning board's demands.

"My nurse will call you with Alicia's appointment," Dr. McGregor said as he accompanied us to the waiting room, where we took our leave.

*   *   *

Dr. Sullivan's office stood as a testament to medical professionalism. Whereas Angus McGregor's office conveyed a down-home quality, the immunologist's workspaces were substantially more formal. Prints of seascapes and idyllic meadows decorated the walls. Every item in his exam room looked to have been positioned for maximum efficiency. Even the tongue depressors in the glass container on the counter had been strategically arranged with their flat sides together.

Dr. Sullivan, on the other hand, was in a state of disarray. His striped shirt was wrinkled, and one of his shirttails was untucked. I noted that one pair of his shoelaces was untied. The knot of his necktie was a half-inch off center. And his wire-framed spectacles appeared to have been bent; one side rode higher than the other, giving his face a lopsided appearance.

Even more noticeable, however, was his youthful visage. He seemed barely old enough to have graduated high school, much less medical school. I had to restrain myself from asking if his mother had dressed him for work that morning.

Alicia emerged from behind the movable curtain, where she had changed out of her exam gown and into her street clothes. She climbed back up onto the exam table. Rachel sat beside me in one of the room's two armless chairs. Dr. Sullivan had seated himself on a wheeled stool near the computer terminal in the corner. *Did all doctor's exam rooms share a standard layout?* I wondered.

Scrolling between pages of information displayed on the computer screen, Dr. Sullivan said, "I've reviewed the records Dr. McGregor provided. He's done a thorough workup. In my opinion, the diagnosis of Lascaux Syndrome is confirmed."

Forty-eight hours had elapsed since our second visit with Angus. During that time, my wife and I had nurtured the faint hope that our family doctor had made a mistake and that we would soon wake up from the horrible nightmare that had beset us. To hear the diagnosis confirmed sent a chill racing along my spine. The truth was now unavoidable.

For ten minutes, Dr. Sullivan discussed Lascaux Syndrome with us, reviewing its etiology, likely progression, and ultimate outcome. Although he spoke primarily to us as parents, from time to time, he made sure that Alicia was following along. He specifically invited her to interrupt if there was anything she didn't understand. All the while, he did his best to soften the impact of his diagnosis.

I had nearly balked at the idea of having my daughter present. Yet, during our discussions regarding her illness, Alicia had insisted that she should be part of any decisions in the future.

The doctor drew a thumbnail sketch of how the immune system works, then told us something we didn't know: "Lascaux Syndrome typically evolves in three stages. The first, or acute stage, lasts between three to six weeks. In stage 1, the patient's symptoms are generally like those associated with a nonspecific infectious disease—low-grade fever, muscle aches, fatigue, and so forth. Stage 2 is a latent phase, lasting anywhere from six to nine months, rarely longer. During stage 2, patients feel well, and the disease, for all intents and purposes, is inactive. With the onset of stage 3, we begin to notice progressive damage to the heart. The time course can be variable, but the outcome is inevitable after the onset of stage 3. That's why if we are to treat this malady, we need to act while the patient is still in stage 1 or stage 2."

"Then it can be treated?" Rachel and I exclaimed simultaneously.

Dr. Sullivan nodded. "There is a therapy that, in some cases, has delayed the progression of genetically mediated immune disorders. As far as I know, it has never been tried in Lascaux Syndrome. There are so few patients, you see. Don't let me mislead you. This isn't a cure, but maybe we can buy this young lady some time."

"What kind of therapy are you suggesting?" I said urgently.

"A stem cell transplant from a genetically compatible donor." Dr. Sullivan described what was involved with collecting, harvesting, and infusing stem cells, plus the risks involved.

As the immunologist spoke, I observed his mannerisms. Reading between the lines, I could tell he was not enthusiastic about the procedure.

We finished our consultation by agreeing that both Rachel and I should be tested as potential stem cell donors. Appointments were made for us to have our blood drawn at the Drummond Memorial Lab.

As we left Dr. Sullivan's office, I quietly asked Alicia, "Are you okay with all this?"

"I'm not worried if that's what you mean."

"You're not?"

"No, I'm not." Alicia smiled. "God will take care of me. Isn't that what you're always saying?"

"Yes, that's right. He will. All we need is faith."

Reminded of my spiritual beliefs, I resolved to redouble my prayers, seeking God's favor and soliciting His mercy for my daughter.

*   *   *

Rachel and I were back in Dr. Sullivan's office two days later. Rather than accompany us on this visit, Alicia had felt well enough to go to school. At first, she had protested that she wanted to be with us, but we had emphasized the importance of continuing her education. Reluctantly, she had agreed.

I was so proud of my daughter. From the beginning, her attitude had never wavered. Without complaining, she had remained stoically accepting of whatever the future might bring, which was more than either Rachel or I could manage.

When Dr. Sullivan entered the exam room, he seemed disheartened. I could tell immediately that he was not the bearer of good news. After greeting us both and asking about the current status of Alicia's symptoms, he confirmed my suspicions.

"I've spoken with the lab at Drummond Memorial," he said as he sat on the low stool. "They've completed their testing. I'm sorry to tell you that neither of you is a match. We can't use either of you as a donor for a stem cell transplant."

"Are you sure?" Rachel exclaimed. "Maybe they should test us again."

The doctor graced my wife with a comforting look. "I understand how distressing this news must be, but the lab has done a thorough job. Actually, they ran the tests twice to confirm their original results. I'm sorry."

I spoke up. "Is there anything else we can try? Surely, we can't just quit. What about other donors?"

Dr. Sullivan responded, "Sometimes that is an option. However, harvesting cells from an unrelated donor isn't feasible in this situation. It's too risky. This isn't like treating leukemia. The complications could be horrendous. Tell me, does Alicia have any siblings?"

"No." Rachel shook her head. "She's an only child."

"Are either of your parents still alive?"

I answered first. "My parents died in an auto accident nine years ago, just before Alicia was born. Rachel lost her father to a heart attack and her mother to breast cancer."

"What about siblings? Do either of you have any siblings?"

"I have an older brother," I volunteered. "Like Alicia, Rachel is an only child."

"Your brother, is he consanguineous? I mean, he's not your half-brother or stepbrother, right?"

"No. We share the same parents."

"Do you think he might be willing to be tested?"

"I'm sure he would. Franklin loves Alicia. He'd do anything for her."

"Then we should speak with him. There's a remote chance he might be compatible."

"We can call him now if you'd like. I have his number." I dug my cell phone out of my pocket.

After I placed the call, the doctor spoke with Franklin. As predicted, without hesitation, my brother consented to become a stem cell donor, not knowing what the procedure might entail. Arrangements were made to have his blood drawn that afternoon.

When Rachel and I left the doctor's office, we desperately clung to our last glimmer of hope.

On the way home, Rachel looked at me from the passenger seat. "This is not good. Not good at all. What if Franklin isn't a match? What will we do then?"

"I don't know. I can tell you one thing: I'm not giving up. I'm going to fight this with everything that's in me."

"Do you have any miracles left? Or have you used up your allotment?"

"Only God knows the answer to that question."

*   *   *

Dr. Sullivan called forty-eight hours later. It was early Sunday afternoon, an hour after our family arrived home from church. Apparently, the doctor had returned to his office to catch up on some paperwork and had noticed Alicia's chart lying on his desk. On a hunch, he had called the Drummond lab, and indeed, the technician had just finished processing Franklin's blood.

The immunologist confirmed our fears with a professional demeanor and concern for our fragile emotions: Franklin was not a match. Like ours, my brother's blood contained some factor that would make stem cell transplantation too dangerous.

Rachel took the news hard. Tears began to flow as soon as I relayed what the doctor had said. They continued for some time thereafter. I too, felt devastated. And angry.

Because of my ire, my first impulse was to blame God and demand to know how He could abandon my daughter to such a terrible fate. Then I remembered something Franklin had mentioned: that we should always honor God and give Him the reverence and respect that are His due. I also remembered his question: *"Are you living your life by faith, or are you relying on the strength of your own abilities to solve the problems that confront you?"* I had memorized his exact words because the question haunted me fiercely. With great difficulty, I struggled to put my anger aside.

I supposed that only when no hope is left can you genuinely learn to trust God and rely upon His mercy. Given the current circumstances, I resolved to stop complaining and focus on what I could do. Determined, I set out to scour the internet in earnest, looking for anything related to treating rare genetic disorders.

Two hours later, I found a website that caught my attention. After twenty minutes and three phone calls, I set off to find my wife. I finally tracked her down in our bedroom. She was lying on her side on our bed, fully clothed, with her back to the door.

"Are you asleep?" I whispered.

"Just resting," she responded in a soft, gravelly voice.

"Roll over. I have something to share."

Rachel sluggishly complied. When her face turned toward me, I noted that her eyes were red-rimmed and puffy, and her usually well-groomed hair was tousled.

"I think I'm on to something," I said with an edge of excitement.

"What? Another miracle?"

"I'm serious. Look at this." I presented her with the information I had printed out.

"What is all this?" Rachel said as if unable to make sense of what she was seeing.

"I've been researching genetic therapies and came across this place." I pointed to the banner printed across the top of one of the pages. "This is a clinic in Austin, Texas. They're working on an experimental process that takes a different approach. By reverse engineering certain viruses, they can replace mutant DNA with normal DNA. From what I've been able to ferret out, they are the only ones in the country perfecting this technique. In several cases, they've had some amazing results."

"What are you telling me?" Rachel became more fully alert. "What is this about viruses?"

"They call it genetic remodeling. I don't understand the scientific details, but apparently, it can reverse the effects of certain genetic mutations."

"Have they tried it on patients with Lascaux Syndrome?"

"Not yet, but the doctor I spoke with couldn't imagine why it shouldn't work, given that certain considerations fall into line."

"What considerations?" Rachel said with skepticism.

"The patient's age and disease state, for instance."

"You spoke with a doctor?"

"I did. He was the on-call guy covering their clinic. It took some doing, but he finally agreed to speak with me. When I explained why I was calling, he seemed really interested. The more we talked, the better the program sounded. There is a catch, however."

"There's always a catch. What is it this time?"

"As we anticipated, genetic remodeling is horrendously expensive."

"How expensive?"

"For a complete course of treatment where they custom-design an operant virus tailored for a specific patient, the costs can run upward of half a million dollars."

"Let me guess. Because the therapy is experimental, insurance won't pay the bill?"

"That is, unfortunately, true."

"So why are you excited? We don't have that kind of money."

"Not yet, but we've talked about this, remember? The Spirit Wolf partnership is near securing final approval for our subdivision plat. Then, it's simply a matter of laying in the infrastructure and building houses. In three to four months, we could have enough to pay for this treatment." I fluttered the papers in my hand.

"Are you serious?"

"Completely."

"Half a million dollars?"

"Or more. Believe me. I intend to research this clinic thoroughly. I need to learn more about what they offer. It's too soon to get our hopes up, but initial indicators seem promising. Tomorrow, I plan to meet with Logan Smallwood and ask the planning board to sign off on our subdivision."

* * *

When I entered the planning board's suite of offices, I stopped at the first cubicle in the large central area. The lady seated at the desk glanced up in surprise.

"Sorry to disturb you," I said apologetically. "I'm looking for Logan Smallwood, but his office is empty."

"He's out inspecting a property. When he left, he indicated that he wouldn't be gone long. Should be back soon. You can wait in his office if you'd like. I doubt he'll mind."

Though I questioned Logan's hospitality, I figured I would accept since she had offered. If the chairman had a problem with me being alone in his office, he could take it up with his underling. I thanked the young woman and headed for the room's far corner.

The chairman's inner sanctum was as cluttered as it had been on my previous visits. Piles of paper littered his desk. I drew my cell phone from its holster and summoned my voice memo app. After clearing a small space at the corner of Logan's desk, I set the phone down but did not activate the record function. Waiting for his arrival seemed prudent rather than filling the phone's memory with background noise.

I sank into an armless chair to wait. With little else to do, I couldn't help but look around. Nonchalantly, I inspected papers and forms scattered here and there, those that I could see. Then, a folder lying by itself on the drafting table caught my attention. I craned my neck to read what was typed on the folder's tab. To my astonishment, it read *Spirit Wolf Estates*. I struggled with the impulse to step over, throw open the folder, and study what was inside.

Then, I noticed a handwritten memo paper clipped to the front of the folder. The memo was embossed with an ornate design. I rose partway out of my chair for a better view. The message read: *Property acquired. Feel free to impose the last condition at your discretion.*

The memo's meaning was an enigma, but the handwriting seemed familiar. A moment later, I realized where I had seen the flowery script before. I had come across it often enough at real estate council meetings. Helen Dunn had written the memo. Of that, I was confident. On impulse, I grabbed the slip of paper off the front of the folder and hastily shoved it into my pocket. Later, I would tease out its meaning.

Then I heard a voice behind me. I twisted around in my chair. Logan Smallwood was chatting with the woman in the first cubicle. Suddenly, I remembered the paper clip still attached to the front of the file. It would be a dead giveaway—a clear sign that the memo was gone. In a flash, I rose from my chair, slipped the paper clip off the folder, and tossed it onto Logan's desk.

As I sat back down, Logan finished his conversation and turned toward his office. I monitored his approach to determine if he had witnessed my actions. Drawing near, he gave no indication that he had. Instead, he kept his gaze cast toward the floor. I breathed a huge sigh of relief.

"Oh, it's you!" he exclaimed when he realized I was waiting. He glanced around suspiciously. "What do you want?"

"I'm here to discuss my project, of course." I activated the record function on my voice memo app.

"Do we have to do this again? Oh, very well. Wouldn't want you to miss anything important." The chairman stepped around behind his desk. "So, what's on your mind?" He sat down in his high-back executive chair.

"I'm here to let you know we are now in compliance with the board's requirements. We've sprayed for noxious weeds, the excavation of the ponds will begin tomorrow, and the partnership has posted a bond guaranteeing the paving of Argyle Road."

"Well done. I'm sure those conditions weren't easily satisfied." I had the distinct impression that the chairman was displeased with our progress.

"So, when can we expect final approval? We're anxious to begin laying in the subdivision's infrastructure."

"About that. The board has reviewed your application again. You see, it's our duty to ensure everything is in order. As a result, it's been brought to our attention that your access easement on the north side of the property is only forty feet wide."

"That is correct." A seed of trepidation blossomed within me.

"That's a problem. I'm afraid we will require a sixty-foot easement for a development of this magnitude. Who knows? Someday, the residents might need to bring in heavy equipment or such."

"Really?" I could not believe what I was hearing. "You intend to hold up our approval over an additional twenty feet of access?"

"It would seem so. You can let me know when you're in compliance." The chairman's lips curled into a faint smile as he picked up a form from the corner of his desk and began reading. He ignored me as I gathered my phone and switched off the record function.

Am I ever going to be done with this guy? I wondered as I left Logan's office.

Before returning to my car, I stopped by the plat room in the basement of the administration building. The desk clerk helped me track down the appropriate documents. According to the most recent deed on file, a man named Walter Drake owned the sliver of land across from our northern easement. It was then that I recalled Ian Campbell having mentioned his name.

Well, Walter, I thought *you're the fellow I need to visit next.*

*   *   *

The sun had descended only halfway to the western horizon when I pulled in and parked in front of Walter Drake's big red barn. Unlike the mature forests on the Spirit Wolf property, large sections of Walter's land had been cleared to grow alfalfa and soybeans. In addition, several grassy pastures were set aside for raising cattle and a few horses.

As I started walking toward Walter's two-story log home, I heard a noise that seemed to come from the barn. I turned in that direction. The man I wanted to see was up to his elbows, working on the engine of an old Allis-Chalmers tractor. I introduced myself and stuck out my hand in greeting.

Walter looked down at his own hands, which were smeared with grease. "Might be best if I just say howdy."

"Indeed." I withdrew my hand and grinned. "That's a smart-looking tractor. You don't see many like it anymore. Have you had it long?"

"Nearly forty years. She takes a lot of fixing, but she gets the job done. How can I help you?"

Walter was a tall, loose-jointed man who walked with a slight stoop. It was hard to be specific, but he appeared to be on the far side of seventy. Years of farming out-of-doors had weathered his skin to the texture of old boot leather. He had an infectious laugh, and his deeply furrowed face radiated good cheer when he smiled.

"I'm here to introduce myself," I said in my most affable manner. "I represent the guys who bought the Campbells' property. As you probably know by now, we plan on developing the land. It's a big project, and I thought I might stop by to see if you have any concerns."

"Ian told me what you plan on doing. I suppose all those houses will increase the value of this place. It might cause my property taxes to go up. We'll have to wait and see. Otherwise, if the new neighbors behave themselves, I can't imagine why it should be a problem."

"I'm glad you feel that way."

Walter and I chatted about various topics for another fifteen minutes, including the price of soybeans and who would win the mayoral race. I intended to build rapport, but I also enjoyed talking with the man as we went along. His earthy genuineness reminded me of country life when I was a kid.

At last, however, it was time to address why I had come. "Ian told me how you, and he cut in Argyle Road."

"That we did, with old Gertrude here." He reached out to pat his tractor. "I named her after my wife. After she passed away, of course. It's as if we still get to spend time together."

"That's sweet," I said with sincerity.

"Yeah. My wife wasn't pretty either, but she was a good worker like this old beast."

"Ian also told me how when you surveyed for the road, you lopped off a section of your own land."

"A damn fool mistake it was. Neither of us had any experience working a surveyor's thingamajig. What do you call it?"

"A theodolite?"

"Yeah. That thing."

"They can be tricky."

I was about to bring up the subject of the easement when Walter said, "That sliver of dirt has been a thorn in my side all these years. It's barely large enough to farm, and its shape makes plowing a royal pain in the rear end. That's why I jumped at the chance to sell it."

"Excuse me?" I said with alarm. "You sold the sliver next to the Spirit Wolf property?"

"I did, just a couple of days ago."

"To whom, might I ask?"

"Some real estate lady. I think her name was Dunn. I have her card in the house."

"Did she say why she wanted to buy it?"

"She said she was working with Ian and needed it to finalize the sale of his land."

"She told you that?"

"She did. I probably would've sold it to her anyway, but helping Ian out seemed like the right thing to do."

"When you sold her the property, was it her name she put on the deed?"

"It was."

Softly, I muttered, "So Helen Dunn now owns that sliver of land." I recalled my visit to the plat room. In my experience, recording a deed takes upward of two weeks. Yet Walter had sold his sliver of land only recently, which would explain why the most current deed on file listed him as the owner.

"Mind if I ask how much she paid?"

"Can you believe it? It was $100,000. It seemed a lot of money for sure, but that was another reason I sold it. I figured that it must be important if Ian needed it that badly." The furrows in Walter's brow deepened. "Is something wrong?"

"I regret telling you this, but you've been deceived. I am Ian and Eva Campbell's real estate agent, their only real estate agent, and we finalized the sale of their property six weeks ago."

"Is that a fact? Then why would—"

"I don't know, but I intend to find out."

*   *   *

The next evening was Tuesday, so I was again back at the Maranatha Gospel Fellowship, helping serve food to those less fortunate than myself. I had committed to the church and felt inclined to keep my word. Even so, I arrived late, and Franklin was actively greeting hungry people as they filtered down the stairs and into the basement from the vestibule above. We nodded in passing as I set to work.

After the meal was served and the kitchen cleaned, it was time for the volunteers to eat. Franklin and I grabbed a tray and headed to a corner to talk. The fare that evening was chicken fried steak with mashed potatoes and peas.

Franklin chose the folding chair beside mine. It wobbled when he sat down. "One day, we will have to replace these when funds become available." He positioned his tray on the round table in front of him. "I see that Rachel and Alicia chose not to come this evening. Is everything okay?"

"They wanted to, but Alicia spiked a fever of 101.5—"

"That's not good. How sick is she?"

"She said she felt flushed but otherwise was okay. Rachel felt she needed to stay home and care for her. She will call me if there's any change."

The previous evening, I had spoken with my brother to bring him up to speed on Alicia's condition. We had discussed genetic remodeling, plus other aspects of her illness.

"This must be excruciating."

"It's like I'm holding a bomb in my hands, and the fuse is lit."

With deep sincerity, Franklin said, "I am truly disappointed that I wasn't a match for her stem cell transplant. It would have been an honor to serve as her donor."

"And we appreciate your willingness, but it may be for the best that we couldn't find a match."

"Why would you say that?" Franklin exclaimed.

"I thought the immunologist wasn't keen on the therapy. He spent a considerable amount of time listing the risks. It seemed he was trying to talk us out of considering the procedure."

Franklin sipped his iced tea. "Choosing the right path is hard when there are so many unknowns."

"Truly, it's agonizing."

"What happens next with Alicia?"

"We're working on it."

Changing the subject, Franklin said, "So where do we stand with the property?"

I filled him in on my meeting with Logan Smallwood, including the subsequent developments. His eyes widened when I informed him that Helen Dunn had purchased Walter Drake's sliver of land.

"Do the limited partners know?" he said with a look of apprehension.

I shook my head. "They'll have to be told soon. But not today. First, I need to meet with Helen Dunn and find out what she has in mind."

"You know what this means, don't you?"

"Indeed, I do. She's going to tie on a mask and stick a gun in my face."

The conversations from other tables created a background buzz throughout the room. We ate in silence for a time.

Then Franklin looked at me. "I've been thinking about your theory. It's an interesting hypothesis that what we think becomes what's real."

"I know. It was a screwy notion. Our thoughts control our actions, and to some extent, our actions shape reality, but that's as far as it goes."

"I agree. Over the years, I've imagined many scenarios, both good and evil, that never came to pass, and there have been lots of events I completely failed to foresee, yet they happened. There is one corollary to your theory, however, that intrigues me."

"What is that?"

"I'm intrigued because it parallels the Christian concept of faith in some respects."

"How so?"

"Faith, the cornerstone of our spirituality, compels us to believe in things that cannot be tested or proven. We accept them as real things that do not exist yet because we are convinced that one day they will. As Hebrews chapter 11, verse 1 says, faith is being sure of what we hope and certain of what we do not see."

"You're not implying that faith calls reality into existence?"

Franklin shook his head. "Not at all. God alone shapes reality. Faith is simply trusting in Him and waiting to see what He has in store for us."

"No doubt, but do you think that sometimes God gives us an inkling of what's about to occur to prepare us for what's to come?"

My brother squeezed his eyes shut. "Enough. All this makes my head hurt."

"You're the one who brought it up."

"Remind me never to do that again." Once more, changing the subject, Franklin said, "By the way, when do you plan on confronting Helen Dunn?"

"Tomorrow morning. That's when I'll beard the lioness in her den."

Chapter 9

I was in a foul mood as I drove toward Helen Dunn's real estate office. The morning was overcast and gloomy enough to fit my state of mind. A drizzle had fallen earlier, leaving the roads dark and glistening. The feeling of fulfillment that had lifted my spirits the previous evening was gone. Something about feeding the hungry had fostered a sense of purpose within me. But worrying about my impending confrontation with my nemesis had robbed me of my good humor. One bright spot, however, was that Alicia's fever had abated, and she could go to school.

The previous fall, Rimdale Properties had relocated to a newly constructed business park a half mile from the center of town. It was a serviceable location with a CPA on one side and an attorney on the other. Yet, for me, the stucco-and-tile motif was too politically correct. The complex lacked the charm of Trinity Falls Realty.

"Is Helen in?" I asked the receptionist as I glanced around the waiting area. I had visited the premises several times, with Helen representing one side of a deal and me the other. The place seemed the same.

I'd noticed that many professionals decorated their offices according to a specific theme. Helen's theme was modern architecture, which I found a bit cliché. Pictures of austere buildings hung on the walls. Most of the images were stark and foreboding. My theme was gardening. Pictures of flowers and landscapes decorated my offices, with an occasional fish thrown in for contrast. It wasn't chic, but my clients seemed to appreciate the ambience.

"May I say what this is regarding?" the receptionist asked cordially.

"I think she already knows. Just tell her I'm waiting."

The young woman spoke into her headset. Less than a minute later, I was escorted toward a room at the rear of the building. Helen's office presented the same motif as the reception area.

"I've been expecting you," Helen announced without offering a greeting. She remained seated behind her desk.

"I imagine you have."

Helen's office was larger than mine and much more lavishly appointed. In one corner of the room, a leather-upholstered loveseat and matching armchairs formed a conversation group. A pair of bronze figurines decorated the dark walnut end table.

I remained standing, gazing down at my adversary. "It seems you've been busy."

"You spoke with Walter Drake. He called me. He wasn't happy. I can only imagine what you told him."

"Unlike you, I told him the truth, that I was the Campbells' agent of record, and you weren't."

"I never said I was. He must've misunderstood. Some people become confused in their senescence, and Walter is what, nearly a hundred now?"

"Not even close. Besides, he didn't strike me as being demented."

"Even so, it's his word against mine." Helen smiled—a dark, humorless reconfiguring of her facial features that lacked warmth.

"How much do you want?" I said, cutting straight to the chase.

"For what?" Helen replied with feigned innocence.

"I'm in no mood to play games, Helen. How much?"

"You are such a bore."

"How much to widen my right-of-way to sixty feet?" I demanded.

"Very well. One million dollars."

"You can't be serious."

"Oh, but I am. Deadly serious."

"That's highway robbery."

"Perhaps, but it's my price."

"Have you no sense of honor?"

"What's honor got to do with anything?" Helen seemed genuinely perplexed. "This is business. Look, you don't have to pay, you know. You could go out and try to scrounge another access to Argyle Road, right?" The wicked smile again spread across her face.

"Why are you doing this?"

"Money. Why else?"

"Helen, I know you. This isn't about money. Something else is afoot. You're a spiteful, vindictive woman who must always get her way. So, what have I done to you that you would repay me like this?"

"What have you done? Are you really so dense? Do you remember the Nelsons' farm and how I attempted to have it rezoned as an outdoor shooting range? You opposed me before the county commissioners and squelched the deal."

I protested in my own defense, "There were major safety issues. It was Nelson's neighbors who objected."

"You were their spokesperson. And when I tried to put together the Flint Ridge project, you refused to sell me the last lot I needed. That complex would've been spectacular, but no. Instead, a multimillion-dollar deal disappeared right down the drain."

"That wasn't my doing. I tried to convince him, but the owner refused to sell. It galled him to think you were about to turn his ancestral home into an industrial center."

Helen snarled, "You can be very persuasive when it suits you. You could have changed his mind had you tried. Well, now it's your turn to know how I felt. One million dollars. That's my price. Take it or leave it."

Before I could reply, the sounds of a disturbance in the front part of the building reached us. In short order, the receptionist materialized at Helen's door. She seemed flustered.

"Excuse me, Ms. Dunn," the woman stammered. "It's Mr. Fuller. He has some, eh, questions…about your commission."

"Tell him we were forced to charge three points above the standard rate because his house was a mess. Even so, it was almost impossible to find a buyer. He's damn lucky we got his garbage dump sold."

The receptionist replied meekly, "I tried to explain, but he wouldn't listen. He says he will start busting the place up if he can't speak with you personally. Those were his words."

Helen looked to where I was standing but said nothing.

"Client issues?" I mocked, feeling a small but satisfying sense of retaliation.

Helen stood up from behind her desk. She looked at me in passing and commanded, "You wait here." Then, she followed the receptionist toward the front of the building. The uproar out front grew louder.

I glanced around while savoring the harsh words being bantered back and forth. This was the first time I was left alone in Helen's office. Surprisingly, her workspace seemed neat, with everything in its place. It was not nearly as cluttered as my own digs. Unexpectedly, something caught my attention. A box of expensive-looking stationery sat on the corner of her desk. The notepaper's texture and color resembled the memo I snatched from Logan Smallwood's office. On impulse, I grabbed half a dozen sheets and slipped them into the breast pocket of my sports coat for later comparison. Feeling suddenly guilty, I glanced behind me and was relieved no one had noticed.

As I stood there, it occurred to me that I had no reason to hang around. Even if I could, I would never submit to Helen's extortion, and there was no point in attempting to negotiate. Helen was a stubborn woman. It was a violation of her nature to back down. Besides, she had me over a barrel. I needed that expansion, and she knew it.

I turned on my heel and left her office.

In the reception area, I couldn't help myself. As I passed the irate man, who stood with his chin thrust forward and his fists balled, I offered in a conspiratorial whisper, "I hear Trinity Falls Realty often sells homes for a three percent commission." The man literally screamed with rage.

*   *   *

The Spirit Wolf investors were already assembled and awaiting my arrival when I entered the conference room at the Byrne River Bank. I could tell they were displeased at having again been summoned so precipitously. Besides, it was six in the evening and no doubt they had come straight from work with no opportunity to eat dinner. Their scowls reminded me of how grouchy I could become when not fed on time.

"What is this about?" Winston Fordyce III demanded from the head of the table. "I thought we'd solved our cash flow issues. So why are we meeting again? You weren't at all forthcoming on the phone."

"That's for sure," Judge Tolliver declared sourly. "It's not as if we can drop everything and come running every time you send up a flare. I have another meeting this evening, so can we move this along?"

I advanced to the center of the room and set my briefcase beside the empty chair where I customarily sat, but I remained standing. "Gentlemen, again, I appreciate your forbearance. Like you, I abhor unscheduled meetings. Yet, as was the case last time, something important has come up, and it's my duty to keep you informed."

After steeling myself, I succinctly laid out the problem: the partnership owned a forty-foot easement on the property's northern boundary. The planning board had decreed that we must expand it to sixty feet. Purchasing an additional twenty-foot right-of-way would cost a million dollars. The telling took all of two minutes. When I finished, there were howls of discontent around the table.

"You can't be serious," Winston fumed. "Is this some kind of sad joke?"

"It is not. I assure you," I replied.

Marcus leaned forward. His eyes narrowed. "How did this happen?"

"I'm still trying to sort that out."

Even Angus spoke up. "Paul, does this mean we don't get our subdivision plat approved?"

"Not without an additional twenty feet of right-of-way." What I found most astonishing was that no one asked the name of the person demanding such a high price. I wondered if the investors had already been told about our predicament.

My suspicions were tweaked even further when Judge Tolliver said, "Right from the beginning, I've had my doubts about this project. Every time we turn around, there's another obstacle to overcome. I'm beginning to think I made a huge mistake, and perhaps it's time to walk away."

I looked directly at the judge. "What are you saying?"

"I've been approached by someone who has taken an interest in the property. A real estate agent I know has a buyer who will take this white elephant off our hands for seventy-five cents on the dollar. That would be a hard pill to swallow, but at least we'll have something in our pockets. Otherwise, we'll have nothing but a two-hundred-acre hobby farm."

I cocked my head to peer at the judge. "When did this agent approach you, if I might ask?"

"This morning. Before court."

"And would this agent happen to be female, I wonder?"

"As a matter of fact, yes, not that it has anything to do with anything. My point is that it's time to get out and cut our losses."

"Perhaps you're right," Winston said. "After all, we're talking about spending another million dollars." He turned his face toward me. "Like I told you the last time. I'm not prepared to sink any more money into this project. If a buyer is willing to take it over, maybe it's time to take a vote."

"Hold on." Still standing, I gave a calming gesture with my hands. "Before you rush into something you might later regret, can I make a suggestion? It was only yesterday that I learned of our conundrum. I've had less than twenty-four hours to work on finding a solution. Give me a chance. Let me see if I can piece together a way out of this mess."

"How much time do you need?" Angus said.

I desperately wanted to ask for at least a month but instead suggested, "Today is Thursday. Give me until a week from next Monday. If I can't find a solution by then, I'll agree to look at cashing out."

A heated discussion ensued. I could tell that Angus and Marcus weren't as enthusiastic about selling as the other two. Ultimately, the investors reluctantly agreed to grant me the requested time. It was now up to me to figure out what to do about Helen Dunn.

* * *

A brisk breeze rippled the leaves of the sycamores and red oaks nearby. Seeking solace and a quiet place to think, I returned to the site where Ian Campbell had considered building his home. I was inclined to agree; it was a delightful location. With a view of the Byrne River and Lake McDougall farther on, the spot was visually appealing, tranquil, and emotionally soothing, which was exactly what I needed.

I had begun my visit to the property that morning by inspecting the northern easement and stewing over how to widen it to sixty feet. The more I reflected on the challenge we faced and the deadline imposed by the investors the preceding evening, the more distressed I became. My frustration had ratcheted upward when it occurred to me that my life was a sequence of deadlines: the deadline for Jack to pass his exam, the deadline to close on the Campbells' property, the deadline to dredge the ponds, the deadline to widen the easement, and most important of all, the looming deadline to raise the money I would need for Alicia's care. Unlike when I was young, time seemed no longer my friend.

The log upon which I sat faced east, toward the rising sun. Rays of sunlight reflected off waves on the distant lake. I was reminded of a day before Alicia was born when Rachel and I had borrowed a friend's boat to sail. We had spent the morning cruising leisurely, laughing and enjoying each other's company. Those had been carefree, halcyon days. Life had been simpler then.

A thought came to me unexpectedly. *Perhaps I'm going about this the wrong way. Rather than stare at the problem as a whole, maybe I should tease apart individual elements and search for hidden relationships. So, what do I know?*

I constructed a mental timeline from the project's inception to the present day. I considered my visits to the planning board and how one requirement had been heaped upon another, each more severe than its predecessor. *Was that a coincidence,* I wondered, *or is that how property developments are usually treated? Or could there be another more sinister influence in play?* One thing seemed especially significant: the planning board's last two requirements could not have been better crafted; it was as if they had been specifically tailored to cripple the Spirit Wolf project.

And then there was the matter of the memo I had found paper-clipped to our file in Smallwood's office. Helen Dunn had written the memo. Of that, I was now sure. The memo's color and texture had matched the notepaper I had swiped from her desk, and its flowery script was identical to several of Helen's handwritten documents filed away in my office.

More to the point, there was the memo's text to consider: *Property acquired. Feel free to impose the last condition at your discretion.* Considering subsequent developments, there could be little doubt about which property the memo referenced. It had to be the strip of land Helen had acquired from Walter Drake.

From there, I was drawn to consider that the planning board's edict had been issued *after* Helen had acquired Walter's land. Meaning she must've known in advance that the edict would be forthcoming. Otherwise, why spend so much money on a worthless strip of property? She had used confidential information to place the Spirit Wolf project in jeopardy. Confidential information that could have come from only one source: Logan Smallwood. *How much leverage had been required for Helen to extract that kind of information?* I wondered. *How deep does their relationship go?*

More was going on than I had imagined, but what to do about it?

Still seated on the log, I mulled over a list of options: confront Helen directly, or Logan, or both; raise a public stink and hope the truth would come out; reassemble the investors and seek their counsel. In thinking over the alternatives, each had its flaws. One glaring limitation was my lack of definitive evidence. I could offer strong suppositions but no incontrovertible proof. I needed more.

I stood and began pacing, trampling the forest duff underfoot. The frustration I had experienced earlier returned. No clear plan came to mind. What I truly needed was divine inspiration.

On impulse, I knelt. Pressing my palms together in front of my face, I prayed. "Dear God, I implore You. Shower upon me Your wisdom and guidance. Help me correct the wrong that is being perpetrated against us. Grant me victory over my enemies. Please give me the strength and the resolve to prevail. Show me the path I am to follow."

I was reminded of being lost in the woods as I spoke that last sentence. The image of the wolf came to mind, my guide and my companion. I pictured him trotting ahead, leading me toward my deliverance. In my mind, I followed him as he noiselessly trod the forest floor.

Feeling acutely self-conscious, I looked around. What I saw startled me so severely that I toppled over onto my backside. There, thirty yards away, sat the beast on his haunches. He was just as I had remembered him: his fur lighter at the roots and darker at the tips, and his almond-shaped eyes like sunlight shining through blue ice.

I froze in place and stilled my breathing. We stared at one another for what seemed an inordinately long period. Neither of us flinched; neither made a sound. Then, the wolf rose and trotted off into the forest. Just like that, he was gone without a trace.

The same questions that had haunted me before arose again. Had I just witnessed an aberration? Was I hallucinating? If not, what had triggered the wolf's return? Was God sending me a message?

The other miracles I had experienced came to mind—provision and protection—the bag of cash and my sojourn over Trinity Falls. The enormity of these events prompted me to consider my relationship with God and how it was evolving.

Out of the blue, I recalled a Sunday sermon my brother had delivered earlier that month. His topic for the day had been the many facets of faith. One theme stood out in my mind. From the dais in the church's sanctuary, Franklin declared, "Faith is strength. Faith empowers believers. It allows us to accomplish beyond the limits of our abilities. By focusing perception, faith lets us discover the truth when others conspire to hide it."

And there it was, the inspiration I had been seeking. At that moment, I knew what I would do.

*   *   *

Bright and early Monday morning, I paid another visit to the planning board's offices. City hall was only open Monday through Friday from 8:00 a.m. to 5:00 p.m. As a result, I was forced to spend the entire weekend worrying. The waiting had been excruciating, especially in the hours since waking that morning. As the time to put my plan into action drew near, my nervousness had become almost unbearable. I'd always considered it a cliché, but my knees shook when I again spoke with the young woman in the first cubicle.

I'd spun a few falsehoods in my time, primarily little white lies with an occasional whopper thrown in, but I had never set out to deceive anyone intentionally. I had no idea if I could carry it off.

"Excuse me," I said, my speech somewhat garbled because my mouth was dry. Yet my palms were moist. *Odd how stress works*, I thought tangentially.

The woman turned away from the keyboard upon which she had been typing.

I eased half a pace closer to read her name tag. "Hi, Karen. I don't know if you remember me. I stopped in to see Mr. Smallwood. It was about a week ago."

"Yes. I remember. I'm afraid he's in a meeting. He won't be available for an hour or two."

"It's not him I've come to see. I was wondering if you might do me a huge favor. I kept a copy when I submitted our subdivision application for the Spirit Wolf project. Last night, while working at home, I accidentally knocked over my coffee mug. What a mess. My copy of the application got completely soaked. I'm afraid it's ruined. I was wondering if there is any chance you might shoot me another copy. I'd be ever so grateful. I'll happily pay whatever the fee might be."

Karen glanced at the pile of correspondence on her desk and then looked back at me. "Sure. I can do that. There won't be a charge. Would you happen to know where your file is?"

"Probably in Mr. Smallwood's office. It was lying on his side table the last time I saw it."

Karen rose from her desk and headed toward Logan's office. I watched her retrieve the file and carry it toward the room that housed the planning board's servers and a bunch of other computer equipment. Through an open door, I noticed an industrial-sized copy machine. She set about feeding pages into its hopper.

As soon as her back was turned, I made a beeline for Logan's inner sanctum. From the inside pocket of my sports coat, I extracted the handwritten memo I had previously prepared. Over the weekend, I had spent hours practicing Helen Dunn's flowing script. When satisfied that I could match her handwriting, I had jotted a note on one of the sheets of high-quality stationery I'd swiped from Helen's office. My note read: *Urgent that we meet. People are suspicious. If anyone finds out, it's your neck in the noose, not mine. Be at the pavilion in Fitzgerald Park at 6:00 p.m. tonight.* I'd left the note unsigned.

After positioning my missive in the center of Logan's desk where he would surely see it, I began rummaging through desk drawers. In a bottom drawer, I found what I was seeking: a box of embossed stationery with matching envelopes. Both bore the planning board's official logo. I collected three of each and hastily slid the drawer shut.

Looking around, I strained to see if I was being observed. I wasn't. After sequestering the stationery in my coat pocket, I hurriedly exited Logan's office. As fast as I could without attracting notice, I returned to the first cubicle just as Karen emerged from the computer room.

"Here you go." She handed me a neatly stapled duplicate of our subdivision application.

"Thank you ever so much. You're a lifesaver. Now, I won't have to admit my clumsiness to my investors."

"Not a problem."

Karen returned to her desk, and I beat a hasty retreat from city hall.

*　*　*

The message I delivered to Helen Dunn turned out to be less problematic. After leaving city hall, I returned to Trinity Falls Realty. I typed the following text on Logan's stationery: *Urgent that we meet. I'm not going to let you set me up. Be at the pavilion in Fitzgerald Park at 6:00 p.m. tonight.* I also typed a word, *Helen*, on the envelope but left the note unsigned.

Epistle in hand, I drove to Rimdale Properties. Helen's Mercedes occupied its usual place of honor in the parking lot. After visually scouting the lot to ensure no one was around, I slipped the envelope under the windshield wiper blade on the driver's side. I knew Helen was a creature of habit. She would discover the note when she took her usual two-hour lunch break.

With the first stage of my plan completed, I headed for McLaren's Hardware. That was the store where I had purchased my drone. It was time to equip my aerial reconnaissance platform with several significant upgrades.

*   *   *

The pavilion in Fitzgerald Park was a spacious open-sided structure erected on a single concrete slab. Its wood framing gave it a rustic feel suitable for picnics, family gatherings, and such. More to the point, the pavilion's beam ceiling and exposed rafters were perfect for what I had in mind.

I set my drone's carrying case on one of the sheltered picnic tables. After loosening its latches, I opened the case to reveal the drone. The upgrades I had purchased had cost a tidy sum, money Rachel and I would miss when paying bills. The miniaturized directional microphone and the high-resolution telephoto lens with zoom capabilities hadn't come cheap. My fervent hope was that they would soon prove worthy of the expense.

I carefully lifted the drone and its controller out of their foam packaging.

It was the first week in July, so we were well into the long days of summer. The sun still rode far above the horizon. Daylight would continue for several more hours. I had stewed over the possibility that Helen and Logan's confrontation might occur too close to dusk. Although of excellent quality, the camera was not equipped with a night-vision mode.

I switched on both the drone and its controller. That afternoon, I confirmed that both sets of batteries were fully charged. It would not do for either device to die during my clandestine surveillance.

With a delicate touch, I activated the drone's motors. The six propellers hummed. The sound, although merely a faint whir, would be audible at thirty feet, which was a problem. I had at first envisioned hovering the drone some distance away from their meeting with its camera zoomed to maximum resolution. Several test flights, however, had revealed that I would need to fly uncomfortably close to record a satisfactory facial image. Moving closer would increase the risk of discovery, and being discovered would scuttle my entire plan.

After considering the matter, I had settled on a different approach, which was precisely why I had chosen the pavilion.

Adjusting the levers only a millimeter at a time, I commanded the drone to lift off from the picnic table. It rose three feet into the air. I then set it to hover while I studied the underside of the roof. I had already decided that the best vantage point would be from a corner, with the camera lens pointed toward the pavilion's center. Such placement would offer my subjects the most excellent chance to be in view. After briefly examining the building's architecture, I identified a crossbeam at the westernmost edge of the pavilion. With the camera looking eastward, the sun would be behind the drone, reducing the glare risk.

With great care, I commanded the drone to fly incrementally higher until it hovered just above the selected crossbeam. It was tricky business, ensuring the six propellers avoided the rafters and the underside of the roof. On my second attempt, one propeller did graze a rafter. The drone wobbled and began sinking toward the floor. I regained control just in time to keep it from crashing. Then, I could have brought along a ladder and positioned the drone by hand.

On my third attempt, I succeeded. Feeling a tremendous sense of relief, I exhaled a grateful sigh. When I tested the camera and the microphone, I could monitor virtually every square inch of the pavilion's floor space. I switched off the drone's motors and placed the camera and the microphone on standby.

My watch told me it was five o'clock. I had an hour to wait, assuming my ruse would work.

Another concern had troubled me earlier. There was a small but definite possibility that other people might intrude on what I desperately needed to be a solitary confrontation. The Trinity Falls Parks and Recreation Department had assured me that no one had reserved the pavilion for that evening, which meant no large gatherings were scheduled. If individuals did happen by, I could do nothing about that.

Chuckling to myself, I reached for the package I had prepared earlier, an empty shoebox wrapped in Christmas paper and tied with a big red iridescent bow. With an evil grin, I placed the package on a central picnic table. Then, I gathered up the drone's case.

Carrying the case and the controller, I retreated to a spot a hundred yards distant, to a vacant picnic table not far from the horseshoe pits.

The second stage of my plan was complete. All that was left to do was to wait.

*   *   *

My stomach was beginning to growl as I sat monitoring the pavilion. Worry had consumed me earlier that day that I had forgotten to eat lunch. Now, I was famished. *You should have thought to bring a snack*, I chided myself. The defiant part of my mind retorted *I'm kind of new at this. Next time, maybe I'll get it right.*

For an hour, I watched half a dozen people come and go. Fortunately, none had lingered near the pavilion or found the gift-wrapped shoebox I had placed there. Had it been a weekend day rather than a Monday, the park's visitors would've been more numerous.

A figure emerged from the parking lot near the bandstand at the park's far side. Even at a distance, I recognized Logan Smallwood's slender frame. He looked around apprehensively, surveying his surroundings to confirm that he was unobserved. I kept my head down, and my eyes focused on the controller I held, much like I was reading a book. Without looking up, I activated the hexacopter's camera and high-gain microphone.

The camera's eight-gigabyte memory would accommodate at least four hours of high-definition video.

Logan strolled to the pavilion but stood just outside, again studying his environment. He seemed like a man with a guilty conscience. I followed his gestures on the controller's display. He was well within camera range, but his facial expressions would be easier to interpret if he moved closer. I thought, *Perhaps you should mosey on over and ask him to step up to the camera.* The contrary part of my brain replied, *wait.*

Then, Logan spotted the shoebox I had placed on the central table. Several times, he looked away and back again. Soon, his curiosity became overpowering. With obvious caution, he stepped forward to inspect his discovery. Upon lifting the shoebox's lid and finding it empty, he again scanned his surroundings, perhaps expecting a prankster to jump out and yell, "Gotcha!" To my great relief, he did not look up toward the rafters.

I struggled to refrain from whooping with delight. Logan was now in a perfect position for video surveillance.

"Why would you think I was setting you up?" a female voice demanded from somewhere off-screen. Helen Dunn then stepped into the camera's field of view.

Rather than emerge from the parking lot, she had approached from a more clandestine direction. *Clever girl,* I thought, *but your caginess won't help you.*

"Because it's my neck in the noose!" Logan exclaimed. "As you so correctly pointed out. I'm the one taking all the risks."

"Keep your voice down," Helen cautioned with a snarl. She advanced to where Logan stood waiting. "I'm as vulnerable as you are."

I could not believe my good fortune. Both perpetrators were now perfectly placed for a video shoot.

"Like hell!" Logan roared. "All you've done is buy up a strip of land. I'm the one who's shredding the board's policies and procedures."

"It's how I got the land that would be a problem were anyone to find out. Remember, I had to persuade old Walter that I was the Campbells' realtor? The real estate council considers misrepresentation tantamount to fraud, a serious felony offense." Helen pointed to the shoebox. "What is that?"

Logan shrugged. "I assume it's a stupid gag of some sort. I found it here on this table. It's empty."

Helen scowled. "It's amazing how many people have a distorted sense of humor."

And some have none at all, I thought. Again, I tried not to chuckle.

Logan waggled a finger in Helen's direction. "When you first came to me with this crazy scheme of yours and promised we could make a fortune, I should've listened to myself. I knew what you were proposing was wrong, but I was greedy. I should have walked away, but no. I had to take the money. I was an idiot. Know this: the fifty thousand you've paid me is not enough. If word gets out, I'll be ruined."

Helen hissed, "Will you lower your voice? I don't want to have to tell you again. If you keep your cool, we'll come out of this okay. There is no way Langdon can raise a million dollars. Besides, even if he does, I'll never let him have his expansion. The partnership will be forced to sell the land to me."

"Why you? How do you know they won't sell to someone else?"

"I have an in with one of the investors. After I own the land and you approve my subdivision application, we can move straight to building homes. That's where the real money is. From that point forward, it's just a matter of raking in the cash."

"You make it sound so simple, but like you said, it's my neck in the noose."

"Where did you get that notion? I've never said that."

"Yes, you did. It's right here in your demand that we meet." Logan pulled a sheet of high-quality stationery out of his pocket. He showed it to Helen.

"I didn't send that. I'm here because you sent me this." She fished in her purse and retrieved a sheet of paper embossed with the planning board's logo.

Logan thrust his hands out, palms up. "I've never seen that page before in my life. I have no idea where it came from."

"Someone stuck it under my car's windshield wiper."

"I swear I have no idea where that came from."

Helen growled menacingly, "What's going on here? Are you trying to pull a fast one? You're not wearing a wire, are you?" She began scanning the park with her eyes. I kept my head down until she looked away.

Dusk was falling. The sky was growing dimmer, and the trees' shadows were lengthening. Soon, darkness would make it difficult to notice the drone in the rafters. Even so, I needed the perpetrators to leave before they discovered my surveillance.

I picked up a rock and hurled it as hard as I could toward the pavilion. It traveled seventy yards and landed with a thud.

"Somebody is hiding out there," Logan squawked. He turned and fled toward the parking lot.

Helen reached out to stop him but changed her mind. Instead, she turned and hustled off in the direction from which she had come.

I waited until I was confident that both parties were well away. After returning to the pavilion, I toggled on the drone's motors. I eased it off the crossbeam with great care and guided it down for a smooth landing on the concrete slab. Holding my breath, I checked to ensure the culprits' conversation had been adequately recorded. The digital counter on the drone's display suggested everything had gone as planned. The video was evident when I played back a short segment, and the voices were audible.

With the drone and its controller safely tucked into the hard-sided case, I returned to where I had parked my car several blocks away. A new question demanded my attention as I hurriedly strode the sidewalks: *How can I best use the evidence I now possess?*

*   *   *

Late the following evening, I pulled in and parked in Helen Dunn's wide circular driveway. I had spent twenty-four hours reviewing the file I had recorded, making backups, and thinking about how to leverage the damning material it contained. At length, I had settled on a direct approach, and since time was of the essence, there could be no further delay.

Helen Dunn resided in a palatial, two-story antebellum mansion with an expansive front balcony and towering columns. Painted white with gray shutters, the house was one of Trinity Falls Township's most imposing. By my estimate, it had to have at least twenty rooms. The odd thing was that Helen lived alone.

Over the years, I had learned a great deal about my nemesis. Born into a middle-class family, she had been raised in Queens. In her mid-twenties, she had married a wealthy financier from Brooklyn Heights. Their stormy marriage had lasted barely three years. After abruptly filing for divorce, Helen had taken her ex to the cleaners. Suddenly, a wealthy woman, she had moved upstate and into the home she now occupied.

Bored and seeking a vocation to occupy her time, Helen dabbled in real estate. A bright and attractive woman, she had advanced rapidly in her new profession. Within weeks after passing her agent exam, a broker named Dale Remington invited her to join his staff. Eighteen months later, once Helen had earned her broker's license, Dale was gone, and Helen Dunn was the new sole proprietor of Rimdale Properties. How she had engineered such a rapid takeover had become a matter of intense speculation.

Standing on Helen's front porch, I quickly prayed: "Lord God, be with me this night. Give me the strength to undertake this righteous quest. Protect me from the slings and arrows of my enemies."

The upstairs lights were on when I rang the front doorbell. I held my laptop tucked protectively under one arm. When there was no response, I rang again and again after that. Then, the lights came on in the foyer. When Helen answered the door, I noted that she was wearing a floral dressing gown. Her hair was done up in curlers. There was no makeup on her face, causing her to seem at least ten years older than her daytime self.

"Do you have any idea what time it is?" Helen snapped.

"By my reckoning, it's time we settle accounts."

"And just what is that supposed to mean?"

"You and I have business to conduct."

"Are you nuts? If you wish to discuss your easement, make an appointment. Now go away, or I'll call the police."

"Don't bother. Unless you let me in and we settle this here and now, I will personally go to the police. I'm sure they would love to watch a certain video I recently recorded. It's most compelling."

Helen paled. I could tell she sensed my underlying meaning, but rather than panic, she feigned ignorance. "I'm in no mood for silly games. Now go away, or I will have you arrested for trespassing."

"I think you'll find this video quite enlightening, and it's of rather good quality. At least, that's my opinion. Still, I'm confident you will be impressed." I flashed a wicked grin. "If you choose not to watch it now, you can watch it tomorrow because it will be on all the local networks. After that, who knows? Maybe the national stations? What do you say? This will only take a bit of your time. My video file is all set up and ready to roll."

Helen waffled but then relented. I could tell she was growing increasingly alarmed but was doing her best not to show it. "Very well. I'll watch whatever it is you think is so important. But then you will leave. If you don't, I will double the price of your easement expansion."

I stepped inside the foyer. A large crystal chandelier hung high overhead. A spray of cut flowers decorated a vase on a side table. A Persian throw rug carpeted the hardwood floor.

I looked at Helen. "You might want to save your threats until you've seen what I have to show you."

Helen led the way toward a room beyond the large central staircase without commenting. Numerous books populated several floor-to-ceiling bookcases. I set my laptop on a round claw-foot table and lifted its screen. Helen stood beside me.

I nodded toward one of the armchairs nearby. "You might wish to sit down. This video contains material that some adults might find distressing." I chuckled softly.

After waking up the laptop from its standby mode, I pressed the play icon on the screen. Helen's eyes grew wide as she watched the tableau unfold. She was hanging on to every word of her conversation with Logan Smallwood. Halfway through the video file, she reached for the arm of the chair I had indicated. She sat down, visibly shaken.

When the video ended, I returned the laptop to its standby mode. Neither of us spoke. The only sound in the room was the grandfather clock ticking beside an antique writing desk.

Then Helen said quietly. "How did you…?"

"Magic. The magic of modern technology."

"What do you want?" Her voice registered barely above a whisper. I had to strain to hear her words.

"We'll get to that. First, I want to be certain that you understand what's happening here. I need to know that you appreciate the seriousness of your predicament. The scheme you and Logan Smallwood concocted is highly illegal. Your involvement makes you guilty of multiple felonies. Your own words stand as evidence against you. I'm certain that the county attorney would eagerly prosecute you for fraud, bribery, extortion, and conspiracy. Your own testimony will convict you, and you will grow old and ugly in prison."

Helen struggled to retain her composure. She sat up straighter in her chair. "Do you really think you'll get a conviction? On what basis? That illegally recorded video file? Perhaps you weren't aware. Recording a conversation without at least one participant's permission is illegal in New York State. My attorney will move to suppress your video. Your so-called evidence will never see the light of day."

"I thought you might object. Allow me to play a voice memo you need to hear." I again activated the laptop and keyed up one of the recordings from Logan's office. I turned to face Helen. "The next voice you hear will be Logan Smallwood's."

Logan's surly utterances issued from the laptop's speakers: "Do we have to go through this every time? If you feel it's imperative that you record our conversation, go ahead. In fact, from this point forward, I give you permission to record any and all of my conversations without limitation. Does that satisfy you?"

Holding up an index finger, I hastily interjected, "And then I respond…"

"Yes, Mr. Smallwood. Thank you."

"There. You see. I even address the man by name so there can be no confusion about who's speaking." I powered down the laptop. "I think that takes care of the permission issue."

Helen slumped in her chair. When she looked up at me, she seemed defeated. The fire had gone out behind her eyes. She sighed heavily. "Like I said, what do you want?"

"I want you to sell me the property you purchased from Walter Drake—not an easement expansion. The property itself."

Helen's eyes narrowed as if evaluating an investment opportunity. Always the calculating businesswoman. "For how much?"

"One dollar."

Despite her dejection, Helen burst out laughing.

I remained utterly deadpan.

"You can't be serious." Helen's laughter faded. "I paid $100,000 for that worthless splinter of ground."

"I know, but you're going to sell it to me for one dollar."

"And if I don't?"

"Walter Drake will sue you. He will have the sale voided based on fraud. I will then buy the land from him. The process will take longer, but the outcome will be the same. Oh, and while defending yourself against Walter, you'll also be defending yourself in criminal court against the county attorney."

"And if I agree, your video evidence will disappear?"

"With one additional proviso. You will resign from the real estate council and surrender your broker's license. You are wealthy enough that you don't need to work. It's time for you to retire. Do these things, and your criminal activities will be forgotten. You have twenty-four hours to decide."

"Who else have you told about this?"

"Only you so far. Oh, and if you have any notion of doing me harm, copies of this evidence plus my notarized deposition will be automatically sent to the county attorney's office." I gathered up my laptop. "Don't get up. I can find my own way out." About to exit the library, I halted to look back. "Let me know what you decide, but don't take too long. I wouldn't want to get the impression that you were trying to pull a fast one."

"What about Logan?" Helen asked numbly.

"Don't you worry about him. He's not your concern." I turned and stalked out of Helen's mansion with my head high and shoulders back.

"Thank you, Lord," I whispered as I started my Jeep and drove away.

*   *   *

More than fourteen thousand souls resided in Trinity Falls Township. Ridge County's population was nearly double that number. We were what demographers called an agrarian society. Our primary industries were farming and its supporting enterprises. Many of our retail businesses had a "down home" feel. As a culture, we endeavored to treat others as neighbors and valued things like hard work, personal responsibility, and community service. All in all, we were a conservative bunch. So when it came to dining out, our selection of cuisines could be somewhat restricted. Such was the case with the Prairie Pantry, a country diner with a Western ambiance.

I had followed Logan Smallwood from his office when he stepped out for lunch. As I watched him pull into the diner's parking lot, my thoughts were still very much on my encounter with Helen Dunn the previous evening.

In business dealings, selecting the right venue to initiate contact is essential to securing an agreeable outcome. Therefore, I sincerely hoped that Logan would be dining alone, and wasn't planning on meeting someone for lunch.

When I entered the diner, I saw that I was in luck. Logan was seated in the corner booth with his back to the dining room. He was alone. I stepped up and, without an invitation, sat down on the opposing bench.

"You don't mind, do you?" I set my laptop down on the table. "We have business to discuss, and the ambiance here seems much more sociable than in your office."

Logan scowled. "You followed me?"

"Yes, I did."

The waitress stepped forward to take our orders.

I deferred to Logan. "You first."

The planning board chairman opened his mouth as if to protest my intrusion but then seemed to think better of it. He said mildly to the waitress, "I'll have a Reuben with fries and a glass of iced tea."

The waitress looked at me. I responded brightly, "Make mine the all-American burger with onion rings and a chocolate shake." When she had gone, I commented to Logan, "You really should try their milkshakes. They're some of the best in the state."

"Why are you here?" Logan demanded.

"There is something I need you to watch." I opened the laptop, summoned the video, and positioned the screen so that he alone could see it.

Logan blanched as he recognized his own image. "For God's sake, turn that thing off."

"No need to be embarrassed. Personally, I think you're rather photogenic." I let the video play all the way through.

"You had no right to record that," Logan stammered.

"You know, that's exactly what Helen said. So I played this for her…" I pulled up the audio file.

The chairman's face grew red. He sputtered, "I never meant that you could record my personal conversations."

"Perhaps not, but I'm pretty sure that's not how the court will interpret your words."

Our food arrived. Logan pushed his plate away as if he had lost his appetite. I, however, took a hearty bite of my hamburger. It was delicious.

"Whatever you think you're doing," Logan snarled, "you're not gonna get away with it."

"You tried to ruin me. Now I'm fighting back the only way I know how."

"What is it you want?"

"Three things. First, you will void the requirement that the Spirit Wolf partnership expand its northern easement to sixty feet. Second, at the planning board's next meeting, you will see that our subdivision plat gets its final approval. Third, after these things have been accomplished, you will resign from the board and never again work for any governmental agency at any level. It's time for you to enter the private sector."

"I won't do it. Do you know how hard I've struggled to get where I am?"

"I know the crimes we've just watched you admit to. I ticked them off on my fingers: bribery of a government official, fraud, conspiracy. Helen is also guilty of extortion, but you weren't part of that. When the district attorney reviews all the records, including the audio and video files I've just shown you, he'll put you in jail. Ultimately, the outcome will be the same, but the process will be messier. Do it my way, and you may avoid being sent to prison."

Then, I made the mistake of rapidly downing half my milkshake. A cold-induced headache formed behind my right eye. I squeezed my eyes shut till the pain abated.

"I hate when that happens," I said, my eye still watering. "So, what's it gonna be? Oh, and by the way, if you're considering contacting Helen, don't. If this goes to trial, she'll stand as a witness against you, and you wouldn't want to be charged with witness tampering, would you?"

Logan sank back on his bench seat like a defeated man. The starch seemed to bleed out of his posture.

"Good," I said. "It would appear we have communicated effectively. I expect a letter rescinding the easement expansion on my desk by tomorrow morning." I switched off the laptop and lowered its screen. Tapping its case, I said, "At the next planning board meeting, I'll bring this along just in case there's a delay in granting us the approval we need. Oh, and of course, I've made backup copies with instructions on what to do with them if something happens to me or my computer."

I took a last bite of my hamburger and stood up. "You know, except for your bureaucratic mentality, you seem like a reasonably decent guy, though your personality could use a little work. Perhaps a move to the private sector will do you good … make you realize that the customer should always come first."

I turned and strode away. In passing, I noted that Logan still hadn't touched his meal.

The more I reflected upon what had just transpired, the more pleased I became. I had instigated two confrontations and had emerged victorious from both. *Who would ever have thought that could happen?*

Chapter 10

The leaves of a nearby sycamore had begun fading from pink to brown. Farther off, stands of mountain ash, red oak, and dogwood trees were in full autumnal display. It was the third week in October, and there was a chill in the air, a bleak warning of winter's relentless approach, though the heart of the fall season was still months away. In anticipation of frigid days to come, work on the Spirit Wolf project was pressing ahead at a feverish pace.

I stood beside Franklin, gazing at what I had regarded as my favorite spot in the entire project. In a landscape graced by any number of beautiful vistas, this one was special. I had returned numerous times over the last three months to meditate and enjoy God's handiwork. On each occasion, I had kept my eyes open for the wolf, but he had not reappeared. The presumption that he was gone for good haunted me. Fear that I would never see him again filled me with sadness.

"Why so glum?" Franklin commented. "You should be relieved, considering how things are working out."

"I am. I was remembering a departed friend."

"Aw, yes." Franklin nodded solemnly as if having read my mind. "It's probably best you know that he's gone. Focusing on mystical phenomena will distort your perceptions of the natural world."

"Yes, but they also heighten awareness and make you appreciate God's subtleties."

Franklin tilted his head to regard me with a look of curiosity. "How so?"

"In my dealings with Helen and Logan, there were too many coincidences to ignore. Looking back, I'm forced to believe that God was involved all along."

"As He always is, but what coincidences?"

"Well, for instance, my finding Helen's memo paper clipped to the front of the Spirit Wolf folder. If you were a conspirator, would you leave incriminating evidence like that lying around? I don't think so. So why did Logan leave the folder in the open for anyone to find? The most rational explanation is that he intended to put it away but was distracted. And if that is the case, how did that distraction come about? Did God engineer events so that the folder would be in plain sight? And why was I allowed to wait in Logan's office alone? See what I mean?"

"I admit, it is intriguing." Franklin gazed out across the property. We had already visited the ponds now stocked with fingerling trout. We had also walked the length of Spirit Wolf Trail, the central road, which, along with Argyle Road, was completely paved. "You said coincidences, plural."

"When I was in Helen's office, there was a disturbance in the reception area. The ruckus drew her away, allowing me to pilfer several sheets of notepaper. How was it that an angry client should show up at precisely the right moment? Was it chance, or was something else in play?"

Franklin tugged on an earlobe. "I see. Anything else?"

"Actually, yes. There is. How did I deliver my messages to Helen and Logan without being observed? I was trying to act nonchalant, but I wasn't invisible. In the planning board's offices, there were lots of people. Someone should have noted that I was poking around in Logan's desk, but they didn't. And in the gazebo, why didn't either Helen or Logan look up to find my drone? It was in plain sight for anyone to notice. All they had to do was lift their eyes, but they didn't. See what I mean?"

"You think God participated in your victory?"

"You tell me. After a while, don't so many coincidences begin to defy the laws of probability?"

"More miracles, do you imagine?"

I shrugged. "Like I said, when you tease apart the big picture, you begin to appreciate the subtleties of God's divine providence."

Franklin reached down to retrieve an acorn. He smiled as he held it up between his thumb and index finger as an object lesson.

I nodded in agreement. "You're right. We get so caught up in the ebb and flow of life that we fail to appreciate the little miracles that surround us every day. By the way, I stopped in to see Helen Dunn. Did you know she's opening a travel agency?"

"I heard something to that effect." Franklin's smile vanished. He tossed the acorn aside.

I admitted, "Actually, I went to see her."

"Did you?" Franklin seemed surprised.

"I wanted to tell her I forgive her. It wasn't easy, but I invited her to church."

"Do you think she'll come?"

"Perhaps not, but it was worth a try. Who knows? Maybe she'll repent of her evildoing and throw herself on God's mercy. It's never too late."

"True. What about Logan? I heard he left town."

"I think he's somewhere in Northern California, as far as I know. Anyway, I wanted to speak with you today to bring you up to speed as to where we stand."

"Good," Franklin said. "I've been wondering how the project is progressing."

"We've finished laying in the infrastructure. The utilities, the wells, and the access roads—they're all done. Most building sites have been graded and are ready to go. The really good news is that the first ten houses are under construction. Several are near completion. Three have been presold. As a result, I've gotten a better handle on our finances. When the dust settles, your payout—including the return of your initial contribution—will add up to around $105,000—before taxes, of course."

Franklin gasped. "Are you serious?"

"Dead serious, but there's more. I've persuaded the investors that having a church on the property would be in their best interest. It would foster a sense of community. At first, they hesitated, but I convinced them to sell me the four acres upon which we now stand. They're going to sell it to me at cost. I'll donate the land to the Maranatha Gospel Fellowship when the sale is complete. After that, raising the funds to build a sanctuary will be up to you, though I'm confident you can make it happen."

"This property? Where we are right now? This lot is absolutely beautiful. I don't know what to say."

"You needn't say a thing. All I'm doing is paying God back for His generosity."

"What about you? Are you guys going to come out of this okay?"

"I trust we will. I've been speaking with Winston Fordyce III. We're finally to the point whereby, drawing upon the equity I have in the project as collateral, I can apply for a generous line of credit. It's been tough waiting for this moment to come, but going forward, there should be money enough to cover Alicia's medical care. In anticipation of being approved, I've scheduled an appointment for her at the Warmview Center for Genetic Research in Austin, Texas. We fly out tomorrow at noon."

"That is great news. I think. She's still in her latent phase, stage 2, right?"

"She is, but her syndrome could activate at any moment. That's why we've been pushing people to press ahead with construction."

Franklin seemed troubled. "Is Alicia up for this? Genetic therapy—it's so brand-new. I mean, it's like something that's never been tried before."

"Trust me. Your niece is more than ready. We're both expecting another miracle. So is Rachel, for that matter."

"You do realize there are no guarantees—"

I reached out to touch my brother's arm. "Stop. Don't finish that thought. Believe only that God will see us through. Keep your faith strong and pray that He will increase it as needed." Then I chuckled. "Will you look at me, preaching to the pastor? Talk about chutzpah."

Franklin became very serious. His voice was barely audible, "How much faith would be required, I wonder, to bring about such a wondrous miracle?"

Abruptly, I pictured the chaos of my headlong rush through Trinity Falls and how the experience and other events impacted my spirituality. Softly, I replied, "A torrent of faith, I would imagine."

* * *

Clean white sheets and a thin cotton blanket covered Alicia as she lay in bed. She had been admitted to a private room in the pediatric wing of the Warmview Medical Center. This was the second day after we arrived in Austin, and she was already exhausted.

"How you doing, sweetheart?" I said, stepping fully into the room. Rachel and I had just come over from a nearby motel where we had booked lodging.

Alicia responded with a brave smile, which was mainly for our benefit. "I'm good to go. Did you see Dr. Davenport out in the hallway? The nurses said she was making rounds. She should be in soon."

Rachel stepped forward to smooth a lock of hair away from Alicia's forehead. "Did you sleep okay?"

"Yeah, except when they woke me to take my temperature. The nurses are nice, though. They tried not to make much noise."

I noticed a meal tray with several empty juice cartons on the bedside table. "You've already eaten, I see."

Alicia made a sour face. "Liquids only. I guess I'm not supposed to have solid foods on the day I get treated."

I nodded. "Just a precaution, I would imagine."

We had arrived late Wednesday afternoon and immediately checked Alicia into the medical center. Her admission—having been prearranged—was handled with great efficiency, as was the battery of lab tests scheduled for that evening and most of Thursday. Apparently, genetic reconstruction was an exceedingly complex process that required an amazing amount of information to complete successfully.

Rachel and I had also had our blood drawn. Healthy DNA would be extracted from our white blood cells. Since we were heterozygous, they would use the normal genes we carried to nullify Alicia's mutation. Needless to say, all three of us were feeling the strain of anticipation.

I moved closer to the bed and held my daughter's hand. "How are you feeling about what's going to happen today?" I said tentatively.

That brave smile reappeared. "Really, I'm good to go. Do you think I'll grow fangs and a mass of hair like a freaky werewolf?"

I chuckled. "Webbed fingers and flippers wouldn't be so bad. I know how much you like to swim."

Rachel chimed in, "Or wings with feathers. You could fly. Wouldn't that be cool?"

A knock sounded at the door, which opened slowly. A nurse's aide wearing scrubs stepped into the room. "I'm here to collect your breakfast tray. Are you all done?"

"Yes, thank you," Alicia responded.

The aide picked up the tray. "Did you get enough to eat?"

"No," Alicia replied dryly. "How about some scrambled eggs and toast?"

"Sorry. Not on the menu. Maybe tomorrow, depending upon how you feel." The aide turned to leave.

I spoke up. "Do most patients generally eat a full meal the day after treatment?"

The aide paused to look back over her shoulder. "It depends. Some do. Some don't. It's hard to predict. Younger patients seem to do better. They have fewer side effects. I'm sure your daughter will do fine." She left the room.

"That was good to hear," I commented to my family. "Another benefit of being young."

Rachel had already seated herself on the edge of Alicia's bed, leaving me the chair on gliders in the corner. I sat down just as another knock sounded at the door.

A middle-aged woman stepped inside. She wore a long white lab jacket and a stethoscope draped around her neck. Her sandy-blonde hair was braided around the crown of her head. She peered at us through a pair of tortoiseshell spectacles balanced on the end of her nose.

"You must be the Langdons, Paul and Rachel, right? I'm Dr. Davenport, and I'll be your daughter's treating physician. And how is our patient today?"

"Except for being hungry," Alicia responded, "I'm good."

"Splendid."

A nurse appeared in the doorway.

Dr. Davenport explained, "I've asked Ms. Sutton here to help Alicia collect another urine specimen." The doctor looked at our daughter. "Do you think you could do that for us?"

"Sure, after all the juice I've had to drink." Alicia slipped a robe over her hospital gown and departed with the nurse.

Dr. Davenport's mood became more taciturn. "I'm glad you're both here. There's something we need to discuss." She positioned herself so she could address us both. "I'm sorry to tell you this, but a problem has arisen. I'm afraid it's significant."

"What sort of problem?" I asked with alarm.

"There's an issue in the lab." Dr. Davenport set the chart she carried down on the bedside table so she could gesture with both hands. "As explained, we use a modified Epstein-Barr virus to transfer healthy DNA into a patient's cells. This transfer can mitigate or eliminate the defect in a patient's native DNA. Unfortunately, we've had a problem coaxing the virus to link with your daughter's DNA. We've tried both of you as donors. For some reason, the virus becomes inert after we add your DNA. The technicians have been working on this problem throughout the night. As you probably know, we've never attempted genetic reconstruction on a patient with Lascaux Syndrome. We are in uncharted waters."

"What does all this mean?" Rachel asked urgently. "What will happen to our daughter?"

"For now, nothing." Dr. Davenport pressed her palms together in a pleading gesture. "I am so sorry to have to give you this news. The entire staff has had such high hopes for her treatment, but unless we can find a way to reanimate the virus, there's nothing we can do. As it is, there's no reason for Alicia to remain in the hospital. She might as well be at home while we work on this problem. If a solution can be found, we will call you immediately."

"You're sending our daughter home to die!" Rachel exclaimed.

"I'm sure the techs will eventually overcome this setback. It's just a matter of time." Dr. Davenport did not sound the least bit convincing.

In that moment, I experienced what most people would call a crisis of faith. I had been one hundred percent certain that God had facilitated Alicia's journey to Austin and had ordained the experimental therapy that would restore her to a healthy life. Now, it was beginning to seem like my hope had been in vain. The faith I had so diligently nurtured was shattered in an instant. An unbearable emptiness flooded my heart.

Darkly, I asked, "What happens now?"

Dr. Davenport responded with a look of sympathy. "I'll arrange for Alicia's discharge. We'll copy her lab studies so you can take them to her primary care physician—"

"Dr. Angus McGregor," I interjected.

"Right, Dr. McGregor. I'll also dictate a letter explaining the medical issues we've encountered and our recommendations for supportive care. I'm afraid this is the best we can do at this point."

"Supportive care?" A look of shock registered on Rachel's face as if the full weight of what was being discussed was sinking in.

I rose from my chair to put my arm around my wife's shoulders. "Thank you, Doctor. I'm sure you and the rest of the staff have done your best. If you would, please tell us what we have to look forward to. We've heard from other physicians, but I'd like your opinion."

"Of course. Alicia's been in stage 2 for almost three and a half months. Sometime before the end of the year, she should begin showing increased signs of cardiac involvement. You already know what symptoms to expect. There is no reason to enumerate them in detail, but as her heart fails, she'll grow progressively weaker, and she will have increasing difficulty breathing. There are therapies that can ease some of her symptoms and temporarily strengthen her heart, but I'm afraid her disease will progress steadily. At some point, her heart will stop. I'm sorry."

Rachel began to sob. Tears formed in my eyes as well.

I looked at the doctor through blurry eyes and tried to be brave. "Thank you. When our daughter returns, we'll get her ready to leave."

Dr. Davenport recovered the chart from the bedside table. "If you have questions or if there is anything else we can do for you, don't hesitate to call. And as I indicated, we will contact you immediately if there's a breakthrough and we can activate the virus."

She turned and left the room, leaving us to deal with our anguish.

* * *

The jumbo-sized chili pot was clean, scrubbed to a bright luster. I set it in the drainer to dry and looked around the kitchen. The other pots and pans had already been washed, dried, and put away. Only a few dinner plates remained, and I made quick work of those.

Franklin finished sweeping the kitchen floor. Using a dustpan, he gathered the refuse to dump into a trash bin. He then returned the broom and dustpan to the corner closet.

My brother and I were the only volunteers; all others had departed. Alicia and Rachel had elected to stay home. Alicia had pleaded to come even though she was feeling drained. Rachel, however, had considered it best not to overtax our daughter's endurance. For all of us, the trip home from Austin had proven physically and emotionally exhausting. In the two weeks since our return, Alicia was only now beginning to recover her stamina.

Rachel and I had been trying to keep our daily routines as normal as possible for our daughter's sake.

"It's a shame Betty couldn't make it tonight," Franklin said, referencing an elderly congregation member.

"George wasn't here either," I noted. "His arthritis must have flared up again."

Betty and George were sometimes prevented from attending the Tuesday supper because of their poor health. I was surprised to discover how many other people with infirmities were in the same boat.

"I worry that they're not getting the nutrition they need," Franklin commented. "I wish there was something we could do. Maybe I could fix a couple of plates of leftovers and drop them off when we're done here."

"Good idea. I'll give you a hand."

Except for the missing in action, the Tuesday supper had proven quite a hit. As usual, many had expressed their appreciation. We served chili with cornbread and green beans. More than a few had requested seconds. Several had come back for thirds. Their expressions of gratitude had done little to warm my heart. I was still coping with our disappointment at the Warmview Medical Center.

When two plates of leftovers were sealed in plastic wrap, Franklin punched his fists onto his hips. "Looks like we're done. Thanks for your help."

"My honor," I replied automatically. I finished drying my hands on a dish towel and hung it on its rack. "Are you in a hurry to get out of here?"

"Not especially. What do you need?"

"Just to talk." I led the way to one of the round tables in the multipurpose room. We sat down facing one another.

I said candidly as I leaned forward with my elbows on the table, "I'm not sure what I'm supposed to do."

"About…?"

"Everything."

Franklin arched an eyebrow.

I restated my dilemma. "Mainly, I'm not sure how I'm supposed to feel."

"That's understandable, considering what you've been through. How do you feel, in plain English?" Franklin regarded me keenly. Earlier, I could tell he had sensed my distress but had said nothing.

His question vexed me until I realized I had not yet untangled the emotions roiling within me. I paused to think. "I'm sad. I'm hurt. I'm scared, and I'm angry. Mostly angry. In fact, I'm furious. There's a rage I can't release. I can't let it go. I want to lash out. I want to hurt something. It's a terrible feeling."

"And you're angry because…?"

"Because of the way things turned out. Alicia never got her chance to see if the therapy would work. She deserves more than being told, 'There's nothing we can do.'"

"Being rejected might have been the inciting cause, but I suspect your anger stems from something far more primal."

"And just what might that be?" I snapped.

"You're mad because God failed to deliver the miracle you expected."

I looked up with a start. "That is exactly right. It's like He set me up. If He had no intention of healing my daughter, why did He ordain those other miracles? Just to get my hopes up?"

"You think God is being mean to you?"

I snarled, "Well, He certainly isn't being compassionate."

"How do you know? Can you foretell the future? Can you judge how alternate outcomes would have unfolded? What if Alicia had gotten her therapy, which had done more harm than good? Or suppose a genetically modified virus with dangerous capabilities had been created. What if such a horror had been loosed upon the world, causing countless people to suffer? How would you feel then? As a species, we're clueless as to the long-term effects of most of our actions. You only have to look at the havoc reaped by well-intentioned but misguided efforts to know what I'm saying is true. History's highway is littered with man's mistakes."

"All very philosophical. What's your point?"

"My point is we don't know. No man can fathom the mind of God. Faith is our most important attribute, and faith requires trust. We must trust that God is in charge and that He has our best interests at heart. Romans chapter 8, verse 28 promises, 'And we know that in all things God works for the good of those who love Him, who have been called according to His purpose.' The passage doesn't say that everything will be good. It doesn't claim there won't be pain, suffering, or heartache. What it says is that if we truly love Him, all things will work together, and the outcome will be good. So, the question is, do you truly love Him?"

I gave my brother a look of rebuke. "You know I do."

"Then trust Him."

"How can I trust when there's no hope? Don't you understand? We're out of options. My daughter's future is written in her DNA. Soon she's going to die."

Franklin tapped the table with the tip of his index finger. "This is precisely the moment when God invites us to put our faith in Him when we're at the end of our ropes and can't see any way forward."

I rocked back in my chair. "You know what's ironic? I trusted God to help me with the Spirit Wolf project. Like you said, I put my faith in Him, and He engineered a great outcome. In a few months, I'll be a wealthy man. I'll have more money than I ever imagined, but I would surrender it all in a heartbeat to have my daughter well again. All the time and energy I put into the project, all the anxiety and worry. If my daughter dies, it will all have been for nothing."

I bowed my head and broke down. The strain of the last several weeks finally found its release.

*   *   *

Two months later, as I sat beside my sleeping daughter's bed, I monitored the rise and fall of the thin sheet that covered her fragile body. For the time being, she seemed comfortable and at peace. However, her breathing could become labored and strained with any exertion or excitement, as if driven by an unquenchable hunger for air.

Dr. McGregor had reminded us that her breathing troubles were due to the weakness of the heart muscle and its inability to clear fluid from her lungs. Medications had been prescribed. At first, they had seemed to help. Less so in the last several weeks.

As I sat quietly in my chair, I watched the flickering lights on the small Christmas tree we had positioned in the corner of my daughter's room. Decorated with tinsel, ornaments, and colored garlands, it was supposed to be a joyous reminder of the holiday a week away. We had agreed to let Alicia have her own tree because navigating the stairs had become a struggle for her. Other decorations were also displayed: a tiny manger scene, greeting cards from friends and well-wishers, and a framed picture of Jesus holding a young child in his arms.

I watched the twinkling lights and was reminded of Christmases past when the season's joy had been undiminished by mounting sorrows, and one year stood out in my mind when Alicia was seven. She had pleaded without ceasing for a new bicycle, and when, on Christmas morning, she had discovered her gift under the tree, her delight had been titanic. What a glorious thing it had seemed, bringing happiness into a young child's life by offering such a simple treasure as a bicycle. I remembered wishing with all my heart that such good cheer would fill her days for a lifetime, which was now about to be cut short.

Tormented by anguish, I shifted my gaze away from the Christmas tree.

"Daddy? Are you here?" said her small voice.

I looked at the bed. Alicia turned her face toward me. "What time is it?" she whispered.

"It's early. Not even five o'clock yet. You should go back to sleep."

"I don't know if I can."

"Are you okay? How do you feel?"

"I'm all right," she said bravely.

"Is your breathing…?"

"No. My chest isn't tight at all." Alicia shifted her body to sit up a bit. I positioned an extra pillow to support her shoulders. She smiled in gratitude and said, "Have you been here all night?"

"Off and on."

"Mostly on, I'd bet. Daddy, you needn't worry. I'm going to be okay."

"I know you are, sweetie. I like watching you sleep. You seem so at peace. Tell the truth. How do you feel?"

"A little weak. Otherwise, I'm good. At least I'm no worse than yesterday." Again, she smiled.

Rachel and I had discussed with our daughter the process of dying. We had explained how when someone passes on, Jesus takes the person's soul to heaven even though their body stays behind. With as much compassion as we could summon, we had spoken of how it was like falling asleep and waking up in a beautiful, wondrous place with no more sadness, and no more suffering. She had seemed to accept our description, though it was hard to gauge the true impact of our words. Having never witnessed death, a child's concept of what it was like could be limited.

"What do you need?" I said. "Is there anything I can get you? It's too early for breakfast, but you could have a glass of warm milk or juice."

"I don't need anything. I really am fine."

For another twenty minutes or so, Alicia and I continued talking. We talked about her days in school, her favorite memories of early childhood, and other topics intended to shift her attention away from the present.

At length, she looked at me and said solemnly, "Daddy, I know what you're trying to do, but there's no need. I'm going to be okay. I can feel it inside." She tapped the center of her chest.

"I know, sweetheart. I, too, believe you will be all right."

"Do you?" My daughter regarded me with a perceptive stare as if measuring my sincerity.

I could not respond to her question; my agony was too compelling. Instead, I replied, "Look, you need your rest. Lie down and close your eyes. Maybe you'll fall asleep again. I'll come and wake you when it's time for breakfast."

"Okay," Alicia said simply.

I withdrew the extra pillow, tucked her in, and tenderly kissed her forehead before quietly exiting the room.

Alicia soon fell asleep.

Troubled by my daughter's simple yet profound question, I tiptoed downstairs. Before heading out into the backyard, I listened to hear if Rachel had awakened. There were no sounds to indicate she was beginning her morning routine.

Outside, dawn was emerging. A line of lavender light lit the eastern horizon. The air was crisp with December's chill. An inch of fresh snow had fallen during the night. I stepped out onto the covered patio and looked up. Only a few stars remained visible in the heavens.

I had come to the end of myself. There was nothing more I could do to deflect the future I dreaded. All that was left was to admit defeat.

"Almighty God," I said softly but firmly, "I surrender. I've petitioned You, I've cajoled You, I've pleaded, and I've begged. I have even addressed You in anger. I've said all I can say. Now, all I can do is accept whatever fate You have in store for me and my family. I'm ready.

"But I don't understand why You went to all that trouble blessing me with three miracles. Whatever message You intended to convey, I must have missed it. True, they drew me closer to You, and I will be eternally grateful for that. Yet, as far as I can tell, they've done nothing to lessen my heartache. You know what my daughter means to me. You know how much I love her and treasure the joy she brings me and my wife. Alicia is the light of my life. When she's gone, that light will become darkness.

"Even so, it is not for me to judge Your ways or question Your purposes. You alone are sovereign. I bend my knee to Your will." I knelt on the patio's cold paving stones. "All I ask is that You sustain me during the black days ahead. Give me the strength to endure the unbearable burden that will soon be mine: the loss of my only child. Be with my wife as well. Her needs are as dire as mine. Hallowed be thy name, Father. Thy will be done."

After speaking my peace, I rose and went back inside.

* * *

In the wee hours of the morning in the first week of January, I was again back in my daughter's room, as I had been on many nights. Rachel and I had been taking shifts standing watch by our daughter's bedside. It was again my turn. Despite my wife's reticence to leave, I had packed her off to bed, hopefully, to garner some much-needed rest. Rachel's exhaustion was undeniable despite her protests to the contrary.

The factor that made this vigil so horribly agonizing was that Alicia was in the process of dying. The previous afternoon, Dr. McGregor had stopped by, as he had every day for a week. After taking Alicia's vital signs and doing a short physical exam, he had announced that the end was drawing near. It would now be only a matter of hours, perhaps days, till her frail circulatory system finally ceased its valiant struggle.

On several occasions, Rachel and I had considered admitting our daughter to the hospital. After lengthy discussions, we had made the difficult decision to keep her at home. With no new medications to administer and no new therapies to try, there had seemed little reason to expose her to a harsh hospital environment. Even Dr. McGregor had agreed that she would rest more comfortably in her own bed.

Filled with unbearable grief, I monitored the rise and fall of her shallow breaths. In sleep, my daughter seemed at peace. It was apparent to me that we had made the right decision.

The holidays were over. Christmas and New Year had come and gone. Times that should have been full of joy and gladness had been heavy with sorrow. Rachel and I had done our best to keep a supportive frame of mind and shut out the terror of our impending loss. Yet, as hard as we had tried, we could not hide our grief. It was impossible to ignore a horror of such magnitude as the imminent death of a child.

Even so, a tenuous peace was emerging in my soul. After allowing myself to acknowledge God's sovereignty and submit to His will, the anger that had once raged within me gradually cooled. Trusting in God's righteousness made accepting the inevitable easier. I had deliberately suspended my will so that He might prevail. Letting go, I discovered, had brought a sense of solace. Sustaining such a mindset, however, was proving tricky. My natural tendency was to hand a problem over to God only to immediately take it back so I could solve it myself.

From time to time, I had again considered the three miracles. In so doing, a different train of thought had occurred to me. Without faith, it would have been impossible to recognize the miracles for what they were: manifestations of the supernatural. Without faith, the miraculous events would have become flukes of nature, distortions of my perceptive abilities. I would have regarded them as delusions or worse. Yet the miracles had nurtured my faith. The miracles had bridged the gap between what I knew and what I was willing to believe.

Reminded of my faith, inexplicably growing more assertive, I closed my eyes and whispered a prayer. "Father God, as before, I bow my will to Yours. I will accept whatever You have in store for me and my family. However, as You know my heart, I again seek Your mercy and compassion. Be with my daughter now. I ask that You would heal her. Strengthen her body. Take away this genetic infirmity that is ending her life. Yes, I am seeking another miracle. Even so, Thy will be done. In the mighty name of Jesus, I pray this from the depths of my being. Amen." It was the sincerest prayer I had ever prayed.

When I opened my eyes, I had the odd impression that a faint golden glow had cocooned Alicia. When I peered closer, she was still asleep, and her breathing was unchanged.

I touched her wrist and measured her pulse as Dr. McGregor had taught us. Her heartbeat was still rapid. I drew my fingers away from her wrist. The glow seemed to shimmer ever so slightly. I wondered if I might be hallucinating.

Alarmed, I began to rise to summon Rachel, but a sudden stupor descended upon me, a heavy tranquility that lay like a blanket over my awareness. Unable to resist, I lowered my head to the crook of my arm as it rested upon Alicia's bed, not unlike a youthful student napping at his desk in school.

When I opened my eyes, I was unsure how much time had elapsed. Alicia was sitting propped up in bed, watching me. She smiled and seemed utterly untroubled. The glow was gone.

"What just happened?" I said with a profound sense of apprehension.

Alicia shrugged.

"Are you okay?" I touched the back of my hand to her forehead and her cheek. The low-grade fever that had afflicted her for a week was no longer evident.

"I'm fine. I'm hungry. What time is it? Is it time for breakfast?"

I consulted my watch. "It's not yet three in the morning."

"Do you think I could eat something anyway? I'm starving."

"What about—?"

"No. I'm fine. My breathing is fine. My chest doesn't hurt. I feel really good."

"Honey, do you remember anything from when you were asleep just now? Did you have any sort of a dream?"

"Not really. I remember I was warm, and there was this light—"

"What sort of light?" I said urgently, interrupting her.

"It seemed to come from everywhere and nowhere all at once. That's all I remember. I really am hungry. Would it be okay if I had some toast or something?"

I studied my daughter intently. The color had returned to her cheeks, and her breathing was slow and steady. Gone was the evident fatigue apparent whenever she moved. Something had changed, but I was afraid to speculate for fear I might be dreaming.

"How about pancakes if you're sure you're up for them?"

"Oh, yeah." Alicia reached for her robe, draped across the foot of her bed. Gaily, she put it on and bounded to her feet. "Come on. I'll race you downstairs. Last one to the kitchen has to wash the dishes." She hurried out of the room.

I had to hustle to catch up.

*   *   *

Six months later, on the Fourth of July, the Maranatha Gospel Fellowship members were gathered on the four acres of land they had acquired from the Spirit Wolf partnership. It was a beautiful summer day. A potluck feast had been organized, and everyone was in a festive mood.

Franklin and I stood off to one side, away from the crowd. We watched as people helped themselves to various casseroles, bean dishes, salads, bread, and a big pot of Swedish meatballs, not to mention a host of desserts.

I leaned closer to my brother and said softly, "Are you ready to do your thing?"

The church's formal groundbreaking ceremony was scheduled to begin in an hour. In response to taking ownership of the property, the congregation had launched a fundraising drive to finance the new sanctuary. Participation was enthusiastic, and as a result, construction was to start six months ahead of schedule.

With his hands folded behind his back, Franklin gazed toward the picnic tables that had been brought in by truck. "I believe I am, and let me say again how grateful we are for your generous donation. None of this would've been possible without the land you acquired for us."

"Please. It's an honor to be able to help. Besides, it's time the church had a new home, not to mention that it will make a tremendous tax write-off."

"Which you deserve," Franklin added.

Before arriving at the potluck, my brother and I had toured the property, noting how the Spirit Wolf project was progressing. Around eighty percent of the estates had been completed, and construction was well along with the rest. More to the point, nearly every home had been sold. Demand had been much more substantial than anticipated, meaning revenues were above projections by a significant margin. Franklin was almost speechless when I told him his profits would be higher than predicted.

Similarly, the investors had expressed their gratitude. They had even talked about keeping the partnership going and pursuing another project. I had politely but forcefully declined. At length, they formally voted to dissolve the partnership and distribute any residual monies after the last estate was sold.

My brother regarded me out of the corner of his eye. "What will you do now that your project is winding down? What are your plans for the future?"

"I was going to tell you later, but now seems as good a time as any. I'm going to retire from selling real estate. I've worked a deal with

Jack Flashman. He'll take over Trinity Falls Realty now that he has his broker's license. We've agreed that he can buy me out with a portion of the commissions he'll earn selling homes. It's a win-win scenario for both of us."

Startled, Franklin turned his head to gape at me straight on. "You're getting out of real estate?"

"I am."

"What will you do? True, you'll have enough money that you'll never need to work again, but I know you. Without something to do, you'll go out of your mind."

"I don't plan on being idle if that's what you think. On the contrary, I'll probably be busier than ever with this project. I'm going to launch a new company. I think I'll call it Food Flight. Rachel will be quitting the library to work with me. She'll help me develop a new technology to deliver hot meals to shut-ins using drones. Not surprisingly, many food bank networks throughout Upstate New York have expressed their support. I've also been in touch with several large corporations, primarily restaurants and major grocery store chains. They're interested in sponsoring us. Ultimately, my goal is to take the enterprise to a national level.

"Imagine how much good a drone delivery service could do. Automated aerial platforms can provide hot meals faster and cheaper than ground transportation, especially in large cities. Think of the man-hours saved. I hope that this endeavor will serve as a pilot program. If it succeeds, businesses in the food sector might consider using drones to deliver meals to their customers at home. The growth potential is enormous."

"Sounds like a cool idea." A look of apprehension spread across Franklin's face. "Does this mean you'll be moving?"

"Not at all. I may have to travel at first, but our family will stay here. I'll hire a manager after the business gets off the ground—no pun intended. He can do the traveling."

"Speaking of family…?" Franklin thrust his chin toward where women and children were serving the potluck meal. "Alicia seems to be doing well."

I nodded. "To look at her, you'd never know she came within hours of dying."

"Are you sure she's completely well? There's no chance that someday the syndrome might…?"

"None at all. We've had her tested twice. Her DNA is normal. There is no trace of the Lascaux mutation anywhere in her body."

Franklin tilted his head to peer at me. "How does that make you feel?"

"How do you think? Humble, thankful…awestruck…amazed." Then I realized my brother might be asking something other than what I first perceived. "What do you mean exactly?"

Franklin turned to face me. "You've been blessed by four unique and undeniable miracles. I guess what I'm asking is how they impacted you. Not how you feel about them, but how have they changed you? How are you different?"

"One way I'm different is I'm overcome with gratitude. My heart is full every time I look at my daughter. I mean, she was dying. Now she is alive. That's why I'm launching Food Flight. I want to give back to God for what He's given me."

"Yes, but how are you changed? You're my brother. I've known you all your life. In these last six months, you've become a different person in a very good way. I want to know the what and the why of your evolution. Can you tell me? Are you able to put your finger on what's different?"

I thought about my brother's inquiry. He was right. I was becoming a different person. As I tried to sort out what was happening, I recognized something inside myself I hadn't appreciated before. Serenity was the word that best explained my new state of being.

I laid my hand on my brother's shoulder. "Do you remember when I described my river transit through Trinity Falls and how I emerged with a deep and abiding sense of peace at the end of my headlong rush? Perhaps another way of sharing what I felt is to say I was filled with pure, unfiltered joy. Since Alicia's recovery, that sensation has grown even stronger. I can no longer doubt God's love. I now trust Him at the core of my being. I can tell you this, having experienced four miracles. The greatest gift I've been given, and the power that is changing me from within, is faith. God has seen fit to bestow upon me an abundance of faith, and it's reshaping my life."

Franklin grinned. "How much faith would you say you've been given?"

"A torrent of faith. Enough to last a lifetime and all eternity."

The End